D0408837

DISCARDED

BY

BERTHOUD COMMUNITY
LIBRARY DISTRICT

Beyond
the
Desert Sands

Books by Tracie Peterson

LOVE ON THE SANTA FE
Along the Rio Grande
Beyond the Desert Sands

LADIES OF THE LAKE
Destined for You
Forever My Own
Waiting on Love

WILLAMETTE BRIDES
Secrets of My Heart
The Way of Love
Forever by Your Side

THE TREASURES OF NOME*
Forever Hidden
Endless Mercy
Ever Constant

BROOKSTONE BRIDES
When You Are Near
Wherever You Go
What Comes My Way

GOLDEN GATE SECRETS
In Places Hidden
In Dreams Forgotten
In Times Gone By

HEART OF THE FRONTIER
Treasured Grace
Beloved Hope
Cherished Mercy

THE HEART OF ALASKA*
In the Shadow of Denali
Out of the Ashes
Under the Midnight Sun

SAPPHIRE BRIDES
A Treasure Concealed
A Beauty Refined
A Love Transformed

BRIDES OF SEATTLE
Steadfast Heart
Refining Fire
Love Everlasting

LONE STAR BRIDES
A Sensible Arrangement
A Moment in Time
A Matter of Heart

LAND OF SHINING WATER
The Icecutter's Daughter
The Quarryman's Bride
The Miner's Lady

LAND OF THE LONE STAR
Chasing the Sun
Touching the Sky
Taming the Wind

*All Things Hidden**
*Beyond the Silence**
House of Secrets
*Serving Up Love***

*with Kimberley Woodhouse
**with Karen Witemeyer, Regina Jennings, and Jen Turano

For a complete list of Tracie's books,
visit her website www.traciepeterson.com

LOVE *on the* SANTA FE

Beyond

the

Desert Sands

TRACIE PETERSON

BETHANYHOUSE
a division of Baker Publishing Group
Minneapolis, Minnesota

Berthoud Community
Library District
236 Welch Ave
Berthoud, Co 80513

FICTION
PETERSON
LOVE ON T
V. 2

NB/4 84

142579

8/2022

© 2022 by Peterson Ink, Inc.

Published by Bethany House Publishers
11400 Hampshire Avenue South
Minneapolis, Minnesota 55438
www.bethanyhouse.com

Bethany House Publishers is a division of
Baker Publishing Group, Grand Rapids, Michigan

Printed in the United States of America

All rights reserved. No part of this publication may be reproduced, stored in a retrieval system, or transmitted in any form or by any means—for example, electronic, photocopy, recording—without the prior written permission of the publisher. The only exception is brief quotations in printed reviews.

Library of Congress Cataloging-in-Publication Data
Names: Peterson, Tracie, author.
Title: Beyond the desert sands / Tracie Peterson.
Description: Minneapolis, Minnesota : Bethany House Publishers, a division of
    Baker Publishing Group, [2022] | Series: Love on the Santa Fe
Identifiers: LCCN 2021057109 | ISBN 9780764237324 (trade paper) | ISBN
    9780764237331 (cloth) | ISBN 9780764237348 (large print) | ISBN 9781493437276
    (ebook)
Subjects: LCGFT: Novels.
Classification: LCC PS3566.E7717 B475 2022 | DDC 813/.54—dc23/eng/20211126
LC record available at https://lccn.loc.gov/2021057109

Scripture quotations are from the King James Version of the Bible.

This is a work of fiction. Names, characters, incidents, and dialogues are products of the author's imagination and are not to be construed as real. Any resemblance to actual events or persons, living or dead, is entirely coincidental.

Cover design by LOOK Design Studio
Cover photography by Aimee Christenson

Baker Publishing Group publications use paper produced from sustainable forestry practices and post-consumer waste whenever possible.

22 23 24 25 26 27 28   7 6 5 4 3 2 1

Prologue

SILVER VEIL, NEW MEXICO TERRITORY
JUNE 1904

Isabella Garcia followed her father into his spacious library, never once stopping her pleading.

"Papi, you must hear me. I'm eighteen years old—old enough to make such a decision for myself. You know how much I hate this place. You forced me to leave the home I loved in California and dragged me here years ago. I have survived it only because you allowed me to spend this summer and last with Aunt Josephina back in California."

Daniel Garcia fixed his daughter with a stern look. It was obvious he was already tired of this topic. "Be that as it may, Isabella, you cannot live with my sister. I will not allow it, and neither will Josephina. She understands the situation and knows that I want only the best for you."

Isabella planted her hands on her hips. "How can this be best? You have forced me to endure this tiny silver-mining town that you created in the middle of the desert. I have lived here for eight years, and the only thing that has gotten me

5

through are the visits to Aunt Josephina back on the family estate." She began to pace. "Honestly, I don't know why you are being so pigheaded, Papi. I have been a dutiful daughter. I have done as you demanded. I endured being torn from my home—the only place I ever loved—and brought here. I have been obedient to my tutors and music teachers. I have done all that was asked of me, and now *I* ask for something, and you refuse. You are cruel and heartless."

"I am neither, Isabella," her father said, his tone betraying his exasperation. He sank into his desk chair and ran his hand through black hair that was turning gray much too quickly. "You aren't even eighteen and hardly old enough to know what is best for your future. You have not yet reached your majority, and as such, you must live by my rules. I have tried to make your burden lighter by allowing you to spend summers with your aunt, but there is much here that you still need to learn."

"Such as what?" She stepped closer to his desk. "And please don't tell me how I need to know the people better and to serve them with greater respect. I care nothing for Silver Veil and the industry you've created. I love California. I love the beautiful people there and the parties and comforts that are at my fingertips. I love Aunt Josephina and the horse-breeding estate that my great-grandfather built. That is home to me now, as it was when I was a girl. Why are you determined to keep me from it?"

He sighed. "In time you will understand. Your mother and I need you here. We want you to know what it is to care for others. The people of Silver Veil are dependent upon us for their jobs, their homes, everything. You must learn to be a good caretaker."

"I don't wish to be their caretaker, Papi. I never asked for that job. I want to live in my ancestral home. It is my destiny—

my legacy from our ancestors—yet you act as though it is something shameful."

"I never said it was shameful. But there is more to it than you seem to understand. When you have wealth and property, you owe a certain amount of your success to the people who help you—who work for you and with you. You act as though money comes up from the ground or rains down from the skies for the taking." He smiled and shook his head. "My dear Isabella, you are a fortunate girl. You have been born to blessings, and as such, you must learn the value of blessing others."

"Then let me bless them in California!" She raised her voice, then lowered it just as quickly. "Papi, I know I seem overly passionate, but that is because it means so much to me. The estate is where I belong. My friends are there. I have no friends here."

"That is how you have chosen it to be. There are people here who would love to be your friend, but you pulled away and hid yourself here at the house or out riding your horse."

"I didn't want to make friends because . . . well, it hurt so much when you took me away from them in California. I don't ever want to hurt that much again."

Her father's expression softened, and for a moment, Isabella thought she'd won him over.

But then he stood and fixed her with a look she knew well: He would hear nothing more about it. "The matter is closed. You will be allowed to spend the summer with my sister, but then you will return in the fall to help your mother as she works with the people of Silver Veil. This is my decision. If you refuse to do things my way, you will forfeit your summer in California."

Isabella said nothing as he left the library. Her hands

gripped her skirts, and her mouth was clamped shut so tightly that her jaw ached. How could he be so heartless? He was impossible.

She wouldn't give up. She would ask again and again, until he let her return to California for good.

"You are a terrible father and a horrible man," she said, shaking her fist at the door.

"I think he's a rather good man."

She startled and whirled around to see a man coming around the corner of one of the bookshelves. She didn't know who he was, but it was clear he'd overheard her conversation.

"And I think you are a rather rude one." As he drew near, she caught a whiff of his cologne. It was musky and sweet, not at all unpleasant, but she decided then and there that she hated it.

He gave her a lopsided smile. "I've been called worse."

"I'm sure you have. You are a terrible person to listen to a private conversation between a father and daughter."

"You are perhaps correct that I am rude—even terrible— for not making myself known. But you, on the other hand, are a spoiled, ungrateful child, and I hardly feel obligated to explain myself to you." He picked up his hat from a nearby table. "Now, I will excuse myself. Your father and I have business to discuss regarding the spur line into Silver Veil. I'm sure your little episode has probably made him forget, but I'm anxious to see our business concluded so I can return to, shall I say, a less confrontational atmosphere."

"You are incorrigible. I hope you do go quickly and never return, Mister . . ."

"Bailey. Aaron Bailey."

"Well, good riddance, Mr. Bailey. I hope never to see you

again." She started to storm out of the room, then paused. "And I hate your cologne!"

He chuckled. "Don't you mean that you hate me?"

She narrowed her eyes and gave him a curt nod. "Yes! I do."

1

Isabella looked from her aunt Josephina to Diego Morales, the man she loved. "I don't want to go. Surely now that I'm twenty-five, I can tell my father no."

"I don't think that would be wise, my dear. He still pays all of your bills and controls the inheritance your grandparents left you." Aunt Josephina smiled in her motherly fashion. "It will all work out for the best, you'll see. I promised your father I would come for a visit once I have concluded some business matters here. We'll soon be together again."

"It's just not fair. I wanted to spend Christmas with Diego." Isabella smiled at the dark-haired man. He was ten years her senior and so suave and sophisticated. Just one look from him gave her a shiver of delight.

She'd had a crush on him since childhood but had known it was true love for the last five years. She anxiously anticipated a proposal and had thought perhaps it would come on Christmas Eve. Now, however, standing at the depot, awaiting the train that would take her to Silver Veil for Christmas, she was more than a little frustrated. Gone were the

11

dreams of a romantic evening by the fireplace with Diego on one knee, promising to love her forever. Her father certainly knew how to ruin her life and had been doing so since she was ten years old. Fifteen years later, Isabella had thought she'd found a way to control her own life and rid herself of her father's interference, but it seemed it was not to be.

Her aunt stepped forward as the train whistle sounded. "You'll be boarding soon. I just want to tell you how much I love you and shall miss you." She embraced Isabella and held her close. "I know we shall be together again, but I want you to remember that God often takes our lives in directions we did not anticipate. No matter what happens, I want you to remember that such a thing doesn't mean God no longer loves us or cares for us."

"What are you saying, Aunt?" Isabella glanced from her aunt to the approaching train. Her father had arranged a private car at the end of the train for her comfort. At least that was something. She didn't give Aunt Josephina a chance to reply. "Lupe, do you have our things?"

Her maid struggled forward, carrying several bags. "I do, miss. I have all but the trunks. The baggageman arranged for those. He said he would see them put on the private car."

"He'd better." Isabella left her aunt and went to Diego. "I wish you were going with me."

He smiled. "That would be quite the grand adventure, eh?"

She wanted to melt into the wooden depot platform. "I will miss you so much. I can't believe it will be six weeks before I see you again. That seems much too long."

"The time will pass more quickly than you realize." He touched his index finger to her chin. "Be brave, my dearest. I will be here waiting for you."

It wasn't a proposal, but it was something of a promise.

Isabella smiled and touched her fingers to his cheek. "You had better be," she teased.

"Isabella, there are people watching." Aunt Josephina was a stickler for proper etiquette and allowed no public displays of affection.

Pulling away from Diego was hard, but Isabella stepped back, knowing it was for the best. "I will return as soon as possible. Father wants me there for the celebration of statehood. I cannot say why, but New Mexico becoming a state is important to him, and he demands it be important to me."

Diego nodded but said nothing more. Isabella studied him for a long moment. He was tall and lean and wore a snug suit jacket that accented his broad shoulders and narrow hips. Most men wore boxier-cut coats, but Diego's was especially tailored to fit him like a glove. Even the dusty-blue color was one that seemed designed for him alone. She'd never seen such a color on any other man.

The corner of his lip rose slightly as his gaze met hers. He no doubt knew that she was admiring him, and she knew he loved her attention. Isabella smiled and looked away. He was the handsomest man she had ever known, and she was delighted by the prospect of marrying him.

The steam train rolled past them, coming to a stop with the passenger cars lined up against the platform. The private car, however, was at the tail end, requiring Isabella and Lupe to descend the platform and walk to the back of the train.

"They could at least pull up far enough for our car to be at the platform," Isabella said in disgust. She hated that she would have to risk her new wheat-colored silk traveling suit by walking along the tracks. She certainly didn't want soot stains on the delicate, expensive material. She kissed her aunt. "I'll return as soon as possible."

Her aunt nodded but seemed to lack her usual enthusiasm.

"Remember, I shall come to be with you. I'm excited to see your father again. Your mother too."

Isabella nodded.

The conductor approached. "Are you Miss Garcia?"

"I am." She looked at the older man with a raised brow, questioning his interruption.

"I will escort you to your private car. Everything is in order and awaits you. I believe you will find yourself quite comfortable."

"That remains to be seen, of course." She looked at Diego. "I will eagerly count the days until we are together."

"As will I, *mi amor*."

She smiled and gave a slight nod, then looked at the conductor. "Please lead the way."

He offered her his arm as they headed down the platform stairs toward the tracks. "The ground is a bit uneven."

She took hold of him, carefully lifting her skirts to keep them from the ground. They reached the car, where a porter already waited with a small step to aid Isabella and Lupe in climbing onto the stairs of the train car. It was awkward, but there seemed to be no other choice.

Isabella mounted the stairs and made her way inside the private car. It was impressive, to say the least. Highly polished paneled wood lined the narrow corridor from the entrance into the grand salon, where expensive mahogany furnishings reflected the glow of lamplight. The shades and velvet draperies had been pulled to allow for absolute privacy—something Isabella appreciated greatly.

"There's a pitcher of iced lemonade on the table," the conductor declared. "A porter will look after you. He'll check in with you every hour on the hour."

"It's all very lovely. I believe we shall be quite comfortable."

The door behind her opened, but Isabella ignored it. No doubt it was the porter, just as the conductor had said.

But in a moment, everything changed. A scent filled the air. She knew that scent. Musky and sweet. It seemed to come with less-than-happy memories, but she couldn't place it. At least not until the man behind her spoke.

"Miss Garcia, it has been a long time."

She turned to find Aaron Bailey smiling at her. He was much handsomer than she remembered from their first encounter. His brown hair was parted on the side and slicked back. Had he always worn it thus? She tried to remember that day in the library. He'd seemed like such a boy then.

"Mr. Bailey, I believe."

"You believe correctly. I am your father's choice of escort for you." He gave her a crooked smile as if amused.

She refused to react. "I'm not sure why he felt the need to send you, Mr. Bailey, but since you are here, you might help Lupe with the bags." She nodded toward her maid.

Aaron didn't hesitate. "Here, let me take those, Lupe. They're much too heavy for one so small." He gave her a broad smile, which irritated Isabella. "Let me show you the bedrooms." He took the bags and moved across the room to a polished wooden door and opened it. "This is the larger of the two rooms, so I presume it will be taken by your mistress."

"*Sí.*" Lupe nodded.

"The other room," he said, moving to the opposite end of the car, "will be yours. It's small but very cozy."

Lupe looked inside and smiled. "It is very nice."

"Which of the bags belongs to you?" he asked.

She pointed, and he placed the bag inside her room. Without further ado, he walked to the larger bedroom and deposited the other things. He approached Isabella just as the conductor announced they were departing the station.

"I will share your company here during the day and evening hours, but I have a berth in the next car for sleeping. It's the last berth and gives me the ability to keep others from pestering you."

"Yes, but who will keep *you* from pestering me, Mr. Bailey?" Isabella's tone was sarcastic, but she didn't care. Aaron Bailey was the last man in the world she wanted hanging around.

Outside, she could hear the conductor calling "all aboard," and she went to take a seat on the plush throne chair by the window. She felt like a queen taking her place at court as Aaron gazed down at her. She pushed back the draperies and raised the shade.

"Comfortable?" he asked.

"Very." She pulled off her gloves as the train gave a little jerk and began to move slowly away from the station. She waved to her aunt and Diego as her car passed the platform. If only Diego were the one accompanying her. If only it could be anyone but Aaron Bailey.

Aaron took a seat opposite Isabella while Lupe occupied herself with unpacking. The train picked up speed, and they soon left any hint of the city behind as the train moved out across vast open land of farms, ranches, and empty fields.

The job of escorting Isabella to Silver Veil wasn't a task he had wanted. He worked for the Santa Fe Railroad, after all, not Daniel Garcia. But when her father asked him to do it, he'd been with the railroad superintendent, who had replied on Aaron's behalf that he'd be happy to do the job and the Santa Fe would be happy to give him the loan of a spacious private car in which to afford Isabella the finest of comforts.

Daniel Garcia was important to the railroad. Not only for all the business he gave the railroad in Silver Veil and a dozen other locations, but also for the stock he held in the railroad. Garcia had made a name for himself and was highly esteemed by the men who controlled the Santa Fe. He was esteemed by others as well. Even the soon-to-be governor of the state and other politicians knew Garcia and respected his opinions and generosity to their projects.

Ever since meeting Daniel years ago, Aaron had admired and liked him as well. Daniel Garcia was smart and industrious, but it was more than that. He was a godly man who lived his faith. When someone was down on their luck, Garcia offered them help and employment. Aaron had seen him put former convicts to work and help them turn their lives around until they became respected members of the community. He was willing to take chances on people, even when everyone else had given up. Aaron had never known anyone with such a sense of kindness and encouragement. Many times he'd advised Aaron and helped see him through a difficult decision. It gave Aaron the utmost respect for him.

It seemed a pity his selfish, self-seeking daughter had to return at this time. For the last few years, she'd lived with her aunt, and although Aaron knew Garcia missed his child, at least there had been peace in the household. Now, Aaron could only imagine there would be change.

"I presume you work closely with my father," she said, breaking the silence, "or he'd never have sent you to protect me on this trip."

Aaron glanced up to find Isabella watching him intently. "I do. I work for the Santa Fe Railroad on the spur leases, and your father, as you probably know, has several. We've become good friends over the years."

"How nice for you both." She turned to look out the

window. "But I hardly need an escort. I'm an adult who is fully capable of seeing to my own safety. I even carry a gun." She looked back at him with a slight smile. "Does that shock you?"

"Not in the least."

She seemed to consider this, but he couldn't tell if she was annoyed or content with his answer. "Well, just so you know."

He chuckled without meaning to. "Is that some sort of warning?"

Her dark eyes narrowed. "Call it what you will."

Aaron nodded and stretched out his legs to cross them at the ankles. He had been about to make a snide comment, then decided against it. He hadn't come here to make war. It was only fair that he give her the benefit of the doubt. After all, seven and a half years was a long time—more than enough time to change from being selfish and mean-spirited to a woman of kindness and grace.

"Have you enjoyed your time in California? I recall that it was home to you at one point."

She looked wary but nodded. "I grew up there on my great-grandfather's estate. It has always been home to me, even after Father insisted on dragging us all to Silver Veil."

"Silver Veil has become quite the town. You haven't been home in nearly five years, as I understand it. A lot has changed there. Your father has been quite industrious."

"I'm sure he has. It has always been his goal to see the town flourish. Silver Veil, along with other small mining towns, is all he cares about."

So much for her having changed.

"Hardly." Aaron couldn't let her get away with that. "He cares deeply about you and your mother."

"What would you know about that?"

Aaron straightened in his chair. "Your father and I have become quite close. Why do you suppose he would send me to bring you back? He trusts me and knows my heart in matters of importance. He's been a good and godly mentor to me."

"Have you no father of your own?"

"I do, but my parents are in Chicago, and your father is close at hand. I believe God knew I would need a friend and mentor and supplied one in your father."

"And my father's wealth isn't a motivating aspect of the friendship?" Her tone was snide and dripped with unspoken accusation as she fixed him with a hard stare.

Aaron shook his head. "Given that my father could buy and sell your father many times over, and that I have an ample savings set up for me by my grandfather, I don't believe the aspect of money ever entered my mind."

She turned to look out the window once again. "You can hardly fault me for protecting my family."

"No, I fault you for not caring enough even to know your family."

Her head snapped back to meet his calm gaze. He had known she would react, and maybe he wanted her to. He had listened all these years to Daniel Garcia's longing for a closer relationship with his only child, never speaking a word against her. Now seemed the perfect time to take her to task for her lacking. It was Aaron's utmost desire to see that she had a change of heart before reaching Silver Veil. Daniel and Helena Garcia deserved better than the heartless, spoiled child they had raised.

"You have no right to speak to me that way. You don't know me."

"I know you better than you think. Your father has been quite forthright in sharing his heartache over you."

19

"I'm sure he's told you all sorts of horrible things about me."

"I didn't say that. In fact, he has only spoken good of you. You and your mother are the most important people in the world to him, and he loves you without reproach."

His words seemed momentarily to silence Isabella, though she continued to fix him with a hard stare. Her harshness didn't bother him in the least.

"I had hoped perhaps the years had changed you—grown you up to see the needs of others," he said.

She opened her mouth to speak, then rolled her eyes and returned her gaze out the window.

Aaron found his irritation with her growing. "Your father isn't healthy. He's been sick for a long time—not that I expect you to know that—but lately it's much worse. You rarely write to them, even though I know your mother sends letters weekly. And, of course, you haven't been back to visit in some time."

"He's always ailed with one thing or another. It's just his weak constitution. My mother said nothing about him being sicker. I think you must be mistaken."

"She wouldn't say such a thing in a letter. Your mother is a compassionate and loving woman. She wouldn't want to worry you."

"But you, on the other hand, don't seem to mind at all."

"I believe in telling the truth. Not only that, but it's something I feel you should know."

Isabella toyed with her gloves. "What is it you hope to accomplish, Mr. Bailey?" She met his eyes. "If it's your desire to shame me, I refuse to be moved. I made my choice long ago, and I do not regret it. I love my parents, but I also love my aunt and my life in California. I see nothing to feel ashamed of or guilty for."

"I'm sure you don't." He shook his head. "You see only what you want to see, Miss Garcia. I knew that even all those years ago, when you acted so heartlessly toward your father."

"Me? Heartless? It was he who showed no compassion. He ripped me away from all I loved as a child. Took me from my friends and family. My beloved grandmother, and aunt, and so many others." She grew thoughtful. "I was ten years old and didn't understand why I had to leave all that I knew and loved. No one consulted me. No one asked me how I felt. He took us from our home and plopped us down in the middle of the desert, where there weren't any other children or family members save him and my mother. I was afraid and alone." She frowned. "But I don't expect you to understand. You know so much more than anyone else about my family and about me. Go right on judging me to be a heartless woman, Mr. Bailey. I simply do not care what you think."

She got to her feet and took an unsteady step against the rocking of the railcar. She grabbed the back of the chair even as Aaron reached up to offer her a hand. Of course, she wanted nothing to do with him and headed for the bedroom.

At the door, she turned. "I do care about one thing. I wish you would stop wearing that ghastly cologne. It gives me a headache."

With that, she was gone, and Aaron was left to sit and wonder if he had falsely judged her. He knew how much she'd hurt her parents, even if they didn't talk about it. The effects were there, nevertheless. Perhaps, on Isabella's part, it was unintentional. Maybe she was coping with her own pain as best she could and had no desire to hurt her folks.

But even if she hadn't meant to hurt them, she had. Aaron couldn't just forget that. Daniel Garcia was dying, and the only thing he wanted was to be reconciled to his daughter before he left this world. And Aaron meant to see it happen. He owed it to Daniel, and he would do his best to see it through, no matter the cost to himself.

Isabella sat on the edge of her bed, considering all that Aaron Bailey had said. The scent of his cologne still hung in the air. She didn't really hate it. She hated what it represented—embarrassment that he'd overheard that argument so long ago, that he knew her heart then and even now.

She hadn't thought about her mother and father or their needs in some time. She hadn't wanted to know how they were doing or what projects they were working on. She hadn't wanted to care about them for fear of what that might mean to her.

"It's not because I'm selfish," she murmured to herself, unpinning her hat. It wasn't selfishness or a lack of caring that drove her. Although some—like Aaron—might suppose it to be so.

She put the hat on the small ledge at the foot of the bed. Her pent-up emotions threatened to spill over. Her eyes dampened. She wasn't a bad person. She wasn't.

Isabella had spent a good portion of her life putting up walls of protection—barriers that created strongholds so she could never be hurt again, like she was when her father took them away from California.

He had never understood her pain and suffering. He had never cared about her little-girl feelings. Losing her grandparents, her playmates, and her pets. Oh, how she had cried to lose her horse, Lucy, and her dog, Mini, who had just had puppies. She had cried in her grandmother's arms, begging her to make Papi change his mind. But he hadn't, and shortly after their departure, her beloved grandmother had died.

Grandfather died a year later, leaving only Aunt Josephina at the ranch. At least her aunt had felt sorry for Isabella and shipped Lucy to New Mexico to be with her.

Then, when Isabella was sixteen, her aunt had invited her to spend the summer in California. Isabella had been so grateful that someone cared about her longing to go home. Silver Veil had never been home, despite the beautiful house her father had built.

Her parents were less than enthusiastic but finally gave in. The woman who had tutored Isabella in music, Mrs. Sanborn, had acted as her escort and traveled with her to California, where she, too, had family. Mama and Papi hadn't even made the time to go with her, and for reasons she couldn't explain, that reopened old wounds.

Being back in California had thrilled Isabella, but things were never the same. She was eventually able to convince her father to let her live there full-time, but even Diego's growing interest didn't make things right. She blamed her father. It was his fault she no longer had her grandparents. His fault that nothing was the same. Why did everything and everyone she had ever loved have to be taken away from her? The things and people of the past were all gone. Her parents had changed, and so had she.

Some would argue that her feeling of losing her parents was by her own hand, but they were the cause of her pain, and she wanted as little to do with them as possible. They hadn't cared about her pain—had never even talked to her about why they had chosen to move to the desert. To Isabella it was clear that they simply didn't care about her feelings, so why should she care about theirs?

She unfastened the buttons of her jacket and eased out of it. The room was a little stuffy, even hot, yet there was no possibility of returning to the main salon without having to deal with Aaron Bailey. She was determined not to do that. Instead, she set the jacket aside and stretched out atop the covers of the bed. With any luck, she might fall asleep and awaken to find this was all just a bad dream.

She smiled, imagining Christmas at the estate, with Aunt Josephina lighting candles on the tree while she and Diego took turns playing the piano. He would sing Christmas carols in his wonderful baritone voice, and Isabella and Auntie would join in. Before long, dinner would be announced, and they would go in and find the table decorated for the season, candles lit to reflect the green garland and gold ribbons that trimmed the room. There would be a veritable feast on the table, with silver, crystal, and china atop Aunt Josephina's best linens.

Isabella sighed. "It would have been so perfect."

2

Aaron spent a restless night in his berth. He kept thinking of Isabella and how beautiful she was—at least on the outside. Her black hair had been carefully arranged for the trip, and her traveling costume displayed her figure perfectly. She reminded him of a statue he'd once seen—a Greek goddess in white marble. It seemed Isabella was just as cold and hard, but also as beautiful. Still, what good was beauty on the outside if there was none on the inside?

He spent time in prayer, seeking God's direction and understanding. He wanted to treat Isabella Garcia with kindness and not just heap coals on her head. After all, she wasn't really the enemy Romans 12 spoke of. That portion of the Bible told him to be at peace with her—to be generous. That was asking a lot. She had caused so much pain for Daniel and Helena Garcia. They didn't have to speak a single word about it. Their feelings were clear in the expressions they sometimes wore on their faces. She was their entire world, and she had left them to muddle through without her, not even bothering to send regular correspondence.

Her absence had left a hole in their hearts and lives, and she didn't care. Or did she? He wanted to think kindly of her. He wanted to do the right thing by her, but nothing about her offered him hope that she cared about anything other than herself.

The train car began to stir to life around him, and Aaron knew he needed to start his day. He made his way to the bathroom and washed up, combed his hair, and considered his clothes. The porter had arranged for his suit to be brushed the night before and his clean shirt to be ironed. They looked amazingly refreshed. He'd have to tip the man extra.

He dressed quickly, then put away his sleeping clothes and tucked the blanket in under the mattress. Certain there was nothing else to delay his joining Miss Garcia, Aaron made his way to the private train car just as the porter was exiting.

"Good morning, sir. I just took the ladies' breakfast orders. Will you be joining them?"

"Yes. Thank you. Bring me eggs and ham, toast, and plenty of butter." Aaron smiled, and the porter did likewise. "Oh, and coffee, please." He reached into his suit and pulled out his wallet. He handed the black man several bills. "You did a remarkable job on this suit. Thank you."

"You are welcome, sir. The Santa Fe aims to please."

Aaron nodded. "I know they do, but you went above and beyond, and I appreciate the effort."

The porter took the money and disappeared down the sleeping car, humming.

Aaron stepped into the private car, determined to have a better time of it with Isabella. No doubt her attitude was difficult due to leaving behind the people she cared for. There had been a man at the station to see her off. The two seemed quite intimate. Perhaps he was a fiancé? And, of course, there was Isabella's beloved aunt. It was bound to be hard to say good-bye. Still, she should care about her parents as well. Where were her feelings for them? They sat silent in their pain, longing for a child who wanted nothing to do with them.

But perhaps she had no idea. What if they'd never said a word to Isabella about their desire to have her back? What if she thought they were as content to have her gone as she was to be absent? Maybe her parents were just as silent with Isabella as they were with Aaron.

"Good morning, Mr. Bailey," Lupe declared, coming from Isabella's room. "Miss Garcia will join you shortly."

"Good morning, Lupe. Did you sleep well?"

She giggled. "I did. I've never slept on a train bed. It was like being rocked in my mama's arms."

"With an occasional jolt that threatened to throw you to the floor, eh?" He smiled at the younger woman, who seemed hardly more than a girl.

"Yes!" She nodded with enthusiasm. "It is true."

"And Miss Garcia, did she sleep well?"

"I did." Isabella swept across the room to the dining table that had already been arranged for breakfast. Orange juice had been delivered to three places. Isabella took a seat and frowned. "I hardly need three glasses of juice."

"I believe the porter presumed we would all share this table." Aaron gave her no chance to argue as he pulled out a chair for Lupe. "Have a seat."

"Oh no, I will eat in my room," Lupe declared.

Isabella picked up her napkin. "At least someone knows their place."

"There's no reason she should have to balance a tray on

her bed," Aaron said. "This table is more than ample for all of us. Lupe, have a seat."

She looked hesitant, but finally Isabella gave a curt nod, and the young woman sat. Aaron slid her chair up to the table, then took his own seat.

"Looks like a lovely day." He motioned toward the desert landscape out the window.

The porter chose that moment to appear with a cart full of food. He positioned the covered plates quickly, then pulled the silver lids from each. Next he put racks of toast on the table, along with plenty of butter, just as Aaron had requested.

"If there's anything else I can be gettin' you, just say so. The name is Abraham." The porter poured coffee for each person.

"A fine name indeed," Aaron declared. "This breakfast looks fit for a king." Along with the eggs and ham he'd requested, there was a side of fresh fruit. It looked most appealing.

Isabella said nothing. She waited until Abraham had taken the cart and gone before picking up her fork.

"Might I offer grace?" Aaron saw the question had taken her by surprise. The look on her face even seemed a little embarrassed.

"Of course." She put her fork down and bowed her head.

Aaron prayed blessings on the food and on their trip, then added special prayers for Isabella's parents and aunt. When he concluded, Lupe murmured *amen*, but Isabella remained silent. She stared at her food for a moment, then reached for the cream. She stirred a generous amount into her coffee, then put the small pitcher aside and reached for the sugar.

Aaron took a sip of his coffee black. He preferred it

that way and knew from the way the Santa Fe had set up their arrangements with the Harvey Houses that the coffee would taste the same all along the railroad. They shipped the water in special tanker cars from back east in order to keep the flavor free of the minerals that were so prevalent in the West.

"Good coffee," he commented.

Isabella had already moved on to her food. Aaron had to smile. She'd ordered the same thing he had. He thought about commenting on it but figured she'd stop eating and order something different if he did.

Between bites of ham and eggs, Aaron allowed himself to glance at the beautiful young woman who graced his table. She was stunning—a real beauty. Her black hair and eyes were reminders of her father's Mexican heritage. She had chosen to wear a salmon-colored skirt and coat with an ivory lace blouse that she'd trimmed with a cameo at the neck. The color suited her complexion perfectly. She was perfection.

"Is there a reason you're staring at me? Have I left food on my lapel?" Her right brow arched ever so slightly.

"I was actually considering whether you looked more like your mother or your father."

She shrugged. "I favor my father's mother, if you must know. There is a painting of her at the house in California that strangers presume is me."

Uncertain what else to say, Aaron slathered butter on his toast. He wondered what he might discuss without causing her to become angry. Should he focus on the house in California, or would that only make her melancholy? Should he ask about the young man who saw her off at the station? Perhaps tell her about his job with the Santa Fe? Nothing seemed exactly right, so he said nothing.

Lupe excused herself to see to some laundry, leaving Aaron and Isabella alone. Aaron thought he heard Isabella sigh.

"Are you all right?"

"I am. Why do you ask?"

"I thought you sighed."

"I did, but it was no signal to you that something was wrong."

"I see." Aaron shrugged. "I suppose a person can sigh for no reason, but generally something prompts it."

Isabella placed her napkin on the table. "Even if there were, I wouldn't mention it to you."

"Why not? Your father sent me to see to your needs."

"Then return me to California, for that is where I need to be." She looked at him for a moment, then gave her own shrug. "You see? You cannot aid me in this matter. I long for home."

"Is Silver Veil not home as well? After all, that's where your parents are located, and if I'm correct in my mathematics, you lived there longer than you have in California."

"Physical presence doesn't always constitute where one's heart resides, Mr. Bailey." She reached for the pot of coffee. "Would you care for more?"

He nodded and extended his cup. Isabella poured until the cup was full, then did the same for herself, stopping about an inch from the top. Once again, she added a lot of cream and some sugar.

"Was there nothing about Silver Veil that you enjoyed?" He knew it was probably a dangerous question but found he couldn't resist.

Isabella surprised him with her answer. "I quite loved the house Father built. The adobe kept everything so nice and cool in the summer, and warm in the winter. I remember the

30

fireplace in the music room. I'm sure there will be a large fire to welcome me home."

"It is a very nice fireplace." He wanted to admit it was a favorite spot of his but figured it would only offend her.

The porter appeared with his cart and a smile from ear to ear. "I see you enjoyed your breakfast."

"We did, Abraham. It was just about the best I've had in some time," Aaron declared.

The porter gathered up the dishes, then brushed crumbs from the tablecloth before folding it up. He removed it from the table and disappeared out the door before anything more could be said. This seemed to be Isabella's cue to move back to her throne at the window. She rose gracefully, and Aaron got to his feet as well. He'd not show bad manners, even if she was difficult.

"Will you be spending every waking moment with me?" she asked, her voice edged with sarcasm.

"I suppose so. Your father asked it of me, and I did give him my word."

"Why?"

"Why what? Why did your father ask it of me? Or why did I give him my word?"

"I suppose I know why he asked it. Why did you feel the need to comply?"

Aaron pulled up a chair opposite her. "I respect him greatly. He's become a mentor to me and has taught me a great deal. Especially spiritually."

She nodded. "Father has always put great stock in his faith and the Bible."

"And what about you?" He braced himself for what he figured would be a rant that he had no right to question her about such things. Instead, she surprised him.

"My parents were always religious, so I grew up attending

church and learning all of the rules and ways of the faith. I know countless prayers and Scriptures." She gazed out the window. "I even believe Jesus died for my sins. What I don't believe is that God really cares about anything I have to say. My prayers have always gone unanswered."

"Why would God give his people a Savior but then refuse to listen to their prayers?"

She considered the question for a moment. "I don't know for certain, but being God of the universe, why should He care what I want or need?"

"As our Father, why *wouldn't* He care? Earthly fathers care about the needs of their children."

"Mine didn't," she said, meeting his gaze. She held up her hand to silence him. "I know you think the world of my father, Mr. Bailey. I understand you have affection for him—that he has been good to you. I suppose I should be happy for you, but instead I find it only compounds my own heartache. Then I remind myself that you didn't have to grow up with him denying you the only thing that ever mattered." She looked back out to the desert.

She sounded so sad that Aaron had little desire to berate her. He felt instead a strange desire to offer her comfort. He folded his hands and followed her gaze.

"My folks were also strong in their faith, but they were silent about it," he said. "They weren't the type to share their thoughts."

"Pity you aren't more like them," she said under her breath. Before Aaron could respond, she continued. "Why did my father really feel the need to send you to fetch me home? Did he fear I wouldn't come? Was he determined to make me feel like a child—to force his authority upon me?"

"I believe he wanted to make sure you weren't accosted. Women traveling alone, especially beautiful women, are often singled out for nefarious purposes. He told me he didn't want you to be alone in case there was trouble." Aaron shook his head. "I'm sure he doesn't know about the gun you carry."

She arched her right brow. "You sound rather upset with me. I asked a simple question."

"No, you and I both know there was far more implied."

Her dark eyes narrowed. "If there is so much danger, then why is he subjecting me to it at all? It seems he cannot care that much about me if he puts me in harm's way."

Aaron could see that convincing Isabella of her father's love was going to be impossible. He leaned back and crossed his arms. "I suppose he could have seen this as a way to get rid of you, but it seems much too questionable. Failure would be too easy, and there's no assurance that you would be eliminated. Furthermore, if he wished for you to be attacked and removed from his life, he most assuredly wouldn't have sent me to accompany you."

She looked momentarily surprised by his sharpness but quickly hid her feelings. "You're the one who said he cared so much. I'm simply pointing out the flaws in your logic."

"Yes, you seem quite good at pointing out everyone else's flaws. Everyone's but your own."

A knock sounded at the door, and the porter popped his head into the car. "We're coming into the station, and you might want to stretch a bit. We'll be here twenty minutes."

Isabella nodded. "I'd like that very much." She rose and headed toward Lupe's room. "Lupe, bring my parasol."

Aaron got to his feet and thanked the porter. Already the train was slowing and giving blasts of the whistle to announce its arrival. Isabella disappeared into her bedroom and returned wearing a coat and hat. She pulled on her gloves and cast a quick glance outside.

Lupe brought the parasol from her bedroom. Apparently there wasn't room to store all of Isabella's goods in one room. The maid crossed the room, extending the parasol to Isabella as the train came to a complete stop. The action nearly knocked the two women to the floor. Lupe reached out for Isabella to keep her from falling.

Once they were both stable, Lupe giggled. "I'm as bad as my uncle after a night of drinking. My feet know where they want to go, but the floor is unwilling to cooperate."

"No one asked for your opinion, Lupe." Isabella snatched the lacy parasol from her maid's hands.

Aaron smiled. "It will be good to be on solid ground, eh?"

"You needn't come with us." Isabella fixed him with a look that might have made a lesser man run for the door.

Aaron simply broadened his grin. "Of course I do. I promised your father I would see to your safety, and I intend to do so. But just remember, if you take your gun along, that I'm the good guy."

For a moment he thought she might argue with him, but instead she heaved a sigh and nodded. "Very well."

Diego Morales was the youngest of six Morales boys. He was also the only one who hadn't proven himself in their father's eyes. Maybe it was because he felt he had no hope of equaling his very successful brothers that Diego didn't even try. Maybe it was because he enjoyed the freedom that came with minimal concern over working. He much preferred the pleasure of a night at the gaming tables or in the company of a willing woman.

Still, his lack of progress and his upcoming thirty-fifth birthday on the twenty-ninth of the month were hanging over his head like the sword of Damocles. Even now he awaited his father, who would no doubt give him another lecture regarding his failings.

As if on cue, the door opened, and his father marched into the room with his secretary following close behind, taking down each of Esteban Morales's instructions.

"Get that letter off to Simon Davenport immediately."

"Yes, sir." The secretary wrote in his book and nodded.

"And check with Mrs. Morales regarding the party she plans for the New Year."

"Yes, sir."

"I'm sure she'll need you to arrange for extra servants."

"Yes, sir."

Diego's father caught sight of him and stopped. "That will be all, Marcus."

The secretary quickly turned and disappeared from the room, saying nothing. Diego thought it rather amusing how fast people could move in order to get away from his father.

"Good morning, Father." Diego remained in place, awaiting his father's instructions.

"Sit down. We need to talk."

Diego nodded and headed for the nearest chair. Once he'd settled, he looked up to find his father watching him. It was almost as if he were judging whether or not Diego was worth the time and effort.

"Son, you have disappointed me in your failure to secure a position that earns you a living and improves the Morales name."

"It seems our name needs no improvement. We are heralded as one of the wealthiest families in the area, as well as generous and trustworthy."

"Yes, but that didn't come about by playing cards every night and taking loose women to our beds. Diego, your brothers have all done well for themselves and this family. There is no excuse for you to do anything less. Any one of your brothers would happily take you under their wing and involve you in their industry. Even Miguel would be happy for your help here with the horses."

"I don't want to be under my brother's wing." Diego toyed with a piece of lint on his custom-made suit. "Besides, you know I intend to marry Isabella Garcia. She is worth a fortune, and I will be needed to manage her accounts and invest her money wisely. I have been studying a variety of investments and have even put some of my own money into various accounts to see what performs best."

His father shook his head. "Her father will never approve the marriage."

"She's twenty-five and hardly needs his approval. As I understand it, she will inherit her grandparents' money when she marries, so she will be a wealthy woman. There is nothing her father can do to stop that."

"And where do you suppose you will live?"

"Most likely with her aunt. Isabella loves her quite dearly, and I would not separate them."

"I see. So you have thought this all through." His father shook his head. "Are you such a waste of a man that you are willing to live off your wife's fortune without having any accomplishments of your own? I find that shameful and disgusting. My son is better than that."

Diego had heard it all before. Since he turned twelve, his father had pounded it into his head that he expected great things from his youngest son, just as he did from the elder five. The others had made good. Miguel helped run the ranch and raised racehorses. He had come up with many innovative ideas and had managed to double the ranch's value in the last ten years. Two of Diego's brothers were lawyers, and one owned several banks. The next-to-last brother, who was just two years Diego's senior, was already wealthier than all the others through his ownership of railroad and shipping stock. He was known throughout California and highly sought after for new investments in transportation. How could Diego ever hope to top that?

"It will take a great deal of skill and intellect to advance Isabella's fortune. I believe I can do so, and in doing that make a name for myself in investments."

"And how will you do that? At the gambling table? You are seldom anywhere else." His father shook his head. "I am finished with these games. You will be thirty-five years old on the twenty-ninth of December. You have until then to show me some step forward—some reason to believe you are worthy of being a member of this family. If not, I will disinherit you and put you from this house."

Diego froze, hardly able to believe what he was hearing. "And Mama has agreed to this?"

"She doesn't yet know about it, but she knows the possibility exists. Not only that, but she will adhere to whatever I say. Just as you should have long ago."

Diego had never hated his father more than in that moment. Esteban Morales had always expected far too much of his offspring—especially from Diego.

"I don't know how you expect me to make a fortune in less than two weeks."

"I don't. I only expect to see something that proves you are moving forward. Secure a position with one of your brothers. Come to work for me. Prove yourself to be a man, and you may remain in this family. Do nothing, and you will be put from our home."

With that, his father stalked out of the room. Diego stared after the old man. It was all he could do not to follow him and beat him to a pulp. He wanted proof that Diego was a man—well, that would certainly show him.

Diego clenched his hands and jaw, as he often did when things weren't going his way. He wished he'd proposed to Isabella before she'd headed east. He'd meant to. He'd been planning to ask her since she turned twenty-five. The understanding was there, just not the formality. He even had a ring. His mother had given him one of his grandmother's emerald rings. It would make a perfect engagement ring. So why hadn't he asked Isabella to marry him?

He shrugged. He enjoyed being single. He liked the freedom it allowed him. He had toyed with half a dozen young ladies from decent families up and down the coast of California. He even had a child or two among women of loose morals. They had no expectations of him, however. They were those kinds of women, and they knew he was that kind of man. There was no pretense. Diego gave them money from time to time but never anything more, and certainly no promises of love or marriage. No. He would marry Isabella Garcia. She was completely head over heels in love with him, and he found her more than tolerable. She was a great beauty, and all of his friends thought him lucky to be in the position to marry her and take over her fortune.

He smiled to himself. He would speak with her aunt about the situation and make plans for a wedding as soon as possible after Isabella returned from New Mexico.

3

SILVER VEIL, NEW MEXICO TERRITORY

Silver Veil, New Mexico, was nestled in the San Mateo Mountains. The first time her father had seen it was when an old Mexican miner had taken him there to talk about silver. Neither Isabella nor her mother had gone on that trip, but when her father returned to California, he was full of stories about the dry air, the haunting beauty of the desolate landscape, and the possibility of wealth beyond their wildest dreams.

Isabella had never known her father to be overly concerned with making money. After all, the Garcia family had old money that went clear back to Spain. There was never any reason to worry about the family's ability to live a life of plenty, and for that, Isabella had always been thankful. It was perhaps the only reason her family didn't suffer as much humiliation and ostracism as one could expect for a people of darker skin. Her father was sometimes snubbed by white men who knew nothing about his holdings, but once they learned who he was, men of every color offered respect. It was absurd what hypocrites people could be.

Complicating their life even more was the fact that her

father had married a white woman whose parents were completely unaccepting of the situation. Growing up, Isabella had often asked about her maternal grandparents, only to be told they were unwilling to be a part of the family. How did one just erase a person or persons from existence? Even in her desire to live elsewhere, Isabella had maintained a relationship with her parents, tenuous though it may be. While it was true she had seldom written to her mother and father, she had always cared about them. She loved them, however mixed up that emotion might be with resentment and disdain.

Her parents were waiting at the train station just as Isabella had known they'd be. They both looked older—tired and maybe even thinner. Hadn't Aaron Bailey mentioned something about her father being ill? She'd have to ask later.

She stepped from the private railcar and marveled at the way her parents' faces transformed at the sight of her. They were clearly delighted to have her home, and why not? She was their only child. Isabella had to admit she was happy to see them as well. It had been far too long.

"Mama. Papi." She embraced them, and they wrapped her in their arms. The day was quite chilly, and their embrace felt good. Isabella clung to them a little longer than she might otherwise have done. For warmth, she told herself.

"It's so wonderful to have you here," her mother said. There were tears in her eyes as she pulled away. "I've missed you so much."

"As have I," her father declared. He stepped back and looked at Aaron Bailey. "Thank you for bringing her home safely."

"My pleasure," Aaron replied, casting a momentary glance her way. They both knew it had been anything but.

They climbed into her father's carriage and made their

way up the mountainside to where the Garcia house sat like a beacon over the town. The orange adobe had faded to a washed-out coral color, but it was still a stunning house.

"Did you notice how the town has grown?" her mother asked. "It's twice, perhaps three times as big as when you left."

Isabella nodded. "It did seem much larger."

"We have three churches and two doctors. Your father arranged for them to share a small hospital for the sick and injured. They have beds for ten people."

"I'm sure that offers much relief to the townsfolk."

Her mother smiled. "It does. It's a wonderful comfort to know that you have help for such a crisis. Last year there was a collapse in one of the tunnels, and four men were injured. They all lived, but I'm convinced if we'd not had the hospital and our dear doctors, they would have perished."

Isabella looked at the passing scenery. The road was much easier to travel than she remembered. No doubt her father had arranged for that as well.

"Our church has a wonderful ladies' group. We do charitable works, and I can hardly wait to introduce you to the women there. Some you will remember. This month we're making blankets for the poor. You can help us."

"I know nothing about making blankets," Isabella replied, shaking her head. "I'm sure it would be best if I did not lend my hand."

"You will learn," her mother replied. "It's quite easy."

They reached the house, and Isabella had a moment of genuine nostalgia. The desert landscaping was beautiful and carefully tended. Of course, it was December, and snow was always a possibility, but it was lovely all the same.

"Your things will be along shortly, I'm sure," her father said, handing the lines to one of his servants. He liked to drive his own carriage but was more than happy to turn it over to someone else to put away. "Aaron was very kind to offer to bring them. I trust he was a good companion on your trip east."

"I was hardly in need of a traveling companion. I had Lupe." Isabella nodded to her maid.

"Yes, but there are always possible dangers for a beautiful young woman traveling alone. I wanted to give myself peace of mind regarding your safety. You wouldn't fault me for that, would you?"

Isabella didn't wish to start fighting. Not when she intended to announce her plans to marry Diego Morales at dinner that evening. "No, Papi. I will not fault you."

"I'm sure you'll want to rest before dinner," her mother said as they moved toward the cobblestone walk. "I have your room ready for you. There are fresh towels and a basin of water if you wish to wash your face."

"I long for a bath. The facilities on the train, even in a private car, were less than satisfactory."

"I'll have the maid draw a bath for you," her mother replied.

They stepped into the house, and Isabella smiled at the scents. They instantly brought back memories. There was something about the aromas here that wasn't present in her California home. Mesquite wood burned in the fireplace, for one. Aunt Josephina preferred eucalyptus for her fires. Where mesquite was a warm, earthy scent, eucalyptus was lighter and almost minty.

Here, her mother and the household staff made wonderful sauces out of various chili peppers. Isabella remembered the house always smelling of spices, just as it did now. There was something comforting about it.

Her bedroom in the east wing of the house was large and

luxurious. Her mother had always given her almost anything she wanted, and Isabella was pleased to find things had remained as she'd left them.

The large four-poster bed was a welcome sight after the narrow and hard berth on the train. Even though the furnishings were better in the private car than what she might have found elsewhere on the train, Isabella was looking forward to sleeping in a real bed.

"This room is very beautiful," Lupe said, her voice betraying her awe.

"There is a room for you, just over there through that door. You'll find there is also a large dressing room and closet for my things."

Lupe nodded and went in search. Isabella heard her give a squeal of delight. "It is very beautiful," the maid called back to her.

Normally Isabella would have reprimanded her reaction, but the place did impress. She smiled to herself and unpinned her hat. Now if she could only find a way to be happy for the next month.

After a hot bath and a nap, Isabella dressed for dinner. During her rest, Lupe and Maria, one of her mother's housemaids, had seen to refreshing her gowns. They had done an admirable job of steaming out the wrinkles and making everything look beautiful.

As Isabella checked out her choice of gowns in the large closet, she was surprised to find several new choices. Her mother had apparently arranged for them. Isabella studied each of the styles, amazed to find that she liked them very much. Her mother had somehow known what would appeal and had spared no expense. Isabella even recognized one of the gowns as a Worth creation.

It was this one Isabella chose for the evening. It was a blue-and-white watered silk. The main section of the gown was robin's-egg blue, while the sleeves and insets on the bodice were white trimmed in several inches of wispy lace so fine that it reminded Isabella of spiderwebs. The overskirt fell to just below the knee in a straight line, as was the fashion, while the underskirt was slightly flared and embroidered with pink rosettes.

"Lupe, I will wear this for supper. Isn't it stunning?"

The maid nodded. "I admired it earlier. The gold-colored gown is also divine. You will be a great beauty in it."

Isabella smiled. "Tonight I will wear this, and we will pin flowers at the waist and in my hair. Run and ask Maria if there are any pink flowers to be had from the hothouse. Something that might match the little rosettes."

"Sí, I will do that right now."

Lupe took off for the door while Isabella further explored the contents of the closet. To her surprise there were shawls, hats, gloves, and even shoes newly made for her use. The gifts touched her deeply. Her mother knew how important fashion was to Isabella. Looking her best had been the most important thing in the world since Isabella was sixteen. That her mother knew this and cared enough to see to her needs touched her.

It also caused a moment of shame. Here it was nearly Christmas, and Isabella had done very little for her parents. She had brought them each a gift, of course, but they weren't anything all that special. She had put very little effort or interest into choosing them, not really considering what her parents might like.

The thought bothered her more than she liked. It reminded

her of things Aaron had said about her being self-focused and selfish. He had accused her of not caring about anyone but herself. Was he right?

"Of course not," she declared to the closet full of beautiful things.

Aaron Bailey knows nothing about me or what I think and feel. He judges me because of one conversation held seven and a half years ago.

Her thoughts grew dark. Aaron treated her as if she were a terrible and thoughtless person, and all because she had no desire to live in Silver Veil. He couldn't understand the pain she had suffered as a child when she was torn from her home in California. The last few years living there again with Aunt Josephina had been her happiest. Why did that make her a terrible person?

"It doesn't," she murmured in a softer manner than her previous declaration.

She frowned. Aaron Bailey had caused her no end of grief. She could only hope—even pray—that he was gone and no longer an issue for her to deal with. She could easily manage the company of her parents for a month, but not if Aaron Bailey was a daily part of it. Surely no one would put that upon her.

But at supper, there he was in the parlor with her father. They were looking over some maps and discussing something intently when she entered the room. Both stopped, however, when they realized she had arrived.

Mama made her way over to Isabella, her own gown of forest green complementing her graying auburn hair. "My dear, you look so lovely. I just knew when I saw that gown that it would be perfect for you."

"Wherever did you find it?"

"A woman in town makes copies of Worth gowns and others. She's quite good, as you can see."

Isabella forced herself not to frown. It really shouldn't matter that some poor Mexican woman had replicated the dress. After all, she hadn't created the design—it was still the artistic creation of one of the impressive fashion houses. "I had Maria and Lupe arrange some flowers at the waist. Aren't they lovely?"

"I like them very much. The ones in your hair as well."

Isabella had fashioned her hair in a bun, then tied a white scarf across her head. Where she had knotted the scarf, Lupe had pinned additional flowers. "Thank you. And thank you for the closet full of presents."

Her mother smiled. "I knew those things would be most important to you." She leaned close. "If you look in the drawers, you will find some more personal articles."

Isabella nodded, but her mother's comment caused her a moment of embarrassment. *She had known those things would be most important to Isabella.* She pushed aside the feeling and turned as her father and Aaron joined them.

"You do look quite lovely," Papi said, leaning close to kiss her cheek. "You remind me so much of my mother. How I miss her smiling face and cheery heart."

"Mr. Bailey wondered who I favored, and I told him about Grandmother's painting at the family house. We had a party there for Aunt Josephina's birthday, and everyone thought the portrait was of me."

"You are the spitting image of her." Papi touched Isabella's cheek. "It's almost like having her with me again. Leaving her and Father in California was the hardest thing I've ever done."

Isabella wanted to ask why he had done it, then, if he felt that way, but Aaron was speaking. He looked at Isabella for an answer.

"What? I'm sorry, I didn't hear what you said."

"I said you look beautiful and that I wish I could have known your grandmother."

Isabella nodded, uncertain what to say or do. She felt a rush of multiple emotions, and none of them seemed willing to settle well with one another.

"She was a grand lady." Isabella managed the words in a clipped tone. She couldn't understand why she felt so confused.

"Dinner is served," an older man declared from the doorway.

Isabella didn't recognize him and looked to her mother in question. "Is he new?"

Her mother smiled. "He is. His name is Ruidoso."

"Noisy?"

Her father chuckled. "Indeed. He said when he was little that he was quite loud and always made more noise than the other children. His parents nicknamed him Ruidoso, and it stuck."

"He seems rather old for a butler."

"He is. He's eighty-four, but there is no other work for him, and he needs to make a living, so we hired him to come work for us a couple of years ago. He only works a few hours each day and then goes home to care for his six great-grandchildren. Their parents died from sickness when they were young, and he has assumed responsibility for them. The oldest, Alana, works here in the kitchen. She's the one who told us about her grandfather wanting work," her mother explained.

"He makes a very good butler when he's here," Papi added.

Isabella wasn't surprised by the story. Her parents had always helped out folks in need. As the silver mine had increased in production, her father had been good to hire newcomers, even giving convicts a job when they asked. He believed in second chances.

Mama took Papi's arm and allowed him to lead her to the dining room, leaving Aaron Bailey to extend his arm to Isabella. Reluctantly, she took it. He walked at a leisurely pace, giving her plenty of time to comment. Unfortunately, she felt there was nothing to say.

He assisted her into her chair, then claimed the place opposite her and remained standing until her father pulled out his chair to sit. At least he had good manners.

Her father offered grace and then motioned for the staff to serve the food. Isabella smiled at the various dishes, food that she had loved as a child. Her mother had apparently given a great deal of thought to her first night home.

"We didn't make any plans for tomorrow," her mother said as the conversation began on arrangements for the days to come. "We knew you would be tired from your trip. However, after that we have so many things going on. There is to be a great town Christmas celebration. The three churches have come together to work as one. Father Eduardo has a wonderful boys' choir and will lead the singing with their help. Pastor Tom from the Bible Church will do the Bible readings, and Reverend Shoal from the Methodist church will offer the Christmas sermon. There will be refreshments afterward, so we have much baking to do. I hope you will help."

Isabella nearly choked on her *pollo a la crema*. She dabbed her napkin to her lips, then took a long sip of water before trying to speak. "I can't bake. I know very little about cooking."

"It will come back to you," Mama said with a smile. "I remember you were very capable at making cookies when you were younger."

"But I haven't done that in years." Isabella glanced at Aaron, who watched her with a hint of a smile. No doubt he was judging her once again to be lacking in any quality that he might find admirable. She squared her shoulders and tried not to let such thoughts control her. "I will do what I can."

She had absolutely no desire to bake or work in the kitchen. That was something she would rather hire out, and once she married Diego, she would have a houseful of staff to do such things. Aunt Josephina kept very few workers, but Isabella already had plans to change that. They would host great parties all the time, and such endeavors would require the proper servants.

She caught Aaron watching her and felt as if he were reading her thoughts. She gave him a nod and returned her gaze to her food. Determined to steer the conversation away from the town's celebration, Isabella put down her fork.

"I know this may seem like a poor time for an announcement, especially since there is a guest at the table, but I find myself too excited to wait. I plan to marry Diego Morales."

Her mother dropped her fork, and it clattered against the china plate. Her father, however, fixed her with a hard look. "That I cannot allow."

Isabella felt as if he'd struck her. She had known they would need to be convinced, but she hadn't expected such a strong reaction from either of her parents.

"Papi, you have always said that you wanted me to marry for love, and I am in love with Diego. He has been a great help to Aunt Josephina and has been there to watch over us both. His father is someone you greatly admire—a good friend, as I recall."

"Yes, his father is a good friend. We correspond often, which is why I cannot allow you to marry Diego. He is not the man you believe him to be."

"He is a wonderful man. You simply do not know him. If you and Mama would come to California, you could get to know him and love him as a son." She smiled and glanced at Aaron. "Diego greatly admires you, Papi, and I know he would love to be mentored by you."

"He doesn't take his own father's direction. Why would he take mine?"

She had not expected any of this. "Perhaps we can speak of it later. I should probably have waited until we were alone, but I was just so excited."

"Has he proposed?" Papi asked, looking at her hand.

"No. But he plans to when I return." She had no proof of that but hoped it might convince her father of Diego's sincerity. "He had planned to propose on Christmas Eve, but you ordered me here."

"We invited you here," Mama said, reclaiming her fork.

"Well, he would have proposed on Christmas Eve had I remained in California," Isabella said with a shrug. "I cannot help that his plans were delayed. However, I assure you that it is what I want more than anything."

"I'm sorry," her father said, shaking his head. "I will never consent. Let us put the matter aside. It causes me great distress."

Isabella had only ever known her father to be this determined on a matter when he moved them to New Mexico and when he refused to let her live with her aunt when she turned eighteen. Isabella felt a sense of dread and confusion mingled together.

Why was he so adamant about Diego? What had Diego ever done to him?

4

The next week passed quickly, with Isabella doing whatever she could to avoid Aaron Bailey. It seemed wrong that he should be staying with them, but Mama had explained that Aaron always stayed with them when he was in town on business. This year he would be with them until Christmas Eve, and then he would head back to San Marcial. Isabella could hardly wait.

On Christmas Eve, Isabella attended the town party along with her parents. Thankfully, Aaron was nowhere in sight. She hoped that meant he had already headed back to San Marcial. She didn't really dislike him—it was just that he was an unpleasant reminder of her fight with Papi. She could admit to herself that she had been quite selfish and ill-tempered at eighteen. She had only cared about getting to California. She wanted never to return to New Mexico and didn't care what Papi wanted. Aaron had witnessed all of that, and she knew he remembered it. But she had changed and was a better person now. Even if she still wished to remain in California rather than conform to her father's desires. They all knew how she felt—especially Aaron—and every time she looked him in the eyes, she felt him pass judgment on her. It just wasn't right, and she didn't want to have to deal with him on this special day.

The Catholic church was the only one big enough for everyone to gather in, so folks set aside their own denominational choices and viewpoints and came to celebrate the birth of Christ as one body.

Isabella found herself very much enjoying the music. The church organist was quite gifted, as were the boys who made up the local choir. Twelve boys who appeared to range in age from ten to fourteen sang in perfect harmony. At one point, an angelic-faced boy stepped forward and sang a solo while accompanied by a lone guitar. "Silent Night" had never sounded so sweet. It was every bit as nice as she'd heard in much grander cathedrals, and for a short time, Isabella forgot about being stuck in Silver Veil.

Pastor Tom Cameron from the Bible Church read a mix of verses from the New and Old Testament. Isabella had heard most of them before, even though she had never paid much attention to any of them. The Bible was boring to her. It lacked any real excitement or interest for her daily life. As far as she was concerned, it was a book for scholars and religious leaders, but not for the common man.

Reverend Shoal finally took his place and began to speak about Mary and Joseph facing the huge responsibility of raising the Son of God. He spoke about how difficult it must have been for each of them to face this task God had put upon their shoulders. So difficult that an angel had to be sent to encourage them. Yet each was willing. He spoke about how each person in the congregation should be willing to take on the tasks God entrusted to them—that it was a trust and must be seen as one. He asked the congregation, "What task has God entrusted to you?"

Isabella pondered the question. She'd always considered

God disinterested in her life. Had He entrusted something to her, something that she had missed?

It seemed to go against everything she believed about God. Why would He need her help with anything? He was God. He could snap His fingers and make the world as He wanted it to be. He spoke and created the entire universe. Why would He need to entrust anything to a twenty-five-year-old woman in New Mexico?

Isabella saw that her parents were in complete agreement with the reverend, as they nodded from time to time. She knew they believed that God was an important part of their daily lives and that He cared intimately for each of His children. Isabella had a difficult time seeing or believing that. To her, God was as powerful and indifferent as her own father. He might care, as she was sure Papi did, that His children obey Him and not question His authority, but she couldn't see the love. Not since she was a little girl had she seen God's love as real.

Perhaps she didn't see her father's love either. He seemed only to think about things that were unimportant to Isabella. He had his own desires and plans, and none of them seemed to take Isabella and her desires into consideration. How could she see Papi or God as someone who wanted only the best for her when neither one even seemed to know what she wanted?

She remembered the terrible fight they'd had when she announced on her twenty-first birthday that she intended to go live with her aunt and never return to New Mexico. She told her parents that she had always hated that they'd taken her from the only place she felt was home. They suggested that home was made up of the people who loved each other as family, but Isabella had refused that idea. She had flatly countered that she loved them but hated Silver Veil and it would never be home to her.

The memory gave her a sense of regret that left her frowning. Why should that thought leave her feeling bad? After all, in the long run, she had won, and Papi had sent her away with his blessing.

"If you don't know what God is calling you to do," Reverend Shoal continued, "ask Him. He has a task for each of us, and He will equip you with the necessary wisdom to complete it. But you have to know what that task is. The first chapter of James tells us that if any of us lack wisdom, we may ask God for it, and He will give it. I encourage you to accept His gift of wisdom as well as the task He has appointed to you."

After the conclusion of the services, the congregation sang more Christmas songs, and brown paper sacks of candy and nuts were distributed to the children. How happy they seemed—so content with their little prize. Isabella wondered if she'd ever felt that carefree and content.

She remembered when she'd been gifted her horse, Lucy. It was such a glorious present, one that Isabella had desired but hadn't expected. How happy she had been. She remembered thinking there was no better gift in the world. That was the way these children responded to a much less costly prize. A thought pricked her heart: Could she have ever been as happy with so little?

Outside, people gathered around Isabella and her parents. The weather was mild but chilly, and the higher elevations had received a bit of snow. It seemed to add extra joy to the spirit of the celebration. Her father had closed the mine and given everyone the day off with pay, and it seemed other businesses had followed suit. What a strange place. Isabella couldn't imagine that happening back in California. The large cities couldn't function if everyone suddenly stopped working. But here, life was slower, less worrisome.

It was easy to see that the townsfolk were grateful to Isabella's parents. Not only was a town gift presented in their honor—two handmade park benches that would be placed on the plaza square as a memorial to their founding family—but small items were given by most everyone. The Garcias were greatly appreciated and loved, that much was clear.

Isabella watched as her parents dealt with their adoring fans. Most were indebted to her parents, and she had heard Mama say that as a Christmas gift, Papi had taken a certain percentage off what was owed to him by each person. No doubt that totaled in the hundreds, perhaps even thousands of dollars. To Isabella it seemed reckless, but at the same time, she could see the sincere gratitude felt by each person who benefitted. Her parents were absolutely loved, and why not? They had been generous to a fault with these people.

"You look troubled," Aaron Bailey said, coming to stand beside Isabella.

She glanced his way. "I'm not in the least troubled, Mr. Bailey."

"Then perhaps your frown was caused by something else?"

She gave him a smile. "Probably the fact that you are still in town."

He laughed out loud, causing several people to turn. He leaned toward her. "That will soon be remedied. I'm heading to San Marcial in a little while to check in with my office."

"Wonderful. Then I shall get to have my parents to myself. That is indeed a lovely Christmas gift."

"Pity you don't want them more often."

Her frown returned. "Safe travels, Mr. Bailey." She turned to go, then stopped. "And merry Christmas."

"Merry Christmas to you, Miss Garcia. I hope you truly appreciate what you have before it's too late."

She snapped around to ask what he meant by that, but Aaron was already several steps away and engulfed by a collection of children who appeared to adore him. She watched as they showed Aaron what was in their sacks. He laughed with them and rubbed their heads. Sometimes he offered a hug. He definitely seemed to be a very affectionate man.

"So why does he treat me so poorly?"

"Did you say something, Miss Isabella?" Lupe asked.

Isabella shook her head. "Nothing that mattered."

That evening Daniel Garcia lit the candles on the Christmas tree and thought of all the years he had celebrated Christmas. There had been happy gatherings when he was a child—entire tables full of goodies and sweets, stacks of gifts wrapped in plain paper but decorated in beautiful ribbons. His parents had been generous with the only two of their ten children who survived. Josephina was three years his junior, but they were as close as any siblings could be. How he missed her. He was so happy she planned to join them next week. He hadn't seen her in such a long while.

"The tree looks lovely," Helena said, coming into the room. "And wasn't the celebration perfect?"

He straightened and blew out his candle. "It was. I was just reflecting on that and other things." She came to him, and Daniel wrapped her in his arms. "This Christmas shall be the best yet. Even without Josephina here."

"But she'll be here in a few days. We could delay our celebration," his wife suggested, as she had on more than one occasion.

Daniel shook his head. "No, it is just as well to celebrate now. I'll be able to rest a little before she arrives."

Helena frowned. "Do you think Isabella has noticed your growing weakness?"

"I don't think so. She hardly notices anything much other than her clothes. She still seems so immature. How can I possibly hope she'll be able to learn about the family business? That is why it's imperative I convince Aaron to give up the Santa Fe and take over as my manager. Then I shall know for sure that you'll be cared for once I'm gone."

She smiled and touched his cheek. "We know God will care for me no matter what. I just wish you could remain with me."

Her eyes dampened, and Daniel touched his finger to her tear as it slipped down her cheek. "We agreed no tears. You'll have plenty of time to grieve once I'm gone." He wiped away the wetness. "We've had a good life, my love. Moving to this dry climate bought us extra time together. It's been perfect."

"Except for Isabella," Helena replied. Her voice was barely a whisper.

"It was our choice not to tell her about my health," Daniel countered. "Now the time has come that there is no choice."

"I hope she'll understand why we kept it from her."

"Even if she doesn't, we will get through this as we have everything else. We must."

She met his gaze and nodded. "I love you so much. I am so grateful for the extra time we've had, and just look at the town you've created. These people had nothing and came from far away to find Silver Veil because of your generosity."

He smiled. "Their hard work has made for the good life here. They will continue to work hard for their town even after I am gone, but I must put someone in place who will love them as we have."

"Aaron Bailey will," she assured him. "I know he will agree

to take on the job. I've prayed and prayed. I believe God will touch his heart."

Daniel nodded. "I will speak to him again after Christmas. The doctor seems confident that I have a few months yet. I will count on that and God's mercy. For now, however, I want to focus on Christmas and my dear family."

She leaned forward and pressed her lips to his. Daniel held her tight for several long moments. He had never loved anyone or anything as much as he loved this woman.

"So how was your trip to fetch the princess and bring her back to Silver Veil?" Aaron's best friend, Jim Jensen, asked.

They had agreed to meet at Jim's for a casual Christmas dinner, and Aaron was glad for the time away from work and the Garcia family.

"It went just about how I figured it would. She was as beautiful and spoiled as I remembered. She wasn't happy to be traveling back to Silver Veil, and she wasn't at all glad to see me."

"And you being so handsome and dapper." Jim chuckled and placed a roasted chicken on the table.

Aaron laughed. "I don't know about that, but if looks could kill, I would be dead about twenty times over."

Jim retrieved a couple of other bowls. One held boiled potatoes and the other what looked to be gravy. "I bought the chicken and the gravy from the Harvey House yesterday. I just warmed them up, so don't be thinking me some master cook."

Aaron nodded. "I figured as much. Hey, if it's edible, it's fine by me. Merry Christmas."

"And to you," Jim said, returning to his little kitchen. He

appeared once again, this time with sliced bread and a pie. "Got these there too. Now we have a feast."

"More than what I would have had at my place."

"But probably much less than if you'd remained with the Garcias. I'm surprised they didn't invite you to stay for Christmas."

"Who says they didn't?" Aaron shrugged. "I had no desire to be there any longer than I had to, however. Isabella Garcia is enough to take away any man's appetite."

"But you said she was beautiful."

"On the outside only. Her beauty is skin-deep and no more. Her heart is as hard as the rock her father mines."

"That's a pity." Jim took his seat. "You want to offer grace?"

"Sure." Aaron bowed his head. "Father, we thank you for the ability to come together to remember the gift you gave us—Jesus. We are very grateful for Him and His salvation. Please bless our families so far away and bless this food. In Jesus' name, amen."

"Amen." Jim pushed the platter of chicken toward Aaron. "Guests first."

Aaron laughed. "I've been here more than my own house lately. I'm almost a regular fixture."

"I'd say it's a toss-up between here and the Garcia house."

"How's it been at the stockyard?" Aaron asked, ignoring the inference. Jim was in charge of the local stockyard, overseeing the shipment of cattle and receipt of new stock.

"Quiet. Most of the shipments went out early. I think folks wanted to spend time with their families or maybe even travel for the holidays."

"I can understand that. I gave serious thought to heading up to Chicago to see my folks. However, I made promises to Mr. Garcia, and the railroad is determined that I see them through. He owns enough railroad stock and leases that the Santa Fe wants to keep him happy." Aaron helped himself to a leg and some breast meat off the chicken before passing it back to Jim.

"Seems to me you want him happy too."

Aaron nodded and reached for the potatoes. "Daniel is a good man and a dear friend. I've never met anyone better. Even my father could learn things from him. The way Garcia works with the people in Silver Veil is incredibly impressive. He has everyone completely devoted to him, from laborers to management."

"Don't worry. Sooner or later, someone will complain or get downright ugly. They always do. Some mean-spirited folks seem to go out of their way to cause problems for good people."

"I just hope Isabella Garcia isn't one of them." Aaron mashed his potato and then poured gravy over the top. "That girl seems to hold no respect for either of her parents. She's disrespectful at every turn and barely cooperates with their requests. She even plans to marry some man that her father completely disapproves of, and she doesn't care to know the reasons for his disapproval. I honestly do not think it matters to her. She doesn't respect her father or esteem him in any way. And don't even get me started on how she treated me."

"I doubt I'd have to work hard at it. You seem more than a little worked up about it."

Aaron stopped with food halfway to his mouth. "Well, she riles me, that's for sure. I've never met anyone more self-ish or difficult. And while she might very well know all the proper manners, she's ill-tempered and rude."

"She's certainly gotten under your saddle. Rubbed you all the wrong ways."

"Discourteous and disrespectful people do that to me. Especially when they have no right to act like that."

Jim nodded as he put butter on his bread. "Why do you suppose she's that way?"

Aaron shrugged. "She's had every advantage. Her parents adore her, and she's all they have. I know they're heartbroken over her unwillingness to come home all these years."

"Just remember, Aaron, they aren't your parents, and you don't know what she's gone through with them."

"I don't have to know to realize she thinks the entire world revolves around her. You should see how she acts toward her maid. The girl does her best to please, but Miss Garcia hardly gives her so much as a smile, much less a thank-you."

Jim took a bite of bread and butter and looked to be considering what Aaron had said. When he swallowed and reached for his glass of milk, he finally spoke. "It seems to me that folks always have a reason for their behavior, Aaron. Sometimes meanness is there to cover up pain or hide a person's own discomfort. Maybe your Miss Garcia is hurting."

"She's not my anything. Thank the good Lord!" Aaron picked up the chicken leg. "That woman would try the patience of Job himself. In fact, if she had been in Job's life, he just might have done as his wife wanted, and cursed God and died."

Jim shook his head. "Merry Christmas, Aaron."

Aaron realized just how worked up he'd gotten. He drew a deep breath and gave a nod. "Sorry about that, Jim. Merry Christmas, and thanks for inviting me to share the day with you."

Jim smiled. "It's always good to have a friend."

"Amen."

5

The smoky office was full of railroad men—most of whom were far more important than Aaron, and yet they were most insistent that he be there. Not only that, but they demanded his opinion. They knew just how close Mr. Garcia had become to their lease agent, and they wanted his opinion on all that related to Garcia's business.

"Now that we're to be a state," one of the men declared, "there will be a boom of industry and newcomers. We have to do our part to encourage people to move to New Mexico. Hundreds of advertisements are being sent to newspapers even as we speak. Some offer information on available property that the railroad will sell or lease to those who wish to come west and settle in the new state. It's important that we do what we can to appeal to folks in the East. The more people we get out here, the faster this state will be settled and fears of Mexican marauders will diminish."

"Perhaps if the railroad were to build houses on some of the properties," an older gentleman suggested. "I find people are far more likely to head into the unknown if there is something awaiting them. I have some figures on the cost of building small but sufficient family homes. They needn't be wired for electrical or plumbing. Simple yet efficient is my suggestion."

"Ralph makes a good point," yet another gray-haired gentleman jumped in. "Wherever we wish to see a town increase in size for the sake of the railroad, we could not only build houses but perhaps aid in bettering whatever town businesses are already in place. I'm sure the Santa Fe can afford to spare the money, especially when it will benefit them in the long run."

"Mr. Garcia has that property near Mile Post 1044, the land close to Engle, where they're building the dam. It would be the perfect location to put money into, with that huge reservoir they're building. We can certainly explore the idea of building a town or expanding Engle. Let's check into it," the superintendent declared, looking closely at his map. "Mr. Bailey, we'll meet after this and discuss the particulars. We'll want you to share the news with Mr. Garcia and see if he'd be willing to put his own money behind it."

"Yes, sir," Aaron replied, dreading what he knew would follow.

"We'll have you go down to see Garcia over the New Year holiday."

Aaron said nothing but moaned inwardly. That was all he needed.

~~~~~

"I think they're right," Jim said as he and Aaron sat eating tamales at their favorite Mexican café. "Settling the state is what's going to prosper it, and this place is just ripe for the pickin'."

"There are plenty of other, more accommodating places to settle. It's hard to live here, Jim. No one knows that better than you. It's dry and difficult to grow crops or raise animals. Storms come along and kick up the sand and grit, and blizzards in the winter kill everything in their paths. There are floods to contend with along the Rio Grande and poisonous snakes and insects. It's a hostile place. I can't see the railroad selling anyone but the hardiest souls on coming to New Mexico."

"Well, someone thinks it's worth the effort; otherwise, why are we going to make it a state in a week?"

Aaron nodded and poured more sauce over his tamale. "They want me to leave tonight and head down to spend the New Year with the Garcias. I knew I shouldn't have mentioned them asking me to stay on after Christmas. Now they're insisting I go, and they want me to escort him to the statehood ceremony. Ultimately, I'm to convince Garcia to put his money behind the settlement near Engle. With the dam going in, they believe it will eventually draw in plenty of people, both for work and recreation."

"They would know."

"I should have asked for time off to go see my folks in Chicago. Then I wouldn't be in the middle of all of this."

Jim laughed. "Now, you know that's not true. You would have been in the middle of it no matter what. I'm sure if you told them tomorrow that Daniel Garcia has asked you to take on management of his estate and dealings, they'd create a titled position for you to do just that. Aaron Bailey, superintendent in charge of Daniel Garcia."

Aaron couldn't help but smile. "I'm already that, I just don't have the title."

"Then you'd better find a way to enjoy it. Now, eat up. You haven't even put a dent in those tamales, and I'm ready to ask for another plateful."

"You work harder than me, so you need the extra fuel."

Aaron drew a forkful of tamale to his mouth and sighed. Just worrying about Garcia and the fact that he'd have to see Isabella again was robbing him of his peace.

Diego Morales awoke two days before his thirty-fifth birthday with a great sense of dread. He hadn't accomplished what his father had demanded, although he had tried. He'd talked to his brother about the ranch, but nothing Miguel offered sounded even remotely of interest to Diego. He'd ventured so far as to check in town to see what might be available, but there was nothing there save manual labor or positions for which he had no training whatsoever.

As he dressed, his utmost desire was to avoid his father and slip out of the house to go speak with Josephina Garcia. He had a proposal for her that he felt convinced she might take him up on. He would offer to oversee her entire property and business affairs. After all, he was going to marry her niece. He would suggest that he move in and be available to her for whatever she needed.

He pulled on his finest suit coat and studied his reflection in the mirror. He didn't want to appear shabby. Josephina Garcia appreciated the finer things in life, and Diego wanted to prove that he could be one of them. He wanted to assure her that he was capable of running a large estate—of being its master.

Luck was with him, as he managed to escape the house without his father knowing he was up and around. Surely that was a good sign. He saddled his own horse, then made his way to the Garcia holdings, which bordered his father's ranch. He went over the words he'd say. He'd make sure Miss Garcia could see him as an asset. From what Isabella had said in the past, her aunt would be more than grateful for his abilities. Diego would show up with the solution to her problem, and all would be well. He'd have his job and a home so that his father could no longer torment him. He'd also be set to propose to Isabella.

The housekeeper admitted him to the Garcia house and ushered him into the large front parlor. There was already a fire blazing in the hearth, and since the ride over had been unseasonably cold, Diego went to warm himself while he waited.

"Señorita Garcia will be here momentarily," the housekeeper told him before closing the doors.

Diego glanced around the room. There was a lot of finery, beautiful things collected over the years and pieces of artwork that he had no doubt were very valuable. The Garcias did nothing by halves. Over the large stone fireplace was an oil painting of Isabella's grandmother. It was uncanny how much Isabella favored her. Both were striking beauties with large dark eyes that seemed to look deep into the soul of a man.

The doors to the room opened, and an older woman stepped inside. "Diego, it's quite early. I wasn't expecting you today."

Josephina Garcia had been a great beauty in her youth. Diego had seen the oil paintings made of her. Even now she was a handsome woman. He smiled in appreciation. "I apologize for the hour, but Isabella told me you are an early riser. I hoped to speak to you before I went to town."

She gave him a once-over. "You look well put together."

"And you look beautiful, Miss Garcia."

She wore an old-fashioned gown with a full skirt and a snug-fitting jacket. Josephina Garcia had not advanced her wardrobe with the times, but no one faulted her for it.

"What can I do for you, Diego? You know that Isabella is gone."

"Yes, but I've come to speak to you. First to ask if you've heard from her, and second to discuss some business."

She frowned. "Very well. Have a seat, and let us get to it."

He joined her near the fire. She chose a wingback chair and perched herself on the edge. Diego chose the large leather chair on the opposite side of the fireplace.

"So, tell me what you have come to say. I have a very busy day ahead of me. I had a brief telegram to let me know Isabella arrived safely but nothing since."

"I am sorry for intruding this way. I was going to wait until Isabella was back and I could propose to her, but I thought this much too important to wait. You see, it's for your benefit that I have come."

She eyed him as if carefully considering his words. "I have no idea what you are suggesting."

"I'd like to help you here at the Garcia estates. I know from Isabella that you have struggled to keep up with everything. I know the staff are only a few now and have difficulty keeping up with their duties. I know you've been unable to find a man to manage things for you—someone you felt you could trust—so my father sent his man to help you. I'd like to offer my own skills in his place. Since Isabella and I are to be married, and because I know she has no desire to leave this house, I would be happy to take the heavy responsibilities from your shoulders."

"I see."

"It's obvious that a lot of things are being left undone," he continued. "I have ideas for making it a great hacienda again. I think you'll be surprised at just how much thought I've given this."

"No, frankly, I'm not that surprised, since I know you've had your eye on my niece. However, I can tell you that my brother will never agree to you marrying her."

"What? How can you say that?" Diego didn't have to feign his surprise. Isabella had always assured him that her parents adored him. Granted, he hadn't seen them since he was a young man, but he had thought they were all on good standing with each other.

"I say it because it's true. My brother knows all about your philandering. He would never accept such a man as husband for his daughter."

Anger stirred deep within him. "I've done nothing wrong. I've merely done as most young men do and enjoyed my youth. How can I be faulted for that?"

"You are long past the years of your youth, Diego. By now you should be settled in your life's work with a home of your own. Instead, you have gambled yourself into debt, if the rumors are true, and fathered illegitimate children, doing nothing to care for them. Your father, in fact, has found it necessary to assist in seeing to those children."

He pressed his hands against his chest. "And left me no need to do anything. Honestly, how can I be faulted? He took it completely out of my control."

"Nevertheless, my brother was appalled by the truth."

"Why did you tell him if you knew it would upset him?"

She looked at him as if he were something to be pitied. "I didn't have to tell him. Your father and he are good friends. They write to each other often."

Diego seethed. How like his father to put an end to his plans once again. "My father is given to exaggeration."

"And my brother is given to honoring God. He's a deeply religious man and would never allow you to marry Isabella with such a reputation. Therefore, I must refuse your generous offer." She got to her feet. "Besides, my brother and I no longer own this property."

For the second time in the course of the conversation, Diego was taken completely by surprise. "You sold it?"

"We did. I've been given permission to live here at the house until my death." She moved toward the door, and Diego jumped up to follow her.

"But why did you sell it? Isabella will be devastated."

"It's true that she loves this place, and for that I am saddened to know this will break her heart."

The old woman opened the parlor door and exited to the hall. Diego followed her, wondering if there was anything he could do to alter the situation.

"But surely you could stop the sale."

She shook her head. "The sale took place over a year ago. I cannot change what has happened."

"But who . . . who bought the property?"

She paused when she came to the bottom of the stairs opposite the front entry. "That's hardly important. The deal is done. Now, I must bid you good day. Please see yourself out."

She started up the stairs, and Diego watched her go. There had to be something he could do. Some way he could best his father and prove himself worthy of Isabella's hand.

He raced up the steps after Josephina. "Wait! Wait! You can hardly live here without help. Let me hire on. I can take care of your needs—act as your driver and care for your horses."

She stopped at the top of the stairs as he came up beside her. "I will not abide this nonsense. Go now, before I call one of my servants."

Desperate, he took hold of her arm. "Please just hear me out."

She looked startled for a moment at his audacity, then jerked her arm away from his grip. Unfortunately, that caused her to lose her balance and fall backwards.

Diego was so shocked that he didn't even try to catch her. By the time his senses returned, the small woman had landed with a soft thud at the bottom of the steps. Almost immediately, a pool of blood formed around her head.

For several long moments, Diego couldn't move. All he could do was relive the last few seconds, seeing Señorita Garcia fall over and over again. What was he to do? It was clear she was dead. No doubt they would blame him if he called for help.

Diego didn't even stop to see if she was still alive. He hurried to the door, careful to avoid the blood on the floor, and quietly slipped out. He mounted his horse and blazed down the drive as fast as the animal could go, determined to distance himself from the Garcia rancho. The last thing he needed was Josephina Garcia's blood on his hands.

"It seems the only time we ever get together is to eat." Jim chuckled and took a seat at the table opposite Aaron. "I guess it's what we do best. Are you headed out on the train for Silver Veil?"

"I am. I have no idea how long I'll be gone."

"It would seem the world is conspiring to put you and Garcia together."

"You don't know the half of it. Every time I go to see Daniel, I can't help but wonder what new plan he'll have for me. Like I told you before, I know he has it in mind for me to take over his affairs and see that things run smoothly after he's gone, but lately he's said things that make me certain he intends me to marry his daughter. The more I think about it, the more I'm convinced that's why he sent me to bring her home. He probably hoped we'd fall madly in love on the trip back."

The waitress came with coffee, and Jim quickly gave her his breakfast order. Once she was gone, he turned back to Aaron. "Let's face it, you're a good and honorable man. Those aren't always easy to find."

"Yes, but his daughter despises me, and I'm not very fond of her. It's a wonder we didn't kill each other on that trip. She's spoiled and difficult. She cares for no one but herself."

"So you've told me. Several times. Look, maybe you could change her."

"My mother always warned me to find a woman I already considered perfect. She told me far too many people go into marriage thinking they can change the other person. Believe me, I don't even want to attempt such a thing. It would take a miracle to transform that woman."

"I can see you've given this a great deal of thought." Jim grinned. "Maybe too much."

Aaron shook his head. "You don't know what it's like with Garcia. He's a good man, but he's dying, and he's desperate to arrange everything properly for his wife and daughter. He wants me to handle his affairs and take care of them."

"That doesn't mean you have to marry either one," Jim said, leaning back as the waitress placed eggs and sausages in front of him. She left a container of tortillas as well, then disappeared. Jim dug right in.

Aaron looked at his own breakfast but didn't feel hungry. He'd tossed and turned all night, wondering why he ever agreed to go.

Because you'd lose your job with the Santa Fe if you did otherwise.

He took a long draw on his coffee. He'd always enjoyed his work with Daniel Garcia, but now that Isabella was there, he felt more than a little apprehension. Part of that was due to her obvious hatred of him, but an equal portion was because of the strange attraction he felt for her. He wasn't about to admit it to Jim, but the beautiful woman consumed his thoughts.

"So, do you think Garcia will want to move forward with building the new town?" Jim asked.

"It's hard to say. He's completely devoted to Silver Veil. He never does anything halfheartedly. If he builds a town, he sees to its every need. With his health failing, I'm not sure he'll want to risk another project. He'd know it would be impossible for him to see it through. He was even commenting on not living to see the dam completed—something he at one time looked forward to experiencing."

Jim nodded. He'd wolfed down his breakfast and was eyeing Aaron's. "You gonna eat that?"

Aaron's stomach tightened. He pushed the plate forward. "No, take it."

Jim didn't have to be coaxed. He started in on the plate of biscuits and gravy. "All you can do is lay out the benefits and let Garcia decide. The Santa Fe can hardly blame you if he doesn't want to go for it."

"Oh, but they will. They seem to think I have some power over him."

"Well, you have to admit you've become Daniel Garcia's right-hand man, despite the fact that you don't work for him."

"A discrepancy that he's always after me to remedy." Aaron sighed. He cared deeply about Daniel and Helena. He wanted to do what he could to help them, but he had also dreamed for some time of working his way up the ranks of the Santa Fe. He could see himself becoming an area superintendent one day. He imagined himself capable of overseeing an entire district and doing it well.

"I'm bettin' he'd pay better than the railroad."

Aaron sighed. "I suppose he would. Still, the railroad was the job I always saw for myself."

"Have you prayed about it?" Jim asked, putting aside his fork for the steaming cup of coffee.

"Not really."

"You know that's not a good way to handle the matter."

"I do, but what if God wants me to give up my plans and go with those Garcia has for me? What if I end up feeling obligated to marry Isabella?"

"First of all, she'd have to agree to marry you as well. You've made it clear she can't stand you."

"True enough."

"Maybe God just wants you to help a dying man without the need to marry his widow or daughter. Pray about it, Aaron. We both know prayer is where you're going to end up anyway, so stop putting it off. Spend some real time seeking the Lord on this matter. He'll show you what He wants from you."

"Yeah. That's what I'm afraid of."

6

Word of Josephina Garcia's death spread quickly. The housekeeper sent one of the groomsmen to town to fetch the undertaker and the sheriff. Shortly afterward, most everyone in town knew of her demise. Diego had purposefully stayed away from home that day, hoping to avoid any conflict with his father, as well as any questioning that might come about from his being the last guest at the Garcia house before the old woman's accident.

It was nearly seven o'clock when he returned. He knew his family would be at dinner, and he hoped he might be able to go upstairs to his room unnoticed. It was not to be, however. The butler greeted him and directed him to the dining room.

"The family is awaiting you there. Your father asked that you come immediately without worrying about dressing for dinner."

That didn't sound encouraging.

Diego drew a deep breath. There was nothing to do but comply. If he dared to ignore his father, Diego risked his anger. He walked slowly down the hall to the dining room. What would he say if questioned about Señorita Garcia? He had thought about this quite a bit. Her house staff knew he'd been there, but no one saw when he left. His plan was to say she was alive and well when last they'd spoken.

He walked into the dining room, and his mother was the first to meet his gaze. She looked worried at first, but a flicker of relief passed over her expression. Maybe things weren't going to be all that bad.

"Sorry I'm late."

"Where have you been?" his father demanded.

"Out seeking employment as you requested. Just as I've been doing every day since you told me I'd be abandoned on my birthday." Diego hadn't meant to say that last part. He hadn't meant to bring up the date at all, hoping his father might have forgotten. He took a seat at the table and waited for whatever was to come.

"Have you heard the news about Josephina Garcia?" his father asked.

"Yes. I heard while I was in town. I saw her just this morning." Diego put on a sorrowful expression. "It's a terrible loss."

"Yes. Her household staff relayed that you were there to the sheriff. He was here to speak with you, but I had no way of knowing where you'd gone." His father's gaze narrowed. "Apparently, you were the last to see her alive."

"I was?" Diego feigned surprise. "I'm shocked. Her house-keeper was right there, and I believe a maid might have been as well."

"Her housekeeper said she left you two alone to talk." His father's tone was laced with suspicion.

Diego picked up his napkin and placed it on his lap. One of the kitchen boys set a plate of food in front of him. Apparently, they were having roast duck for dinner. Diego wasn't fond of duck, and his family knew that full well.

"Yes, we were in the front parlor. She had a lovely fire, as it was quite chilly this morning. I went over early so as to see her before heading to town."

"What for? What did you want from her?"

Diego shrugged. "I thought perhaps she'd heard from Isabella. I know I haven't said anything to either of you, but we plan to be married."

"Bah! Her father will never allow it. Especially now," his father replied.

Diego picked up his knife and fork and gave his father a look of innocence. "Why do you say that? For some time now, Isabella and I have known we would marry. She's already agreed." That was a lie, but one he felt certain would easily turn to truth.

"You should never have even discussed marriage without first talking to her father." Esteban Morales dabbed his lips, then took a long drink of wine. "At this point it's immaterial," he continued. "The housekeeper said she had no idea when you left. She didn't see you go."

"What does that have to do with anything? Why are you acting as though I did something wrong by visiting Señorita Garcia? I didn't leave her dead in the front parlor, if that's what you're trying to find out."

His father kept watching Diego as if trying to catch him in a lie. Diego knew the trick was to keep his story as close to the truth as possible.

"We know that." His father offered nothing more.

"Well, after checking to see if she needed my help with anything, I left for town. I arrived there by nine. The bank was just opening. I had a long talk with Mr. Brewer, the manager there. I thought he might have a job I could do."

"And did he?"

"No." Diego cut into the duck.

"Señorita Garcia fell down her stairs," his father said. "The housekeeper found her at the bottom of the staircase. She'd hit her head and broken her neck. The doctor said she died almost instantly."

"How awful." Diego put down his knife and fork. "Hardly dinner conversation. This will be so upsetting to poor Isabella. I believe I should go to her in New Mexico."

His father studied him. "The Garcia lawyer is leaving tomorrow. I think it would be good to send you out of town. After you speak with the sheriff, of course. There's going to be plenty of talk, and without you here causing trouble, it will die down faster."

"Then, if you might allow me, I'd like to accompany him. I'm sure Isabella will need me by her side. A trip there will allow me to ask for her hand in person and to help Mr. Garcia with anything he might need done at this end."

"There is nothing much to be done. Their personal items will be packed and shipped. The livestock have already been arranged for, as have the grounds."

"Yes, she told me the estate was sold last year. Do you know who bought it?"

"I did." His father's tone was matter-of-fact. "If you spent any time with me and your brother, helping to run this place, you might have known that for yourself."

"Isabella doesn't know about it."

"I've no doubt that's true. Josephina didn't want her to know. She figured her brother should tell Isabella when she returned to Silver Veil."

"I see." But Diego didn't see at all. Why all the secrecy? Why hadn't he realized what was happening right under his nose? "Do we know yet when the funeral will be?"

"Señorita Garcia long ago made her wishes known with

her lawyer. The mortuary drove out this afternoon and took her body to town. The funeral is the day after tomorrow."

"But the lawyer is leaving tomorrow. That makes it very difficult. I know Isabella will need me, but I know too that she'd want me to be at the funeral." Diego shook his head and gave a heavy sigh. "But my place is at her side."

To Diego's surprise, his father hadn't given him a hard time about leaving. He hadn't attempted to put him from the house or even to refuse the money Diego needed for travel. He was totally convinced that sending Diego away would help the entire situation, and that served Diego's plans perfectly.

The sheriff's brief questioning had been nothing to fret over. Diego told him exactly what had transpired that day, right up to the moment Señorita Garcia walked him to the door. Diego assured the sheriff that he had left her with a smile and a wave from the back of his horse. She had been perfectly fine. The sheriff made notes, then got up and left, seeming less than convinced, but there was nothing he could do. Diego was the son of a man who held great power in the valley, and he had absolutely no reason to harm Isabella's aunt. He confided to the sheriff that they were soon to be family, and Josephina Garcia had been instrumental in seeing that come about. He loved her as dearly as if she were part of his own family.

No need to share that he hated his family.

The train trip to Silver Veil was a disappointment, to be sure. They weren't even in first class, and Diego found that appalling. There were people packed all around him and the shabby lawyer.

Mr. Charles Williams sat opposite Daniel with a book in his hand. He was a man of fifty or so, with graying blond hair parted down the middle and slicked back on the sides. He had a thick bushy mustache, as many men of the day sported, and wore small gold spectacles that made him seem scholarly. He was a man of few words and had spent most of the time on their trip reading.

When night fell and Diego asked about their sleeping arrangements, it became clear that Williams had been completely remiss in their travel needs when he arranged passage to include tickets for Diego. They were to go directly from California to Albuquerque without stopping for the night or even having the benefit of a Pullman car. When Diego appealed to the porter, he was told there were no sleeping berths available. Diego had voiced his dismay more than once, but the lawyer seemed unconcerned. Perhaps Father had told him to ignore Diego, that he was of no importance. Diego seethed.

The final night on the train, however, Williams delivered good news. Tonight they would arrive in Albuquerque and stay in a hotel, the Harvey House hotel called the Alvarado. The one-hundred-room hotel was said to be one of the finest of Fred Harvey's establishments, and Diego was quite happy with the arrangement, even if it did mean extra cost. He wanted to be completely refreshed and looking good when they arrived in Silver Veil the next day.

It was imperative that he impress Daniel Garcia. The more he thought about it, the more he was convinced that he and Isabella should marry as soon as possible. After all, once she heard about the sale of her home in California, she would be devastated and hate her father more than ever. Diego figured once they were married, with any luck, he could convince his father to allow them to live at the Garcia house. He could offer to work for his father from that location, and it would win Isabella's absolute devotion. He smiled to himself and caught his reflection in the train window. All he had to do was convince Daniel Garcia that he was worthy of marriage to his daughter.

The telegram had arrived the night before, leaving Daniel and his wife bereft. Daniel Garcia had always presumed he'd die before his sister, and yet here he was, reading of her death.

Charles Williams, the family lawyer, said only that she had died and that he would arrive on the Thursday train with more information and a copy of Josephina's will.

Daniel picked up a framed photograph of his sister and shook his head. How could she be dead? She was healthy and well-off. She'd said nothing about sickness or other complications. He sighed. They'd always been so close, and to imagine her dead was nearly impossible.

A quick glance at the clock confirmed that Daniel should head to the depot. The train would soon arrive from Albuquerque. He and Mr. Williams would go over the terms of his sister's will, even though Daniel was sure he already knew what she had to say. She had told him on more than one occasion that she would leave half of her holdings to Daniel and half to Isabella. If Daniel preceded her in death, it would all go to her niece. Her jewelry and other personal items would go to Isabella immediately, while the money would be held in trust until she married or turned thirty, whichever came first. He wondered if she'd ever discussed it with Isabella.

Daniel walked to the window, and a coughing jag took hold of him. When he withdrew his handkerchief from his mouth, he wasn't at all surprised to find it speckled with blood. Well, *speckled* wasn't exactly accurate. The bleeding was increasing, and so too was the feeling of weakness and being unable to draw a decent breath. The doctors were now suggesting it was a cancer rather than tuberculosis. The dry air of New Mexico had helped buy him time, so perhaps in the beginning it had been neither one. The doctors had no idea. They argued among themselves, and by the time they settled on cancer, it was clear the disease was terminal.

From his window, Daniel could look down on the city of Silver Veil. It was his greatest contribution to the world besides Isabella. When he'd first become sick, it had made his own mortality a reality. He had given much thought to his life and what he had and hadn't accomplished. His biggest desire was to do something good—to invest in the lives of others and give them the opportunity for real change. Silver Veil and his success with the mine had given him that chance. Of course, when silver had been devalued, it had been hard on everyone, but they'd made it through, and their little town found other ways to be productive. With Aaron Bailey's help, Daniel had invested in the railroad and used his profits to create new opportunities for the townspeople to make money. There were now a group of jewelry makers who worked with turquoise and silver, several artisans who wove the most beautiful rugs, and a guild of silversmiths who created elegant silverware and tea services.

He frowned. Who would take care of the people after he was gone?

Aaron was the one he felt most inclined to choose, but the young man seemed wholly devoted to the railroad. Daniel knew Aaron was a good man, a trustworthy and godly man, but Aaron showed little interest in changing his position.

Daniel couldn't help but fear what the end might bring. Most of the people in Silver Veil were unschooled and illiterate.

He feared all were susceptible to being cheated. More than once, card sharps had shown up and taken advantage of his people. For that was how he saw them: they were his people, his family. He was like a patriarch to them all.

The clock on the mantel chimed the hour. He had wasted too much time. Making his way to the foyer, he found Helena just coming down the stairs. She was beautiful, as always. Her eyes seemed to light up at the sight of him, and a smile edged her lips. How she had filled his life with joy.

"Are you ready, my love?"

"I am. I hope this won't be too hard on you." She reached the bottom step and paused for a moment to study him. Finally, she stepped down and came to his side. "You aren't feeling well today. I can see it in your eyes."

"I'm just burdened and sad." He forced a smile. "But I know God is with us and will deliver us. He has a plan, even in my dying."

She nodded. "I know." There was a slight break in her voice. She handed him her heavy shawl. "I think we should go."

Just then Isabella came out of the music room and looked at her parents. "Where are you two headed?"

Daniel stiffened. They hadn't yet told Isabella of her aunt's death. Daniel had wanted to say something the night before, but word had come so late that she was already asleep. He had planned to tell her today, but she had avoided both him and her mother, heading out early for a ride with her maid and one of the groomsmen.

"We have a guest arriving at the depot." Daniel considered telling her the truth then and there, but it would be horrible to tell her and then leave, so he said nothing. "We'll be back momentarily and will then have lunch together. I'll expect you to join us."

She sighed. "Well, since Mr. Bailey is already staying with us, I can't imagine who it might be. Should I dress?"

"Yes, that would be fitting. Oh, and you should know that Mr. Bailey will accompany us to the statehood celebration."

She rolled her gaze heavenward. "Well, at least after that I shall return home and never be pestered by his presence again."

Daniel and Helena exchanged a look but headed for the door at the sound of the train whistle. "We're late."

Isabella was happily ensconced in the music room, reading a book by the fire, when her father and mother returned. She heard Aaron's voice almost immediately. He was speaking with her father. She made her way to the foyer as another man joined in the conversation. He looked vaguely familiar, but she didn't think on it long because behind the little group she saw a face she'd longed to see.

"Diego!" She let out a squeal of delight and rushed to greet him. "Oh, how wonderful to see you. Papi, did you plan this?" She paused at her father's side. "You are wonderful." This was the best of gifts.

Her father shook his head. "I wish I could take credit for anything that makes you this happy. I'm sorry to spoil your reunion, however. We have some news to discuss."

Isabella shook her head. "But Diego just arrived. I long to talk to him."

"Later," her father said in a businesslike manner. "We need to speak in the library. Aaron, I hope you don't mind entertaining Diego while we're gone."

"Not at all." Aaron moved to stand between Diego and

Isabella. "Come with me, Mr. Morales. We can wait in the music room."

Diego looked at Isabella with a helpless expression.

"Wait!" Isabella went to Diego's side. "Why can't he join us in the library?"

"This is a family matter. Now please, Isabella, don't make this any harder than it needs to be." Her father headed down the hallway with Mama at his side. The other man followed obediently, and Isabella knew she had no choice.

"I'll be back soon," she told Diego.

"Close the door, Isabella," her father commanded as she entered the library.

She did and then took a seat at the table beside her mother. "What's going on? Why all the seriousness?"

"We aren't going to delay this," Papi began. "Mr. Charles Williams is the lawyer who has handled our family business in California for some time. His father handled it before him, in fact."

Isabella gave the older man a nod. That was how she knew him. He'd come to the house on one or two occasions. Usually when Aunt Josephina had business of a legal nature, however, she went to his offices in town.

"I remember seeing you at the house," Isabella said, glancing at the somber faces around her. He had obviously come to share bad news. Was something amiss with the family's holdings?

"We got word last night," her father began, "that Mr. Williams was coming." Papi looked to Mama, and it seemed as if his strength drained away. "We wanted to tell you before now, but the moment simply did not present itself. I'm afraid it's your aunt."

Isabella felt her throat tighten. "What do you mean?"

"I'm afraid she is dead, sweetheart. Mr. Williams has brought us the details. Apparently, she fell down the stairs."

"No. No!" Isabella shook her head over and over. "This can't be. She was fine when I left." She reined in her emotions with effort and looked at the lawyer. "What happened?"

"We're uncertain. Diego Morales was the last one to see her alive. He stated that he met with her that morning. After he left, her housekeeper found her at the bottom of the stairs. She had sustained injuries to her head and neck," Mr. Williams answered. "No one understands what might have made her fall."

"Oh no." Isabella clutched her throat. "I think I might know." She could hardly bring herself to speak. "She'd been having dizzy spells. Oh, I should never have left her."

"Dizzy spells?" her father asked. "She said nothing to me about them."

"I know. She didn't want to worry you." Isabella sighed. "She'd been having spells off and on for over a month—maybe two. She planned to speak to the doctor if they didn't go away."

"That would certainly account for the fall," the lawyer said, pulling a tablet and pencil from his case. "I will send a telegram to the sheriff. This will clear up the matter. Knowing that she was experiencing problems, it makes sense that she might easily lose her balance on the stairs. Perhaps the dizziness created a sense of confusion, and she was unable to grab the banister."

"I wish I'd insisted she see the doctor immediately. It's all my fault." Isabella began to sob into her handkerchief.

"Nonsense, Isabella," her father said, shaking his head. "Our life is in the hands of God. If my sister was ill, suffering from these spells, you couldn't have stopped the possibility of a fall."

Isabella couldn't stop the flow of tears. "I can't believe she's gone." She got up. "Please excuse me. I can't bear this sorrow."

She hurried to the door to escape. This couldn't be happening. It simply wasn't possible.

Diego waited until Mrs. Garcia offered to show Mr. Williams to his room to speak to Isabella's father.

"Sir, if you have a moment, I would like to explain why I accompanied Mr. Williams."

Daniel Garcia looked at him. "I already know why you've come."

"You do?"

"You want to marry my daughter."

Diego smiled. "I do. I love her very much, but I also came to offer my condolences. As the last to see your sister, I wanted to assure you that she was fine when I left her."

"I'm confident we've figured out what happened," Mr. Garcia said, taking a seat behind his desk.

"You have?" Diego asked so quickly that he was afraid it would draw attention to himself. "I'm so glad to hear it. Might I ask what conclusion you came to?"

"Isabella said my sister was experiencing dizzy spells. No one else knew about it. She figures Josephina got dizzy while climbing the stairs and lost her balance."

Diego nodded. "That would make perfect sense." He fought to keep from showing any sign of relief. He alone knew she had lost her balance pulling away from him, and that was the way it would remain. "Still, I am very sorry. I know how close you were to your sister and she to you."

"I appreciate your condolences." He watched Diego with a wary eye.

Diego remained standing, as Garcia hadn't asked him to sit. It made him feel like a child, and he resented the man for it. "As you already figured out, the other reason I came was to ask for Isabella's hand."

"I won't toy with you. The answer is no. You have a reputation that could only bring sorrow to my daughter. You have debts and no job. You have nothing of your own, and I know that your father plans to put you from the family now that you have turned thirty-five."

Diego felt his gut tighten. All he could do was admit to his terrible past and assure Garcia that he had changed. That he had come here to prove himself a different man.

"It's true that I was an irresponsible youth, but I have turned over a new leaf, as they say."

"You're thirty-five years old, Diego. That's hardly a youth. Most men your age have long committed themselves to a course of living, are married, and have produced heirs. You've done nothing, as far as I can see, but cause trouble and live off your father's money."

It was difficult not to fly across the desk and punch Garcia in the mouth. How dare he?

"I know I made bad choices." Diego forced out the words. "But I assure you, I have changed. I have come here as proof of that. It is my desire to do whatever you require of me to marry Isabella. We love each other, sir. Perhaps you would allow us at least to court while I show you that I can be the man she deserves."

Daniel looked at him as if he could see right through the lie. "And you would be willing to take a job of my offering?"

"Anything. I was searching for work when I learned of your sister's passing."

Daniel slowly nodded. "Very well. Work in my silver mine for one year. Prove to me you aren't afraid of hard work. I will put you up in one of the mining apartments and feed you as long as you work faithfully each day. You'll also receive a regular salary alongside the other men."

The thought of such labor was unthinkable to Diego, but he desperately needed to buy himself time. His father would disinherit him otherwise, and Mr. Garcia would put an end to him having anything to do with his daughter. At least this way he could offer the pretense of starting over.

Diego extended his hand. "I will do it, Señor Garcia. For the sake of proving to you and to my father that I have changed, and for the hope of marrying Isabella. I will prove to you all that I am not the foolish boy I once was."

7

After taking breakfast in her room, Isabella joined her parents in the library for the reading of her aunt's will. She was strangely relieved that neither Diego nor Aaron Bailey was present. She wasn't sure why, but this seemed like much too private and personal a matter to share with them.

Throughout the night, she'd tossed and turned, thinking of how it was all her fault that Aunt Josephina was dead. She should have made her go to the doctor at the very first spell. If only she'd done that, her aunt might still be alive.

Isabella took a seat at the large worktable in the middle of the library. It was solid oak and so well polished that she could see her reflection in the wood. Once they were all assembled, Mr. Williams began.

"Miss Garcia made her wishes quite clear, and her will is very simple. She wished that her few personal belongings, artwork, and jewelry be given to Isabella, her niece." He looked up and nodded at Isabella. "The large oil paintings of her mother and other family oil paintings will go to Isabella as well." He turned to her. "Those things, as well as your own, are even now being prepared to ship here."

"Ship here? But the rancho is my home." Isabella looked at her father. "Surely you will need someone to stay on to manage it and see to the livestock. I intended to return as soon as possible."

The lawyer spoke before her father could say a word. "The rancho was sold last year to Mr. Morales."

Isabella startled. "Diego?"

"No," the lawyer replied. "His father."

She looked to her father for an explanation. Words wouldn't even form in her mouth. How could they have done this? That was Garcia family land. It was the home of her childhood.

"Josephina sent word to me of his offer last year," her father explained gently, "and we thought it would be good for us to take advantage of it, since neither of us could manage such a large estate anymore. Mr. Morales agreed to let Josephina live there for as long as she desired while he took over the horses. In fact, the groomsmen and stable workers are all under his employ."

"I don't believe this," Isabella said. "How can it be true? You know how much that place means to me. It's my home, and I want no other."

"I am sorry, Isabella. I fully intended to discuss it with you while you were here visiting. Josephina had been talking about taking an apartment in town and knew we would have to arrange for you."

What a betrayal. Her aunt had said nothing—not even a hint. They all knew the California estate was home to Isabella. They had ripped her away from it when she was but a child, and although she had done everything in her power to get back to her home, they were once again tearing her away. This sorrow, on top of losing her aunt, was more than Isabella could bear.

Of course, if she married Diego, there was a possibility his father might let them have the rancho or at least the house as a wedding present. She almost smiled at the thought. Surely that was why it had been allowed in the first place. Her father would never have sought to keep it from her if there was a way to preserve it. No wonder Diego had come. No doubt they were working out the details.

She drew a deep breath and forced her body to relax. "Well, perhaps there is still no reason to hurry with the shipment. Perhaps Mr. Morales would allow me to stay there as he did Aunt Josephina." She gave the lawyer and her father a hopeful look.

"I'm sorry, my dear child. That isn't possible. Mr. Morales's son Miguel is going to build a better racetrack. The house will be used as a hotel for those coming to do business with the horses. He plans to turn it into quite the operation."

"No! This isn't possible. That is my home."

"I'm sorry, Isabella." Her father's voice was soft, almost inaudible. "But it is already done. The arrangement has been made, and the work is already in the process. Surely you saw the men clearing the land around the old racetrack."

"I did, but Auntie told me it was . . ." Isabella tried to remember what her aunt had said. It had been rather confusing. Something about a place to train the horses. She hadn't lied to Isabella. She just hadn't told the whole truth.

"If I might return to the will itself," the lawyer interjected, "there is only one small portion left to discuss."

"Please, Mr. Williams, continue," Isabella's father said.

"For the rest of Josephina Garcia's monies, investments, and bonds, they are to be equally divided between her brother and her niece. Mr. Garcia, you will receive this immediately. Miss Garcia, your money will be put in trust until your thirtieth birthday or your marriage to a man of your father's approval, whichever comes first."

"What?" She shook her head. "What if my father doesn't approve?"

"Then you will wait until your thirtieth birthday to receive the money. I believe your aunt saw this as a safety to protect you from men who might seek to take advantage of your fortune. She trusted her brother to know whether your intended was simply after your fortune, hence the clause of his approval being necessary."

"That's completely unfair. I'm twenty-five and fully capable of minding my own affairs." She looked to her father. "I don't think this is right. You have always tried to deny me what makes me happy."

"Isabella, you know that isn't true," her mother protested.

"That is hardly the case." Her father looked hurt, but Isabella didn't care. God knew he'd hurt her with all of this nonsense.

Isabella pounded her fists on the table. "All of my life you have sought to make me miserable. You forced me here, and now it seems you will strive to keep me here by taking away my home. Why? Why have you done this? Why have you sold our family lands?"

Her father looked momentarily to Mama and then back to Isabella. "Because I am dying."

Isabella heard the words, but they didn't really register. Her father had been sickly for some time, but dying? It made no sense. "I don't . . . don't believe you."

"Isabella!" Her mother's raised voice caused Isabella to quiet. Her mother was never one to shout. Even when Isabella had been small, she never spoke in a loud reprimand.

"It is true whether you believe it or not. It was one of the reasons I agreed to sell the estate. Your aunt approached me with the idea after Mr. Morales asked about the possibility of purchasing part of the land. Eventually, we agreed to sell the entire estate so long as Josephina had a place to live until she chose to move away."

"Why didn't you tell me?" Isabella forced herself to calm down. She folded her hands in her lap. "Why?"

"Because we knew you'd be upset. We hoped you'd remain happy for as long as possible and maybe even return to Silver Veil on your own."

"But this isn't my home. I have no desire to be here, but now you have forced me to stay because I have nowhere else to go." She stared hard at her father. His skin was gray, and his face almost skeletal. Why hadn't she noticed this before?

Am I truly so selfish that I couldn't see he was suffering? She bit her lower lip. Aaron Bailey had mentioned her father being ill, but she hadn't believed him. Was he really dying? Isabella felt awash in shame.

"What has made you ill?" she finally asked.

"We're uncertain. At first the doctors thought it was tuberculosis. It was the reason they wanted me to move to this very arid region. And it did help. My lungs seemed to dry, my coughing and trouble breathing improved."

"That's why we moved to Silver Veil?" She'd never known. To her as a ten-year-old, it just seemed like her father's whim.

"Yes. We were told these southern territories were perfect for healing lung issues."

"Why didn't you tell me?" She was beginning to feel like all her life she'd been left out of a story that everyone else knew the ending to.

"We were worried about you," Mama replied. "You were just a little girl. You were so upset about leaving your grandparents and your horse. We didn't want to further your worry by telling you that Papi was sick."

"You should have told me. I would have understood why

you were taking me away from California. I thought you were just being cruel. I thought you didn't care."

"Of course we cared. You are our child—our entire world. We didn't want you to worry, however. The doctors weren't sure if the move would cure me or even help me," her father replied. "I didn't want you to think I might die."

"But you do now?" She knew it sounded harsh and wished she could have softened her tone.

"There's no keeping it from you now. I haven't much time."

"How do you know?" She shook her head. "Doctors can't tell those kinds of things. You said only God gives life and takes it."

"It's true," her father said with a sad smile. "However, there are obvious signs that things are not going well. I'm coughing up blood. Quite a bit of it. I'm very weak. My weakness grows day by day."

"And what did they decide is wrong?"

"They don't know. One says it must be a cancer, another says it's a bacteria eating away at my lungs. Others still believe it to be TB. We just don't know. We know only that my body can't go on much longer."

Isabella floundered for other options. "Surely there are better doctors in the big cities. We could go to Philadelphia or Boston. Both are known for having great hospitals. Perhaps they would be able to help you more than the doctors in this tiny town."

"I have seen the best doctors, my dear. Again, I didn't tell you because I didn't want to worry you. I wanted very much for you to enjoy your life. But now . . . well, now I need you to be here for your mother and for Silver Veil."

"Silver Veil can take care of itself. As for Mama, she could have easily moved to the ranch in California, but you've taken that from us. Think of what a comfort it might have been for us to have the ranch and our memories there. Even Mama's friends are nearby." Isabella's throat grew tight as she fought off her emotions.

"This home is my comfort now," her mother said, casting a glance at her husband.

"And I will be buried here," Papi added.

Isabella pushed away from the table and stood. "I can't bear this anymore. I must have time to think." She hurried from the room, tears blinding her. How could they have kept all of this from her?

Lupe was waiting for her not far from the library.

"Lupe, please bring my cloak. I want to sit in the courtyard."

"Sí, Miss Isabella."

The younger woman hurried away, and Isabella tried to regain her composure. She wasn't easily given to tears, but all of this news had come as a shock. Why hadn't her parents been honest with her about the sale of the land and her father's sickness? Why hadn't Aunt Josephina warned her? At least that would have given Isabella time to get used to the idea.

Lupe returned and helped Isabella into the cloak. The mauve-colored wool instantly warmed her body, but Isabella's heart felt like ice. She made her way out to the courtyard. She remembered the hours she'd spent here as a child. It had been a place of quiet respite where she could make plans for her future.

The courtyard sat at the very center of the large adobe house. Overhead, the second-floor rooms each had a small balcony that looked down on the carefully tended gardens. In the summer, the scent of flowers would drift in through the open balcony doors. Isabella remembered the enticing smells. It was one of the only things she enjoyed about her home here. At this time of year, however, everything was either dead or dormant. Much like the rest of her existence.

Stepping into the garden area, she made her way to one of the benches and sat down. What was she supposed to do now? Her home was gone. She glanced around the courtyard. This would never be home.

She thought back on the lawyer's words regarding the will. She would inherit Aunt Josephina's jewelry and artwork immediately and half of her money when she turned thirty or married, whichever came first. But marriage was restricted to a man her father approved.

"Am I interrupting?"

She looked up and smiled. "Oh, Diego, I'm very glad to see you. I'm trying to sort through all these thoughts and feelings."

"Perhaps I can help." He smiled down at her. "May I sit with you?"

"Please do." She scooted over so that their nearness wouldn't appear inappropriate.

"How did the reading of the will go?"

"Well enough, I suppose. I'm to inherit Aunt Josephina's jewelry and artwork immediately. I will also get half of her money once I turn thirty or marry a man who has my father's approval."

"I see." He turned toward her. "That was very kind of your aunt."

"Kind, but far too restrictive. She should have just left the money to me unencumbered. I am an adult, after all."

"This is true."

For a long while, neither of them said anything more. Isabella didn't know what to say. She thought about proposing they marry, but she knew her father didn't approve of Diego, so it wouldn't matter regarding the money. Still, she wanted to marry Diego. She'd wanted it for a very long time. She'd been infatuated with him since she was young.

At sixteen, when she'd gone back to California to spend her first summer with Aunt Josephina, she had encountered Diego one evening when they went to the Morales house for supper. He was twenty-six and so dashingly handsome. He had given her a shiver when he'd taken her hand and gently kissed the top of her fingers.

"I asked your father for your hand," Diego said, breaking the silence.

Her head snapped up. "You did? What did he say?" She was hopeful that perhaps her aunt's demise had changed her father's mind.

"He told me no. He said I wasn't worthy of you, and you know what? He's right."

"No, he isn't." Isabella shook her head. "He doesn't know me. He doesn't understand what I want."

"He has good reason to worry about you. You are his only child."

"Yes, but I don't want his concern. Oh, Diego, I want very much to marry you." There. She had spoken her mind and the truth of her heart.

He grinned. "And I want to marry you. Your father said he might consider allowing me to court you under certain conditions."

"And what are those?"

"I have to change my ways—which I told him I already have. I am to work in his silver mine for one year. If I prove myself with that, he will perhaps allow me to court you with marriage in mind."

"A year in the mine? That's such hard work. I wouldn't wish it for anyone, but especially not for you. You weren't brought up to work like that, Diego. It's neither right nor fair. I'm tired of my father making decisions for my life without consulting me. He has no consideration."

"Yet I heard the servants talking. Did you know that your father is ill?"

Her brows knit together. "He's dying."

"Yes. That is what I heard." Diego paused. "I'm sorry."

"I'm sorry for Mama. Papi is her entire world. I don't know how she'll get by without him."

"Perhaps that is why your father wanted you here."

"No doubt it is, but what about what I want? No one ever seems to consider that. All of my life, people have been imposing their will on me. Did you know that your father bought the rancho in California?"

"He told me just before I left to come here. I'm sorry, my sweet. I know that must hurt you greatly."

"It does. No one cared about what I wanted or needed. They simply decided for me. They're always deciding what's best for me and never consider what I desire."

"I care about your desires, my dear. I know this is very hard for you, but I will do whatever I can to make it better, including work in the mine. I told your father I would work for him to prove I've changed."

"It's so unfair that you should have to do that." She was impressed, however, that someone of Diego's standing would agree to such a requirement. He was handsome and his family wealthy. He could surely have any woman he desired for a wife. Isabella was deeply touched that he wanted her.

"Diego, do you think you might write to your father and ask if we could live in the California house?"

"You wouldn't want that once they finish with all their planned changes, I'm sure. It won't be the same, Isabella. We must forge our own way and make a place of our own.

Perhaps we will come to love Silver Veil after I serve my time in the mine."

"I'll talk to Papi. Now that his sister has passed and he's soon to follow, perhaps I can get him to change his mind."

"I don't know how you would do that. My father has told him how foolish I've been. He knows all about my reckless youth."

Isabella nodded. "You're hardly a youth now. I'm sure he's heard things, but it doesn't matter. You've not done those things in a very long time. Look, I will remind him that I'd like him to be at my wedding to give me away. He knows he's dying and hasn't much time. Perhaps that will change his mind."

"Perhaps." Diego nodded. "I can start working for him, and maybe he will see my sincerity, and this, along with your comments, will make him see that it's in your best interest to allow us to marry. We could even promise to remain here."

"No. I won't lie about it."

Diego looked at her for a moment. "Even if it's the only way to get him to approve of us marrying?"

Isabella shook her head. "I despise lying. I'm not going to lie. Papi knows how I feel about this place. If I were to promise to stay here, he'd know it was a lie." She rose, and Diego did as well. "I'll talk to him and plead with him as a daughter who longs for her father to give her away and be there on her wedding day. That will surely touch his heart."

Aaron could hear the entire conversation between Isabella and Diego. Sitting on his balcony for his prayer time, he'd seen Isabella's arrival in the courtyard. He'd assumed she would see him as well, but she never looked up. When she chose the bench closest his room, Aaron almost returned inside. When Diego showed up, he definitely intended to go, but something held him fast.

He wasn't sure what to make of the things he'd heard. Diego had encouraged Isabella to lie, and Isabella had refused—she said she hated lying. But still, she proposed a lie of her own. She would appeal to her father on behalf of her desire to have him give her away, for him to be present at her wedding.

Aaron hated the thought of Isabella making a pretense of it mattering to her that her father be at her wedding. She'd made it very clear that her father didn't matter. His ideals and desires for her were resented and dismissed. She didn't care about him at all. Aaron was confident of this.

"So what do I do about what I've heard?" he quietly asked aloud.

Isabella and Diego had already made their way into the house. Aaron thought he should confront them, but he knew that would only cause more resentment on Isabella's part. Maybe he'd have a chance to talk to her alone. The one thing he wasn't going to do was stand by and let them hurt Daniel Garcia. Not if he had anything to say about it.

He thought about how Daniel had asked him to consider managing things for him in Silver Veil. That management included helping Mrs. Garcia once he was gone and looking out for Isabella. When he'd first proposed the idea, Aaron had quickly refused, reminding Daniel that his life was built around the railroad. The Santa Fe was his employer, and he planned to make his way up into a position of district superintendent. He could scarcely do that while giving Daniel Garcia and Silver Veil half his time.

Aaron glanced heavenward at the pale-blue sky. "What am I supposed to do, Lord?"

8

On the fifth of January, Isabella and her parents boarded a train for Albuquerque and then changed to another train that would take them to Santa Fe for the statehood celebration. Aaron Bailey accompanied them, but Isabella's father had refused to give Diego time away from his new job to join them. She thought him rather cruel, especially given that Papi had given his people the day off to enjoy the statehood celebration. Papi said giving Diego more time would only stir resentment amongst his fellow workers. She supposed she could understand that, but sooner or later they were bound to find out that Diego was a dear friend of the family.

In Santa Fe, they were staying with friends of her parents in a rather grand house not far from the Plaza. The Plaza was where all the celebrations would take place the next day. The sunbaked adobe house was a single-story structure that stretched out in an impressive horseshoe shape. The Garcias were put in the family's east wing, while Aaron was given a room in the west wing, where guests usually stayed. Behind the house were tiny adobe cottages where the servants had their quarters. A large landscaped garden lay between them and the main house.

Isabella thought it all very lovely, including her room. It held a large four-poster bed and a fireplace, as well as a reading area and a dressing salon. Isabella hardly remembered when her head hit the pillow. The bed was so comfortable that it seemed to wrap her in an embrace, and when she awoke the next day, she was hard-pressed to leave it.

For the celebration, Isabella chose a gown of straight lines with an empire waist. The material was layered white muslin and lace, with overlays of peach-colored silk. She had Lupe pin up her black hair and then wrap a peach-and-yellow scarf around it. It made for a very fashionable look. In case the day was too chilly, Isabella ordered Lupe to bring a long, tailored cotton coat.

She glanced at the clock and grimaced. "I'm already late. Come on, Lupe, help me finish doing up my boot buttons."

The maid had them hooked in just a few minutes, and Isabella made her way to the dining room.

Everyone was already assembled when she made her entrance. The smile of her hostess, Anna Greer, assured Isabella she'd chosen well.

"My dear, you are stunning. You will be the envy of every woman there," Mrs. Greer declared as the men rose in greeting.

"Indeed. It's remarkable that you aren't already wedded," Mr. Greer added.

"I hope to be soon," Isabella replied without thinking. She allowed Aaron to help her into her chair—the only one left. Pity it had to be beside him. She breathed in the aroma of his cologne. She supposed it wasn't so bad. There was a definite scent of orange and sandalwood in the musk.

A footman brought her a glass of orange juice. Her arrival,

it seemed, had signaled the table service, and soon there were servants offering platters of eggs, tortillas, grits, and much more.

Once everyone was served, Mr. Greer offered a prayer and blessed the food and the day. "We are so grateful for statehood, Lord. It will mean many blessings to this land, and we praise you for all you have done. In Jesus' name, amen."

"Amen," everyone murmured.

Isabella remained quiet. She wasn't sure where God was in all of this, but she couldn't imagine that He concerned Himself overmuch with a territory becoming a state. What purpose could it possibly serve Him?

Aaron spoke to Mr. Greer as if they were old friends. The older man asked him something about the railroad, and Aaron told him all about it. Isabella nibbled at her eggs, not really having much of an appetite. Everyone else, however, seemed famished, and even Papi ate well. She tried to concentrate on what was being said, but her thoughts kept wandering. How would she ever convince her father to see Diego as a changed man?

Diego had spoken of the behavior of his youth, but he was thirty-five years old now. How could her father continue to hold the past against him? She breathed a heavy sigh, which drew Aaron's immediate attention.

"Are you all right?" he asked in a whisper while the table conversation continued.

"I'm fine. I just have a lot on my mind."

"I'm glad to see you and Aaron talking, Isabella," her father interjected. "I've asked him to act as your escort for the day. Your mother and I have duties to see to, and we'll be tied up most of the morning with the governor."

"I hardly need an escort, Papi. Besides, Lupe can go with me if need be."

"Lupe can certainly accompany you, but I'd feel better if Aaron is also with you. These parties can bring some of the rowdies into town, and I'd hate for you to be accosted."

Isabella could tell by the way he spoke that there would be no arguing with him. "Very well, Papi."

"Aaron also knows his way around Santa Fe. He's been here many times to work on projects with the railroad. Isn't that right?"

Aaron smiled. "Indeed. I know all the finest cafés and where to get the best bargains on Indian jewelry."

Mrs. Greer laughed. "He does. In fact, he helped me bargain for a beautiful necklace. I sent it back East to my sister, and now all of her friends want ones for themselves."

"It was a magnificent necklace." Aaron turned to Isabella. "A squash blossom in turquoise and silver. Have you seen them?"

"I'm not sure I have."

"Then we'll be sure to take a walk to the Plaza, where the Navajo vendors sell their wares."

She smiled in spite of herself. Aaron was such a personable man when he wasn't telling her what a horrible person she was.

When breakfast concluded, Lupe arrived with Isabella's purse and coat, as well as gloves and hat. Isabella secured the large straw hat atop her head. The creation was quite striking, having been dyed the same color as her overlays. There were clusters of bright yellow flowers grouped around the brim to add decoration.

She pulled on her gloves as they made their way out to the carriage. To her surprise, instead of a carriage, there were two automobiles.

"These are my pride and joy," Mr. Greer announced. "New Cadillacs. Aren't they grand?"

"Indeed," Isabella's father declared. "Most impressive."

"I've had the tops put down. It makes for a most comfortable ride. We'll ride in the first car, and your daughter, her maid, and Mr. Bailey can come along in the second." He motioned for the drivers and gave them instructions before sending them back to their cars.

Isabella was intrigued. She'd never ridden in an automobile before. Aunt Josephina had preferred carriages and horses. The driver opened the back door for her. She climbed up and took her place, and Lupe quickly joined her.

"I've never been in one of these," her maid said in awe.

"Me neither." Isabella couldn't keep the excitement from her voice.

"You ladies are in for a real treat," Aaron declared, taking a seat up front with the driver. He turned to smile at them over his shoulder. "I'm sure this Cadillac gives one of the finest rides." He looked at the driver. "What say you?"

"It is a very nice ride, sir."

Isabella wished once again that Diego could be by her side. Spending the day and evening with Aaron Bailey was not what she had hoped for. How wonderful it would be to share this experience with Diego rather than Aaron. Perhaps when it came time for the evening celebration, she could remain with her parents—even suggest they give Aaron the night off so they could enjoy themselves as a family.

The driver put the car in motion, and Lupe reached for Isabella's arm. Normally Isabella would have chastised her for such unacceptable behavior, but not this time. She was more than a little anxious herself.

Aaron looked back at them and grinned. "Here we go!"

Diego was no fan of the silver mine. It was cold and damp, and the job of picking up ore was the lowest of all jobs. With each minute he spent doing the tasks required, his hatred of Daniel Garcia grew. There was even some bitterness toward Isabella. After all, if it wasn't for her, he wouldn't be here.

Yet if not here, then where? He'd wasted too much time, and his father had made it clear that he wouldn't support Diego any longer. His only hope of marrying Isabella and going back to his comfortable and lavish lifestyle was to give her father this year of his life. With any luck, Daniel Garcia would die soon, and the terms of the will would be null and void. Obviously, there wouldn't be any way to assure Isabella married a man approved by her father if he were no longer alive.

"You're lagging behind, Morales," his supervisor, Mr. Briggs, yelled in the open chamber. It seemed to amplify the sound, and everyone glanced over their shoulder to see if Diego would respond.

Diego knew better than to open his mouth. He'd already protested once, and that only served to earn him extra duties. Instead, he picked up the pace and doubled his efforts. For now, he had to do things this way, but in time he'd figure out something else. There had to be a better way.

No doubt Mr. Garcia would write to Esteban Morales and tell him of the arrangement. Diego planned to write his father a letter as well. He would exaggerate the kind welcome he'd received and the generosity of Isabella's father in giving him work. He knew Garcia would no doubt tell his father the details of the job, but Diego intended that his father see it from his prospective as well. He might even add that Garcia had mentioned his illness and the need to have a son-in-law who could take over his business and obligations. Perhaps he could convince his father to advocate for Diego to be given more responsibility. After all, he and Isabella's father were long-time friends.

It was worth trying.

Daniel Garcia stood with his arm around his wife's waist, more to steady himself than to put on a display of affection. Helena was constantly vigilant regarding how he was feeling and whether he might be overdoing it, and she was the one who urged him to take advantage of her being next to him.

"Why don't we sit and have something to drink?" she suggested as a band of musicians began to play.

Daniel nodded and followed her to a bench, where he eased down with a sigh.

She smiled, but Daniel could see the grave concern in her eyes. "You're far too weak to be out here all day and then all evening. I think I'll fetch the driver. We'll go back and rest and then return later when it's time for the fireworks."

There was no arguing with her. Daniel didn't have the strength, and the thought of napping for a while was very appealing. He wondered about Isabella and Aaron. They should be told of the new plan, but that would require additional energy. He knew Isabella intended to consider the Indian wares being sold at the Plaza. Perhaps he could send the driver to find her before they left.

He closed his eyes for a moment. Thankfully, the herbal concoction one of the women in Silver Veil made for him helped control his coughing fits. He'd only had a little trouble that morning before they headed out. The coughing worried Helena, and he hated to do that. He never lied to her about how he was feeling when she asked him, but neither did he volunteer information when she didn't seem to notice.

"I found the driver," Helena announced when she returned. "He's bringing the car closer and will take us home."

"What about Isabella and Aaron?" Daniel took a couple of breaths to gather the strength to stand.

"The other driver is going to find them and let them know." She smiled and helped him up. "I'm sure they're having too much fun to worry about us."

Daniel nodded. He hoped so. He wanted more than anything for Isabella to fall in love with Aaron Bailey. He had considered this for some time, and the only way he could die in peace was if they were together and Aaron agreed to take charge of his affairs. Otherwise, he couldn't let go of life and die. He just couldn't.

9

The driver caught up with them just after lunch and announced that Isabella's parents had returned to the house to rest. Isabella wanted to join them, but the driver said they wanted her to stay. Besides, he couldn't return to the house because he had to attend to further business for Mr. Greer.

Isabella said nothing, but she wasn't happy with the prospect of continuing the chilly day at Aaron's side. Lupe, however, was having the best of times and found it a delight to talk with Aaron about everything under the sun.

"So there are Navajo and Zuni Indians here. Are there others?" the maid asked.

"There are. Sometimes the Hopi come too. Any of the tribes who have things to sell come here to the Plaza in Santa Fe. They also go to the various train stations and sell to passengers, as well as trading posts that have been established with special places for them to set up shop. It's a good way for them to make money, and people from elsewhere are fascinated to meet real-life Indians. They've only heard stories about them back East, and they get very excited to see the Indians in their native costumes."

"I can hardly wait to see the things they're selling," Lupe replied.

Isabella had to admit she was just as excited. Aaron made a good salesman. She supposed there could be a worse way to spend her day.

Multiple displays of handcrafted wares, including jewelry, baskets, and blankets, to name just a few, were arranged atop pieces of canvas on the ground. Down a long row, the owners sat beside their work. They welcomed each visitor, holding up items for them to see and telling them various prices.

"Which are the necklaces Mrs. Greer was speaking of?" Isabella couldn't remember what Aaron had called them.

"These." He pointed to one vendor's wares. "They're called squash blossom necklaces."

The Navajo woman held up one of the necklaces and spoke in broken English. "You buy for wife?"

Aaron smiled, but Isabella shook her head. Aaron took the necklace and let Isabella see it up close. The turquoise stones were polished but not shaped. The greenish-blue color very much appealed to Isabella.

"The Navajo work to fit the silver around the stones rather than reshape or cut the stones. The Zuni, on the other hand, do cut and reshape the stones. They are known for their inlay work, where they create amazing pieces with many colors of stones. I'm a fan of both."

Isabella studied the necklace, admiring the beauty of the natural turquoise. "It's lovely," she told the woman.

"See these stones with the silver flourish coming out?" He pointed to the stones on either side of the lower part of the necklace. "They are supposed to look like little flowers blossoming. At the bottom is the *naja*. That's the Navajo word for crescent. It looks rather like a horseshoe, and most believe that's what it is. However, it comes from the Spanish

Moors, who believed it was a talisman for protection. Some think that when the Spanish came here, the Navajos saw the shape and adapted it for their necklace. Even the flowers are thought to come from Spanish pomegranates."

"It's a beautiful piece."

He handed the necklace back to the woman, and she quickly picked up another and offered it up.

"The silverwork is so lovely," Isabella said, admiring the second necklace. "And look, there's a stone in the center of the naja."

"Some believe that the naja can represent the womb and the extra stone is an unborn child."

Isabella looked at Aaron, surprised by his knowledge.

He shrugged. "I find Indian art quite fascinating. Even their woven rugs and baskets tell stories. I've learned to ask questions over the years."

"Well, they're all quite beautiful."

"Would you like to have one? Your father gave me money to buy you whatever you want. Food, souvenirs, and most anything else you fancied."

She considered the two pieces she'd been shown and nodded, pointing to the first one. "I'd like that one."

Aaron pulled his wallet from his suit coat and paid the Navajo woman what she asked. She started to wrap it in a piece of cloth, but Isabella stopped her.

"I'd like to wear it."

The woman beamed her a smile and nodded. Aaron took the necklace and secured it around Isabella's neck.

"Oh, Miss Isabella, it's beautiful. It looks so perfect with the peach color," Lupe declared.

Isabella felt the stones and silver and smiled. "It's heavy, but I like the weight of it."

They moved on and looked at some of the baskets and

rugs made by the Zuni. Isabella picked one of the blankets that had been done in bands of black, red, and yellow against a dark cream-colored base.

In the center of the Plaza, a musical band struck up, and Isabella followed the others to watch the musicians as they played in the Mexican style. The day was turning out so differently from what she'd expected, and she realized she was enjoying herself.

By suppertime, her parents had returned, and she showed them her treasures. Mama was particularly fond of her squash-blossom necklace.

"I don't know when I've seen one as lovely as this," she said, admiring the piece and lightly touching the stones. "You chose well."

"Thank you for thinking to give Aaron money to pay for these things." She surprised everyone by giving her father a kiss on the cheek.

They joined the Greers at a long table for supper. There was a feast of all sorts of Mexican and Indian foods, as well as foods inspired by the white settlers who had ventured to live in the territory. It was rather like having a large family celebration. Lots of long tables had been put together for the celebration, and a mishmash of chairs lined each side. There was laughter and shouts amidst the eating, and it was a most joyous occasion. Isabella might've even been a bit glad she'd come.

Still, in the back of her mind, she couldn't help thinking of Aunt Josephina and how she would never see her again. She wasn't even able to be at the funeral to say good-bye. And who knew how much longer her father had? How could she celebrate when her aunt wasn't even cold in the ground? Yet Papi wasn't having any trouble with it. Perhaps because his time was short, he wanted to put death from his mind and enjoy life for as long as he could. Isabella could hardly fault him for that. Aunt Josephina would have wanted it that way.

Still, Papi had said nothing to anyone about his sister, and in fact had encouraged them all to remain silent about it. There was no sense in drawing disapproval for their presence or condemnation for not observing a lengthy period of mourning, he'd said. Life was too short to spend it in sorrow. Isabella would have agreed with that at one time, but lately her ability to reason what was acceptably proper and what was not seemed skewed. She forgave Diego even if what they'd said about him was true, but she couldn't excuse Papi for selling the Garcia estate?

I must forgive, she chided herself silently. The Bible said one must forgive others in order to receive forgiveness. She remembered that from a Sunday school lesson. She had to forgive Papi for the past and all that he had done to her recently. The estate was just a place now. All the people she loved were no longer there.

Her exhilaration and enjoyment in the festivities faded as her thoughts continued to darken. She set down her fork without finishing her meal.

Several people took seats on the bandstand stage. One by one, they rose to address the crowd. The governor talked about the new statehood status and what it would mean for New Mexico. There was already protection for the area as a territory, and soldiers stood at the ready to ward off Mexican *bandidos*, but statehood would bring even more benefits. Several other men spoke, but Isabella paid them little attention. She didn't want to care about this new state. Finally they unveiled a map of the United States of America. It had been carved in wood with two pieces missing— Arizona and New Mexico. Someone came forward and fitted the piece for New Mexico, and the crowd cheered. Isabella clapped and forced a smile but wondered when they might be allowed to return home.

Home. She had no home. California was gone now, and tonight they would sleep in a stranger's house. At least a stranger to her. Silver Veil was all that was left to her, but that had never felt like home. Not really.

"I hope you'll dance tonight, Isabella. When you were a little girl, you loved to dance," her father said.

"I'm tired and doubt I will." She hoped the manner in which she'd answered would keep him from trying to persuade her. When he said nothing more, she relaxed and raised her gaze. She found Aaron watching her and for a moment found it impossible to look away.

He eventually turned to answer a question from Mr. Greer, and Isabella contemplated her supper plate. It really hadn't been such a terrible day. If she could keep her thoughts from dwelling on the past or worrying about the future, she might actually enjoy the present. That thought confused her. Was that at the heart of her misery? Did she make herself unhappy pondering things she could never change?

When supper was over, bonfires were lit, and the dancing started. Isabella had to laugh at the awkward way some folks joined in. Especially when older folks danced with the children. But they were having so much fun that she couldn't think badly of them. Actually, this was probably the best day she'd had in some time, despite being tied to Aaron Bailey. He'd been quite cordial. In fact, he'd been rather fun to be with. He knew a lot about the new state and the various people who lived here, and something about the way he told the stories appealed to her.

"Would you care to dance?" Aaron asked her. "I know you told your father you don't intend to dance, but I hoped you might have changed your mind."

Isabella couldn't hide her surprise. "I . . . ah . . ."

"Go dance with the poor man, Isabella," her father said, smiling.

She looked at her father and then back to Aaron. "All right. Let's dance."

They only danced twice before the fireworks began and people stopped to admire the display. The weather had been lovely but cold, and the celebration was a perfect way to spend the day. Isabella found herself almost wishing it wouldn't end. If Diego could have joined her, it would have been perfect.

"You're frowning again," Aaron said.

She turned to see that he looked concerned rather than annoyed. "I'm fine. Really. I was thinking about how it turned out not to be a bad day after all."

"And that made you frown?"

She smiled. "No, I was just wishing Diego could have been here to enjoy the celebration."

"Is he fond of New Mexico?"

She shrugged. "Not that I know of, but then again, there's a lot about him I don't know. At least according to my father."

They walked a little ways from the main crowd. "I've never known your father to lie," Aaron said.

"He's lied to me for at least fifteen years."

It was Aaron's turn to frown. "Because he didn't tell you he was sick?"

"He should have. Instead, he kept it from me."

"Perhaps, but that's hardly the same as lying."

Isabella considered this for a moment. "Even so, he should have told me."

"I think he was a father trying to protect his daughter from unnecessary sorrow."

Isabella shook her head and almost stomped her foot. She barely held her temper. "He didn't care how I felt, otherwise he wouldn't have taken me away from my home. Had he told me he was sick, I would have understood better. I wouldn't have held it against him."

"So now that you know the truth, stop holding it against him."

She fell silent and pretended that Aaron's reasoning didn't prick her conscience. She decided to change the subject. "I think where Diego's concerned, perhaps my father has been fed false information."

"And who would that have come from?"

"Diego's father."

"Why would a father lie about his son?"

"Diego's father has never cared much for him. He's the youngest of six, and his older brothers have all done well for themselves. Diego hasn't found a profession or a way to make lots of money like they have, so his father hates him."

"It seems to me that he's found a way through you." Aaron's tone was accusing.

"I don't mind. I'll need someone to help me manage my inheritances. He's quite good at handling money." Isabella couldn't see it being a problem. Diego had a mind for money and was sure to figure out the best ways to invest.

"Did he say that?"

"Yes," Isabella confirmed. "It hurts Diego that his father puts no trust in him."

"Perhaps his father sees or knows something about his son that you don't. Maybe he's said the things he's said to your father because he wants to protect his old friend's daughter."

Isabella didn't like the way the conversation was going. "Look, it's been a very nice day, and I don't want to end it on a negative note. You've been kind and a better companion than I thought you'd be, and I don't want to fight with you. I know you think that's all I want to do, but I don't."

"I don't think that way at all. I just don't want you to get hurt. Your father feels the same way."

"Why should you care what happens to me, Aaron Bailey?"

Aaron glanced back at the dancers. "I care because of them." He motioned with a nod.

Isabella caught sight of her parents and smiled. Mama and Papi used to like to dance when she was little. When they all lived in California. She could remember relatives and friends showing up. There was always so much food and music and laughter. Now her parents barely moved as they held on to one another and swayed to the music.

Her eyes dampened, and she lost any desire to argue with Aaron. Her father was dying, but even now he was making a memory her mother could reflect on after he was gone. He loved her mother so much. He loved Isabella too. She had never doubted his love, just his judgment and ability to consider her desires.

"I've never met two people more in love," Aaron said.

She could hear the sincerity in his voice. "What about your own parents?"

He shrugged. "They love each other, but what your parents have is . . . something more. I think most people only dare to hope love like that will come into their lives."

"But it doesn't come. Is that it?"

Aaron turned away from the dancers and looked at Isabella. "No. It doesn't."

"And why is that?"

Another burst of fireworks sent their gazes heavenward, and all around them, people gasped and applauded the fine display. Isabella, however, wanted Aaron to answer her question.

"Why do you believe love like my parents' doesn't come for most folks?"

"I don't know. Maybe because people settle for something less out of desperation and fear of being alone. Maybe because someone else arranges their relationship. Who can say? I just know that it's rare." He held up his hands to silence her before she could speak. "Look, I know people fall in love and do have love in their courtship and marriage. I'm not saying they are without love. It's just not the kind of love your parents have found." He glanced back to where they now stood.

Isabella followed his gaze and saw her mother smiling up into her father's face. She always looked at him with such adoration. They did have something special. Isabella just hadn't understood it before. She wasn't sure she understood it now. But at least she could see it for what it was. Instead of making her happy, however, the thought left her feeling empty. What would her mother do once Papi was gone?

"You're frowning again."

She nodded. "I'm just trying to figure out what my mother will do once my father is gone. As close as they are, how can one live without the other?" She looked at Aaron for an answer but knew he wouldn't have one.

"There's only one love more perfect than theirs," he replied. "The love of God for your mother is even deeper."

Isabella considered that. "When I was little and got scared of something, Mama always said that God's love was perfect and that perfect love drives out all fear. She told me God loved me even more than she and Papi did, and therefore I needn't ever be afraid."

"A beautiful thought, don't you think?"

Isabella's parents chose that moment to start walking their way. "I'd like to believe it. Especially now." She glanced at Aaron. "I just don't know if I can."

10

With statehood officially settled and the celebration more than a week behind them, everyone seemed to fall into a routine. Diego got up every morning and made his way to the meeting hall to have breakfast. After this, he headed into the mine as the whistle blew the top of the hour. At noon, another whistle blew, and they stopped for lunch. At six, the whistle blew again and the shift changed, and Diego was free to go home or wherever else he desired. The trouble was there was nothing here he desired. The idea of waiting an entire year while doing hard labor was quickly losing what little appeal it once had.

Diego looked at his torn and bleeding hands and cursed. These were not the hands of a gentleman but a common laborer, something he had never intended to be. Worse still, his father wasn't even here to see his efforts. Mr. Garcia had no doubt written to Father and told him all about it, so Diego was doing his best to look productive, but it wasn't fair. He shouldn't have to prove himself at all.

He pulled on his work gloves and went on with the back-breaking work of picking up ore. With each cart he filled, he thought of being that much closer to his end goal, but it was hard to remember it would take an entire year of this kind of work before Garcia would consider him worthy enough to court Isabella. In the meantime, he was hardly allowed to see her, and he knew better than to seek out others for female companionship. Garcia seemed to have spies everywhere.

"Don't forget to stop by the office and pick up your pay, Morales," Mr. Briggs said as he watched what Diego was doing. "It's payday."

"Sounds good to me. Where does everybody go to celebrate?"

"You'd have to talk to the boys to figure that out. I go home at the end of the week. My wife and children are celebration enough for me." Briggs turned and walked away without another word.

Diego hated his supervisor. He had tried to be friendly with him, but Briggs would have no part of it.

One of his fellow workers came alongside him. "There's a great bar we go to on the far side of town called El Conejo Enojado—The Angry Rabbit. Most folks just call it Conejo's. The beer is cheap and the food, good. You're welcome to join us tonight."

Diego nodded. "Thanks, Rudy. I'd like that."

"We'd better get back to work, or we won't have a job for long." Rudy went back to his place and left Diego to his work loading rock.

Diego wished he'd proposed to Isabella long ago. He wished he'd *married* her years ago. If he'd done that, her father would be giving him a better job than this. No doubt this was to humble him and make him more mindful of the good fortune his position in life had brought him, but Diego already appreciated his position. That was why he resented being forced to work like a peon.

The longer he thought on it, the angrier he grew. He

wanted very much to put Daniel Garcia in his place. The memory of Josephina Garcia just before she fell down the stairs flashed through his mind. She knew the truth about him, and so did her brother. Hopefully, Daniel would soon follow her in death. After all, once Daniel Garcia was gone, he could no longer dictate the course of their lives.

"On Monday I want you to get down to Engle and work on what additional tracks are needed for the new dam," the superintendent declared. "I have word from the construction supervisor that they're nearing completion of the track from Engle to the dam site. We have railcars full of supplies waiting to ship."

Aaron looked at the map he'd just placed on the table while the superintendent continued.

"As best I can tell from his letter, they've laid track to this location." He pointed, and Aaron took note.

"When do you want me to go down?"

"Right away. There was some talk of additional track being laid, and I need a detailed outline of what they have in mind. When you have that figured out, I want you to go to Silver Veil and talk to Daniel Garcia about the new town idea, since you didn't get far when you were down there after New Year's."

"He's dying, and his health continues to diminish. I'm not sure we'll convince him to start anything new. Frankly, it might be best to wait and see what happens."

"What do you mean?"

"Well . . ." Aaron hesitated. He'd never shared Garcia's desires with the superintendent for fear he would demand Aaron agree to them.

"Get on with it, man. I haven't got all day."

Aaron drew a deep breath. "Garcia wants me to quit my job for the Santa Fe and work for him. He wants me to take over managing his affairs."

The older man stared at him for a moment and then smiled. "But don't you see, that's perfect! If you're in charge, you could set things in motion for building the town."

"I know, but it would mean leaving my job with the Santa Fe."

"We could arrange something. I could give you a leave of absence. Or you could continue to work for the Santa Fe from Silver Veil."

Aaron shook his head. "I would have far too much to do for Garcia. I doubt I would have time for anything else."

"Well, that would be fine too. He has a lot of land and money and plenty of business with the Santa Fe. Let me talk to management, but I think we can spare you. It would be worth it to have a man like you managing Garcia's money and stock. I think you should take his offer. In the long run you could really benefit the Santa Fe."

"I'll continue to think about it, sir. However, if I do what Daniel Garcia wants, my focus would be benefitting Mrs. Garcia and her daughter, not the Santa Fe."

"Why don't you make your way to Silver Veil and see what all Garcia would expect of you? Perhaps if you knew the details of the job, you'd find it more appealing. I don't see this as an opportunity we can let go by the wayside."

"I thought you wanted me down at the dam site." Aaron hadn't expected his boss to be so enthusiastic about his leaving. Or maybe he had, and that was the reason he had said nothing about it the first time Daniel begged him to quit his job.

"I'll put Stevens on it. He can manage something that

simple. You're better needed working alongside Garcia. We need him, Bailey. We need to keep him happy, and we need him making decisions that serve our purpose. Go back to Silver Veil and stay for a time. I'll get in touch with you if I need you."

"What about my salary? I still need money to live on."

"You'll continue to draw your pay for now. Obviously, once you're on Garcia's payroll, you needn't be on ours. I'll send the checks to you at the Silver Veil depot. This is important, and you need to keep everything running smoothly. The last thing I need is for that man to die and his widow to cancel out everything he's done or plans to do. We need you to keep the projects focused and moving forward. Encourage Garcia on the Engle project. Perhaps even get him to travel with you to the site. This will greatly benefit him as well as the railroad."

"It's hard to care about financial benefits when you're dying, sir. The trip to Santa Fe was hard on him. I doubt he has another trip in him."

"If he dies, how will things be managed?"

"That's what he wants me to do." Aaron had known it would be a mistake to mention anything about Daniel's desires to have him take over managing his estate. Now he was getting pressure from both sides.

"With you in charge, we could count on you to work with the Santa Fe exclusively. You already understand railroad business." The superintendent's expression was full of surprised excitement. It didn't matter to him that Garcia was dying. He wasn't close to Daniel like Aaron was.

"If I quit to help Mr. Garcia, I will keep the family's needs and desires in mind first. Just as I mentioned earlier."

"Of course, of course. But serving our needs will benefit his family."

Aaron really couldn't argue that point. If he were to convince Daniel to invest in building up another town near the new dam, it would eventually pay for itself and bring additional profit to the family.

"I want you to do this, Bailey. At least for now. Garcia may have another arrangement in mind for after his death, but while he's alive and wants you at his side, I believe that's where you should be.

"Yes, sir." Aaron knew he'd lost this battle. He also knew it was Garcia's fondest wish that Aaron continue to manage his estate after he was gone. It didn't look like Aaron would have any say about it.

The noon whistle blew, and Aaron left the offices and headed to one of the nearby cafés. He had planned only to grab a quick lunch, but when he saw Jim was seated in the back, he made his way through the room to join him.

"Didn't figure to find you here. Thought you were in El Paso," Aaron said, taking a seat at the table.

"Got back late last night on a freight. How'd things go in Santa Fe?"

"Turned out better than I expected." The waitress approached, and Aaron and Jim gave their orders before the conversation continued. "We had a pleasant day even though Mr. Garcia asked me to escort his daughter."

"You had to be with her the entire day?" Jim grinned and took a drink of his root beer.

The waitress returned with coffee for Aaron and the promise that their meals would be out soon. Aaron sipped the black brew and grimaced at the strength.

"You should have gone with root beer," Jim admonished. "You know how strong they make the coffee here."

"I know. I guess I just keep expecting a different outcome."

"Kind of like Mr. Garcia."

126

"Huh?"

Jim laughed. "He keeps expecting a different outcome from you. He keeps after you, hoping to wear you down and get you to take over his job and family. Did you ever think that maybe this is God's plan for you, Aaron? You claim to be praying about it."

"My supervisor just told me to forget about my work with the Santa Fe even though they'll keep me on the payroll until Daniel starts paying me. They want me to go to Silver Veil to see what Garcia's job offer entails."

"See? I'd say you've gotten your answer from God."

"Or at least the Santa Fe."

Jim laughed all the more. "Down here, they're nearly one and the same."

Aaron stepped off the train in Silver Veil and glanced around the little town. Daniel Garcia had taken a desolate spot in the mountains and turned it into an oasis. The people here seemed happy. No doubt there were problems, just as there were everywhere, but Aaron hadn't heard of anything major. There'd never been a murder or a bank robbery.

He supposed part of the reason was the town's isolation. A person traveling on the main line from Albuquerque to El Paso would have to take the spur line up into the mountains. The train to Silver Veil only operated one day a week unless the Santa Fe had a special request or need. So it wasn't like people might accidentally wander into town. They really had to want to be here.

Aaron knew Daniel liked it that way. It had made it so much easier to keep the peace in the early years. As time went by, the town grew, and certain jobs had to be appointed.

Most everyone did double duty. The town's law official, Zed Jones, was also the postmaster and town recordkeeper. Lucas Adams was the bank manager, who was also looking into becoming a leader of the new Boy Scouts of America organization, and he sold jewelry on the side, since his family had a big shop in Dallas. Some of the local artists even arranged with him to sell their wares in his family's store.

Aaron had watched this town grow for the last seven and a half years. He knew almost everyone and understood what Daniel hoped to accomplish. He really was the perfect person to take over. But it was hard giving up on his own plans in order to take over the dreams of another.

As he passed the blacksmith's, he gave Will Jefferson a wave. The big man had been born into slavery back in Alabama but came west with his grandparents after the war gave them their freedom. He'd worked as a cowboy and a wrangler before settling in Silver Veil as a smithy.

Will dusted off his hands and made his way out to the road. "How you doin', Mr. Aaron?"

"Doing good. And you? Did that grandbaby finally arrive?"

Will gave him a broad smile. "He did. Big and healthy, and Mama is doin' just fine."

Aaron nodded. "Congratulations. I'm glad things worked out so well. A boy will carry on the family name."

"Yes, sir. Say, would ya like me to carry you up to the Garcia place?"

Aaron smiled at the Southern phrasing. "No. I need time to think. The walk will do me good."

He smiled. "I understand. Good luck with the thinkin'."

"Thanks, Will."

Continuing up the mountain road to the Garcia house, Aaron wondered what Daniel would say when he showed up.

He hadn't bothered to send a telegram to let Daniel know, and it was possible he wouldn't want Aaron there. But Aaron doubted it.

He pulled his coat a little closer as the breeze stirred. Based on the clouds moving in, they might be in for snow. He quickened his pace just in case.

He was surprised by how enthusiastically the Santa Fe was pushing him toward acceptance of Garcia's job offer. Aaron knew if he accepted it, that would be the end of his career with the Santa Fe. He had always hoped to be put in charge of a railroad district someday. He hadn't assumed it would be the local Rio Grande Division—the Horny Toad Division, as the local workmen called it—but he would have enjoyed that. He had come to love the arid land around him.

But working for Daniel Garcia would change all of that. There would be no going back to rebuild his career with the railroad, despite what his boss suggested. Daniel intended for someone to take over his little town permanently. He needed an honest man to keep the people honest. He needed someone to oversee the mine and silver processing mill he'd created. He needed someone to tend to the needs of the people of Silver Veil, as well as to his wife and daughter. And if Aaron were to be perfectly honest with himself, Daniel wanted him to marry Isabella. The older man had teasingly said, on more than one occasion, that he thought Aaron needed a wife and that he had an unmarried daughter. Jim had suggested Aaron could help Daniel without marrying either his widow or his daughter, but Aaron had a sneaking suspicion that just wasn't true.

Forgetting the weather, he paused in his climb and looked back down on the little town. It had grown considerably over the years. Families who had benefitted from Daniel's plans had encouraged their extended family to join them. Convicts who hoped to be rid of their past had heard about Daniel Garcia's willingness to give a man a second chance. They were perhaps the most stalwart of people who fought to keep the town free of riffraff. They knew better than anyone how, without much effort, a town could change for the worse. When less-than-desirable men came into town, Garcia had found one of two things worked in dealing with them. He either gave them money and a train ticket to leave, or he took them under his wing. He had managed to break through to some of the most hardened hearts.

Oh, to have that kind of influence on a man. Or a woman. Isabella came to mind, and Aaron shook his head. He was not going to marry Isabella Garcia. He didn't love her. He didn't even like her.

Much.

Resuming his walk, Aaron realized this was it. This was his call to make a decision. Daniel Garcia needed him, and the Santa Fe wanted him to help. Aaron wanted to help too. Daniel had come to be a second father to him. Aaron had worked with him since first coming to New Mexico years ago. He had learned all manner of things from Daniel, but most of all, his faith had grown stronger because of him. And Mrs. Garcia had mothered him and cared for him. Once when he'd been ill, she had insisted he remain at the house and recover. They were as much family to him as were his own people.

But then there was Isabella.

Daniel Garcia was hunting for a husband for his daughter and had settled on Aaron. It wasn't that she wasn't appealing. She was beautiful, but that wasn't enough for Aaron. She was troubled and difficult. She lacked respect, and she refused to see her need for God. Aaron could hardly allow himself to be unequally yoked, even if he did find her attractive.

Not only that, but she had no interest in him whatsoever. She fancied herself in love with Diego Morales. Her father had acknowledged this by giving Diego a job to prove himself. What if Diego did exactly as Garcia required? What if in one year Diego completed his task and Garcia believed him worthy of marriage to Isabella? Where would that leave Aaron if he began a real attempt to pursue her?

The house came into view, and Aaron spotted the gardener and his son out working to clear away some brush that was no longer desired. He supposed if Diego proved to be a good man—good enough for Isabella—Aaron would be trimmed away just as easily.

"But it's doubtful Daniel Garcia will live that long," he reminded himself aloud.

And that created the real problem. Time. They had so little time to make these life-altering decisions. Time was what they most needed, but it was also what they most lacked.

"Aaron, I saw you coming up the road from my bedroom window. Whatever are you doing here?" Daniel Garcia asked, meeting him at the door. He leaned against the jamb and began to cough. Aaron waited for the older man to catch his breath and calm his lungs.

This spell, however, was worse than usual. Daniel gasped for air and grew weaker by the second. The handkerchief he used was spotted in blood, although he had done his best to hide it. Aaron could see the sickness was taking its toll, and reached out to help steady the older man.

"Let's at least get you to a chair."

Aaron helped Daniel back into the house and found a straight-backed wooden chair just inside the foyer. He assisted Garcia onto the seat, and when the housekeeper appeared, he suggested a glass of water. She nodded and hurried away. It wasn't but a few moments before she was back with the water. Daniel took sips between the worst of the coughing. Little by little, the irritation appeared to ease.

"*Gracias*, Maya." He looked up at Aaron and smiled. "Thank you. As you can see . . ." He paused to clear his throat. "As you can see, I'm ever closer to the end."

Aaron glanced at Maya and then back to Daniel. "How are you feeling otherwise?"

"Tired. It's a wonder I can still get out of bed, but I just keep driving myself with the reminder that soon I'll have a new body that never tires or hurts and can never become sick."

A smile broke from Aaron's lips. Daniel was always so positive. "I hope you don't mind my showing up unannounced."

"Of course not. You are always welcome here. Why don't we go to the library and talk? Maya, would you bring us some coffee and then send Pablo down to the station to retrieve Mr. Bailey's bags?" He turned to Aaron. "I presume they're there?"

Aaron nodded. "I knew I'd do well just to make it up your mountain road without carrying anything." He laughed, and Daniel smiled.

"Good. Maya, send Pablo. Give Aaron his regular room."

The housekeeper had kept her distance so as not to interfere, but now she stepped forward to take the glass from Daniel. "I will send him and then have coffee waiting for you in the library." She hurried off down the hall.

"And she will too," Daniel said. "Even if I could move fast, she would move faster. I've never seen anything like it. She probably saw you somehow when you got off the train, and put the pot on."

Aaron chuckled and helped Daniel to his feet. "She is a wonder." He glanced around. "Where are Mrs. Garcia and your daughter this fine day?"

"Down in Silver Veil at the church. The ladies have one of their charity events today. They've been gathering clothes and shoes for the poor." He leaned heavily on Aaron and coughed from time to time as they headed for the library. "Helena sent letters to all her friends and extended family and asked them to send what they could. She managed to get ten crates full of goods. Some of it looked brand-new, but her cousins can afford that. Now they are preparing it for distribution."

"I thought Mrs. Garcia's family had nothing to do with her."

"Her mother and father were the instigators of that, and they are dead. As are her aunts and uncles. Her cousins, however, are quite different in their thoughts. They see no problem with our union. A couple of them even came to me for advice on investments."

"I'm glad. I would hate to have my family turn their back on me."

"If they did, you'd always have us." He gave Aaron a weak smile. "So why have you come?"

"There are several reasons, but believe it or not, the Santa Fe wants me to make myself useful to you."

"They know who butters their bread." Daniel chuckled.

Aaron could hear how heavy his breathing had become and stopped. "We can rest a moment if you like. I'm not going to pretend you don't have issues. That wouldn't serve either of us well."

Daniel nodded and leaned up against the wall. "No, you're certainly right about that. It's one of the reasons I esteem you so highly. You aren't afraid of the truth."

"I might dislike it, but no, I'm not afraid of it."

They rested for a moment, and then Daniel pushed off the wall and started again. They reached the library shortly thereafter, and sure enough, a tray of coffee and cookies was already awaiting them.

Daniel pointed to it as Aaron led him to a chair by the fireplace. "I told you so."

"You did indeed. May I bring you a cup?"

"Not just yet, but help yourself."

Aaron poured himself a cup of coffee, grateful to know it would be the perfect blend. The coffee served by the Garcia kitchen was always smooth and nutty in flavor. He made his way to the fireplace and took the chintz-covered chair a few feet from Daniel's.

"Now, just how useful would the Santa Fe like you to be?" Daniel asked, barely giving Aaron time to sample his coffee.

"They were intrigued when I mentioned your desire for me to come work for you full-time. They suggested I could manage the accounts here and represent you to the railroad while still remaining on their payroll. At least for a time."

"That could prove very beneficial for you, but the work I have in mind for you would keep you more than busy. You'd have little time to do anything for the Santa Fe."

Aaron suppressed a sigh. "I figured that would be the case, but I'm ready to discuss it with you. It would seem that the Santa Fe and God are of the same mind."

11

The ladies had just finished sorting the clothes and shoes into groups by size. Isabella listened to the women telling stories while they worked. Most spoke in Spanish, which Isabella spoke fluently. There was much laughter, and they even broke into song from time to time. Praising God seemed to make the work go more quickly.

Isabella was surprised by how easily her mother spoke to the women in Spanish. It used to be that her ability was minimal at best. Now she spoke as if it were a language she'd been born to. Not only that, but she made herself such a part of their company that it was almost as if she were one of them, rather than a lady of means.

When Mama and Papi married, Mama had been living the life of a well-to-do politician's daughter. She spoke some Spanish due to the household staff, but her life was one of high society and the very latest fashions. The shock of a white woman marrying a man of Spanish and Mexican descent caused more than a bit of scandal, and Mama was ostracized from her family. Isabella's grandparents hadn't wanted anything to do with Mama from the moment she'd taken Daniel Garcia as her husband.

Mama missed them but often told Isabella that their prejudice and bitterness had cost them the honor of being grandparents to Isabella. Mama had hoped Isabella could one day mend the gap between families, but her grandparents had died only a few years after her birth, and Isabella never had a chance to meet them, much less help bring the two families together. Isabella sometimes wondered if that reconciliation was the sole reason God had put her on earth. Then she'd reason that if it had been, God would surely have worked out the details and kept them alive.

"Are you ready to go?" Mama asked, pulling on her wool cloak as the mine whistle blew the end of the shift.

"I am. I'm famished." Lunch had been hours ago, and Isabella was used to stopping for tea in the afternoon. Now, as she and her mother made their way to the carriage, the sun was already setting, and it would soon be time for supper.

"I didn't mean for us to be so long," Mama said, waiting for Isabella to climb into the carriage. "But we got so much accomplished." She checked her pockets. "Oh, my gloves aren't here. I'll be right back." She hurried back to the church.

Settling into the carriage, Isabella was surprised to see snowflakes falling ever so lightly. It had been a long time since she'd seen snow fall. Mesmerized by this, she was startled when a man's voice broke the silence.

She turned to find Diego standing next to the carriage. He was filthy from working in the mine, but he gave her a smile and instantly charmed her.

"How are you, my dear?" he asked.

"I'm well. How are you? I feel terrible that you are having to work so hard. I've tried to talk to Papi about it. I suggested he at least let you live in the house, but he said the other workers would treat you horribly if they thought you were his pet."

"And they would, no doubt. They are a ruthless and cut-throat bunch."

Isabella frowned. "Are they dangerous?"

"Yes, very much so, but you shouldn't worry. I can take care of myself. And I would endure anything necessary to win your hand."

His words touched her heart, and Isabella immediately felt guilty for the fact that, of late, she'd not given him much thought. She'd been far too worried about her father.

"Papi's condition is growing worse. He has so little strength."

"What will happen if he dies?"

Isabella shrugged. "I'm not sure. He and Mama expect me to remain here and help with their work. She has no desire to leave Silver Veil, so I'm not certain what will happen."

"But you hate it here," he reminded her.

"I do. Although I suppose it's not so bad, since I no longer have my home in California to return to."

"Once you have inherited, you will have enough money to buy a home in California. Perhaps even buy the rancho back from my father."

"I know, but it wouldn't be the same. I loved that place because I grew up there. My father grew up there too. However, none of the people I love are there anymore."

Diego crossed his arms. "I intend to speak to my father about that. There's no reason with all that land that my brother couldn't set his racetrack elsewhere. They should be glad for us to live on the property. I could even help with the running of the racetrack. It's something I know quite well."

Isabella nodded. "I suppose you do."

"Don't worry, my sweet. We will find a way to make them all listen to us." He reached out his dirty hand and took hold of her gloved fingers. "We will make them listen."

Isabella glanced back at the church. "My mother will return at any moment. Might we meet somewhere tomorrow?"

"Where?"

Isabella considered their options. "I like to go for rides, but since it's snowing, I doubt I'll be allowed to go. Can you sneak onto the property? I could meet you in the storage room behind the stables. No one would have any reason to be there. Come around noon." She frowned. "Or do you have to work extra hours tomorrow? It's Saturday, and I just assumed you'd have the day off." She heard the church door open and pulled her hand back quickly.

Diego smiled and crossed his arms. "I do. And I will come meet you. Never fear."

"Diego. I wasn't expecting to see you here," Mama said as she returned to the carriage, gloves already on.

"Mrs. Garcia, how nice to see you." He bowed. "It's payday, and I must put my money in the bank and save it for our wedding." He smiled at Isabella.

Mama didn't smile. Instead, she climbed into the carriage with Isabella. "I'm afraid we can't stay to talk. As you see, it's starting to snow, and that will make our road slick. Have a good evening, Diego." She picked up the lines and smacked them on the horses' backs.

Mama drove them to where Main Street crossed Washington Street and then turned left. They drove to the next intersection, where she turned left again. Isabella could feel her mother's tension. Was she that upset to find Diego talking to her daughter? Surely not.

The horses seemed to realize they were heading home as soon as they neared the railroad tracks. Isabella waited until her mother directed the horses past the station and up the mountain road before she spoke.

"It was so nice to see Diego. I have missed him so much."

Mama shook her head. "I'm sure you have, but I wish you would put him aside."

"Why?"

"I'll leave it to your father to tell you everything about his past."

"I'm sure he's accused of much, but he's a changed man. He loves me, and I know we'll be happy together."

"Well, that certainly remains to be seen." Her mother looked up at the sky. "The snow has stopped for the time being. I'm certainly grateful for that."

Isabella sensed her mother relax just a bit. Perhaps her tension was more about the roads and weather than about Diego. Nevertheless, Isabella wasn't going to tell her mother about meeting Diego tomorrow.

After lunch the next day, Isabella slipped out of the house and made her way to the storage room. Diego was already waiting for her and embraced her when she arrived.

Isabella wasn't sure what to do. For some reason, his actions made her uncomfortable.

Stepping back, she did her best to conceal her feelings. "Did anyone see you?"

"No. I'm certain of that. I took the road to the mine, then cut across and behind the equipment buildings and onto your property. I'm sure no one could see me."

"I know there would be such a fuss if they found you

here." Isabella glanced around and chose one of several crates to sit on. "I'm glad you could come. I've been so worried about you."

"And I've worried about you." He sat down beside her and took her hand. "I hate this separation."

"I do too. I don't see why you can't live at the house, even if it does make some of the men jealous. You're very nearly a part of the family. They know you are more than just another worker. If there's going to be jealousy, I would imagine it's already in place."

"Yes. There are some who do recognize my attachment to the family, but they've said very little."

"Have you made any friends?"

"Surprisingly, yes. Several. They are far beneath the people I would usually associate with, but it's important to prove to your father that I can bend to his will."

"I met some ladies yesterday at church. They seemed quite nice but of a lower class. Still, my mother treats them like equals. She says it's important to esteem others as better than ourselves because the Bible bids us to do so. I've never really thought much about it, to be honest. There are always people who do the menial jobs and others who are above them and do jobs that require more skill and experience. Above that are people who perhaps own shops or oversee other workers."

Diego interrupted. "And over them all are the people of means who provide the positions that allow them to make a living. We do not all belong in the same society, however. You cannot be a friend to those you must lead. They will not take instruction or direction if they believe themselves to be equals."

"That has always been my thought. I believed it was the opinion of my parents as well, but it is not." Isabella shrugged. "But enough of that. You look so tired. Are you eating enough? Sleeping?"

"As well as can be expected. Your father put me alongside the other workers with no more or less than they have. Which means none of us have much of anything. I sleep on a cot and eat the food of field workers and cowboys."

Isabella shook her head. "I hate that. Father is being cruel. You are a good man, and just because there are supposed mistakes in your past, one shouldn't decide you are unworthy of love and consideration. My father preaches that God is all about second chances and forgiveness. Does he mean that for everyone but you?"

"It would seem." He gave her a sad look, and Isabella felt even sorrier for him.

"I will speak to him again and see what I can do to change things."

"I wouldn't expect anything to change, beloved. He has already made up his mind due to my father poisoning his thoughts. I think we will have to elope in order to marry. Your father's imposed year of work will simply turn into more years or conditions before he allows me to take your hand." He drew something out of his pocket. "I know you are probably worried that I will not be true and wait for you. I want you to have this."

He extended an emerald ring to Isabella. She gasped at the size of the stone. It was a beautiful rectangular cut, and the rich hue of the green gem against the gold was impressive.

"I want to give you this ring as a token—a promise. I want you to marry me, and this will be our pledge to one another," Diego declared.

"It's so beautiful, but I dare not wear it. Please keep it for me. I don't want to lose it." Isabella closed his fingers around the ring.

"I cannot keep it with me. Someone is sure to steal it. Please keep it with your other jewelry. If your mother or father comments on it, tell them your aunt bought it for you."

"Lie to them over a ring? I don't think I could."

He pressed the ring into her hand. "Please take it and pledge yourself to me alone. In fact, let's elope. We could run away, and I could marry you."

"We'd lose a lot. I have so little unless I marry a man my father approves."

"Your father will hardly live long enough to approve me. He looks worse every day, I hear."

Isabella took the ring and held it to her heart. She didn't know why, but his comment left her cold and uneasy. "If we ran away together, we'd have little or no money. My grandparents' money is still under my father's care, and I haven't received my aunt's jewels yet. Although I would never consider selling them. So you see, we would be unable to take care of ourselves, and they would no doubt come after us."

Diego thought for a moment. "Well, we could put on a pretense that would solve all of our problems."

Isabella frowned. "What do you mean?"

"You and I could make it look like you'd been taken. Kidnapped and held for ransom. I could get a couple of friends to help us."

"That sounds dangerous." She bit her lower lip, her uneasiness growing.

"It wouldn't be, because I would be there. The men would be good friends of mine." His words gained speed as he seemed to warm to the idea. "See, we could agree on a place to meet, and you would go to a hiding place with me and my men. We would send your father a ransom letter demanding a certain amount of money and telling him where to leave it. I could even act as the hero and pretend to find you after the money was exchanged. My men would get a cut of the money, but most of it would be ours for our escape." He grinned.

Isabella could hardly believe he was suggesting such a thing. Her father was in such a weakened state that something like this would surely push him over the edge—kill him.

"No. I cannot do that to my family. Besides, Papi would never let you marry me after pulling such a stunt."

"He'd never know. I'm certain I can work out the details and see this through."

"No." Isabella shook her head. "We'll find a way to convince my father to get you out of the mine. I don't want you having to continue with such hard work. Just be patient. I'll get this figured out."

"But my way would be quicker and so easy." Diego drew her to her feet and pulled her close. "Just think, we could be man and wife in a matter of days rather than months or years."

His comment made Isabella angry. He had no consideration for her father or her mother. When Isabella thought of the fear it would cause them, she couldn't stomach the idea in any form. It angered her that Diego considered it a viable plan.

"We are not going to do that," she stated firmly. She saw anger flash in Diego's eyes and reached out to touch his arm. "Don't be angry with me."

"I'm not. I'm just so disappointed. I want to be with you, Isabella."

"And I want to be with you, but not like that. Now, I'd better get back to the house before someone comes looking for me. Will you be able to leave unnoticed?"

"I'll be fine."

He didn't sound fine. He still sounded angry, but Isabella

decided to ignore it. She headed to the storage room door and cracked it open to look outside. "It's all clear. I'll go first. We'll try to meet again soon."

She made her way back to the house, cutting in through the arched opening to the courtyard. She was nearly to the hall door when she heard her name called. She turned to find Aaron Bailey coming from the same direction she'd taken.

"Yes?" she asked.

"Your father is asking for you, and no one knew where you'd gone."

"It's not important. I just needed some time to myself. Where is Papi?"

"In the library." Aaron's expression told her he didn't believe her. "I hope you know what you're doing. Diego Morales is not someone I'd trust, and you may find yourself in trouble if you aren't careful." With that, he turned and left.

Isabella was stunned that he knew she'd been with Diego. She'd been so careful and had been certain no one knew where she'd gone. She stared after him. Would he say anything to her father? She certainly didn't want to explain her secret meeting with Diego.

She sighed heavily. None of this was Aaron's business. He was nothing more than a worker for the railroad and her father. He had no right to chastise her, and at her first opportunity, she intended to tell him to mind his own business and leave hers alone.

12

With the arrival of February, Diego was congratulated for working at the mine for a whole month.
"Many a man has given up before reaching one month," Mr. Briggs told him. "We're promoting you to using a pick. You'll be one of the men who digs the ore out instead of the one picking it up."

Mr. Briggs acted like it was some big honor, but Diego only nodded. There wasn't a job in the mine that he wanted. He was tired of working here, tired of the stench of unbathed bodies, and tired of spending his days working rather than having fun.

He thought about Isabella. Surely by now she'd received her aunt's jewelry. Even so, they certainly couldn't sell it here. Albuquerque would probably be too close to get rid of it too. Perhaps if they caught the train back to California, he could check with former friends as to who might sell the jewelry for them.

He remembered the look on Josephina Garcia's face as she fell to her death. Diego probably could have caught her. He might have stopped her fall. He wasn't sure that this was true, but the possibility had haunted him since the accident.

Even more guilt-inducing was the fact that he'd run away and left her there to bleed to death.

Well, it wasn't his fault. It was an accident. He hadn't caused her to die, and if he'd been caught there, someone would have accused him of murder.

The lunch whistle blew, and the men left the mine to gather in a large common area inside the office building. Garcia had set the place up for meetings and for meals, and he furnished food for each shift's lunches.

Diego grabbed a tray and got in line. The serving women were fast at their job and knew each man. They no longer had to ask if he wanted this or that—they knew. He had to admit he was impressed with their ability to remember that he didn't like overly spiced food or chicken. It didn't always merit him something else to eat, but generally it got him a larger portion of something he did like.

Today they were eating beans and tamales. It was a far cry from the beefsteak Diego preferred, and there were none of the delectable French sauces his father's cook was so good at making.

"*Hola*, Señor Diego," a woman at the end of the line said as she put a glass of iced tea on his tray.

"Hello, Aggie."

She was at least five years his senior but seemed to be sweet on him, though Diego didn't find her at all appealing. He steadied his tray and turned to find a place where he could sit in peace and eat his lunch.

"Diego! Over here," Rudy called. He and Jorge had already laid claim to a small table.

Diego made his way to them and plopped down across from Jorge. They already had half their food devoured. A person learned to eat fast in case there were leftovers. It was always first come, first served.

"I've got something I want to discuss with you two," Diego said before taking a long drink of tea. He always felt like he needed to wash away a mouthful of dirt before he could eat.

"What you got in mind?" Rudy asked.

"A way to make a lot of money."

"Money's good. You got our attention." Rudy even stopped eating for a moment. "What do we need to do to get this money?"

"Not much. Just kidnap the boss's daughter."

Rudy looked at Diego as if he'd lost his mind. He laughed and turned his attention back to his food. "For a minute I thought you were serious."

"I am." Diego ate nearly half his tamale in one bite. These ladies could certainly cook.

Neither man would even look at him, much less speak. Diego chuckled. "I know it sounds bad, but just listen to me and promise to say nothing."

The men glanced up, barely acknowledging his comment with slight nods.

Diego smiled. "You can't have known this, but Isabella Garcia and I are engaged to be married. We were very close back in California."

"If you're engaged to the boss's daughter, why are you working in the mine?" Rudy asked.

"It's an arrangement I made with her father. I want to learn every aspect of the mine because he plans to turn it over to me one day. However, he doesn't want to give Isabella her inheritance. Her aunt recently died and left her a lot of money, and Mr. Garcia won't release it."

"That doesn't sound like him," Jorge said, shaking his head. "He's always very generous."

"Not with his daughter. Look, I talked to Isabella about this, and she's all for it." This got their attention. "She knows her father would be willing to pay a lot to see her returned safely, and that way she could at least get some of the ransom money, as would I, and of course you two. Since we'd be doing it with her help, there'd be no danger of her getting hurt. And, if worse came to worse, we could just admit it was a farce—that we were just joking around. She'd see that we didn't have any trouble."

Rudy grew thoughtful and rubbed his bare chin. "So what would we have to do?"

"Well, we haven't worked out all the details, but she would leave a ransom note and then sneak out of the house. I'd meet her nearby, and we would take her someplace safe."

"Her father has a cabin up in the mountains," Jorge offered. "I've been there a couple of times, helping the boss. I even went up there once on my own when I wanted to get away from everything. I knew Señor Garcia wouldn't be there, so I took advantage of it."

"That sounds perfect. I doubt he would think to look right under his nose. He's going to believe the kidnappers would have taken her away on the train."

"We could make it look like that," Rudy agreed. "We could get on the train in disguise, a couple of us traveling with Señorita Garcia. One of us could wait at an appointed place with the horses, then whoever was on the train could sneak off, and we'd all ride to the cabin."

"It would work too," Jorge added. "There's another road that goes up the back side of the mountain and meets up with the path that goes to the cabin."

Diego nodded. It was starting to sound like a real plan. Now, if he could just convince Isabella to participate.

"But folks would know it was us when we didn't turn up at work," Rudy said suddenly. His expression of interest turned to worry. "How would we explain that?"

"We would show up for work as always. If Isabella is helping us, she can be by herself in the cabin, even for several days if need be. She's very resourceful." At least he hoped she was. He'd never known her to be afraid of much. "We can go to work as usual, and I can go visit her at the cabin after everyone's gone to sleep."

Rudy nodded, looking relieved. "Sure, and you can borrow my horse, Dusty. He's surefooted and shoed. Not like most of the ponies around here that go barefoot. Unless you're rich like the Garcias. They shoe all of their horses."

"Better take the preacher too," Jorge teased. "That's a long way up and back down. You might just want to stay the night."

Rudy laughed. Diego forced a grin. At that moment, intimacy with Isabella Garcia was furthest from his mind. Her father's millions was the thing he wanted to cozy up to.

Isabella sat beside her mother, rolling bandages like the other dozen or so church ladies seated at the table. Mother had explained that each of the three churches did a variety of things to help prepare their community for tragedy or problems, such as a collapse or explosion at the mine. They also worked together to assist the poor in town.

Mama said it was God's will that they should treat each person with care and be helpful to all. These were people who had far less and deserved help. Papi would meet with each family or individual and observe what their needs might be. He had some family housing for mine workers as well as individual apartments that could be shared, like the one he'd put Diego in. Isabella still thought it a shame that Diego couldn't just stay at the house like one of the family. He could surely prove his goodness all the faster if her father were able to oversee his private life as well as his working day.

The women settled on a hymn and broke into harmony as they praised God for His goodness. Isabella had to admit the singing made the day pass much more quickly. The work didn't seem much like work at all when everyone pulled together.

"The women at one of the other churches are sewing baby blankets today," Mama had told her before they left home that morning. "And the Methodist church ladies are knitting wool socks for older people. All of the women are working in spirit as one. Even though we attend separate churches, we are still part of one body."

"What makes us one? Doesn't each church worship in different ways and believe different things?"

"The most important thing is that we believe Jesus came to earth as our promised Messiah—our Savior. He gave His life for us, dying on a cross and taking our sins onto Himself. Then He rose again from the grave to conquer death. Without Jesus we cannot have salvation—He is the only way to the Father. The churches here in Silver Veil are all in agreement on that. We try not to let the rest of it concern us overmuch."

Her mother's comments had remained with Isabella throughout the day. She knew there were great fights over what should and shouldn't be believed. She had even read in the newspapers about problems between local churches when she lived in California. It made her not want to be a part of any church. If they were that ugly amongst themselves, why should she want to join them?

But if Mama was right—and Isabella had no reason to think otherwise—it made more sense. It wasn't their differences that mattered. It was their agreement that Jesus was Lord.

"Your father says that as people read the Bible," her mother had said, "they will soon enough see the flaws in man-made religions. As we study God's Word, we will come to understand what is truth and what are lies. That is why it is important to be in the Bible daily. He will open our eyes to see the truth, and the Holy Spirit will enable us with understanding."

When she was little, Isabella remembered praying with her mother and asking Jesus to come into her heart. Attending church as a young child, Isabella felt a sense of belonging. When she left California for New Mexico, however, that feeling was lost amidst her anger and confusion over why her parents would take her from all she loved. She honestly figured God didn't love her anymore, just as she knew her parents didn't. After all, how could they love her and take her from all that was important to her?

Since then, a hardness in her heart had kept Isabella from even praying. She didn't want to talk to God if He was mean and heartless. Yet something in her kept calling back to those moments when she was little and had prayed that Jesus would be her Lord and Savior.

Now, Isabella felt that hardness giving way. She listened to the women talk about the blessings they'd received or given. They talked about answered prayers, and always they praised God for His provision. Perhaps she would find comfort and wisdom in reading her Bible.

The song ended, and a woman Isabella knew as Señora Julietta stood. "I want to tell you a story," she said softly in Spanish. "When I was a young bride, I prayed for my husband and the children God might give us. I prayed that our children would be a blessing and follow God."

Several of the other women nodded in agreement.

"I prayed," Julietta continued, "that they would remain

close to us and bring us much pleasure and honor. When our children were born, I continued to pray over them, and as they grew, I prayed more and more. When they became adults, some of them left and chose their own way. It grieved me, and I cried out to the Lord. I used to cry, 'But, Lord, I prayed for them. I gave them to Your care. Why are they not doing good and serving You?' I felt that God had turned away, and it made me both sad and angry.

"Then our youngest son got in with bad people. He deserted our teachings. I shook my fist at God and ranted and raved. I thought I could trust Him, but He had betrayed me. I told this to my mother, and she wisely sat me down and said, 'Julietta, God has not betrayed you, your son has betrayed God. He has betrayed his family and the truth that he was taught.'"

Again, many of the women nodded and murmured amongst themselves.

"Then my mother reminded me that God is love. He does not force or impose His will on us. He does not force our obedience but allows us to choose our way. My son chose his path, and it grieved me deeply, but it also grieved God. I learned from that time to pray for my son, to pray that God would reach him—that he would yield himself to God, no matter the cost.

"Not long ago, my son was in a terrible fight, and he was injured so badly that the doctors didn't think he would live. I went to him and knew he would die by nightfall." Her eyes filled with tears. "I told him that it wasn't too late—that Jesus was patiently waiting with open arms."

Isabella's chest tightened. She could imagine the scene, and it moved her in a deep way.

"He said, 'No, Mama, it is too late. I have offended God and sinned against Him and all mankind.' I told him that

God loved him even more than I did, and if I was willing to give him a second chance, how could he think that God's love would not do the same? He cried out to the Lord and asked for forgiveness. He begged Jesus to cover his sins, and in that moment, I saw God's love. My son's eyes widened, and he gasped a little. I thought it was his terrible pain, but then the most peaceful look passed over his face, and the edges of his lips curled up just a bit. He looked at me and said, 'Mama, He's here. He's not going to forsake me.' Those were his last words."

Her voice broke, and she paused to take a handkerchief from her pocket and wipe her eyes. "And you know what?" she continued, sniffing. "He was right. God was there. I felt His presence as I feel it now. He's here with us because we've come together in His name to do His work and offer praise to Him. Many of you wondered where I was these last few weeks, and now you know. We buried my boy in Albuquerque next to his father, but I know I will see him again one day." She smiled. "I just wanted to tell you of my joy."

Many of the women got up and went to her. They hugged her close and spoke words of compassion and love. Isabella had never seen anything like it. The woman's son was dead, yet she had called it her joy.

"'Likewise, I say unto you, there is joy in the presence of the angels of God over one sinner that repenteth,'" Mama whispered.

Isabella turned to her mother. "What did you say?"

"Luke fifteen, verse ten," Mama replied, wiping her own tears. "Jesus has just told the parable of the sheep that went missing and the shepherd who left the ninety-nine to find the one. Then He tells of a woman who has ten pieces of silver but loses one. She searches and searches until it is found and then invites her neighbors to celebrate with her. Jesus then tells the people the story of the prodigal son. Do you remember it?"

"I do."

"Julietta's prodigal son has come home, and all of heaven is rejoicing."

The prodigal had returned. Isabella shifted, uncomfortable at the thought. Had her mother spent years in prayer for her hard heart? When she heard Julietta's story, did she have hope for Isabella?

She looked at her mother and saw tears streaming down her face. She looked back toward Julietta and the other women, most who no doubt had children of their own. They were crying and laughing, rejoicing over the lost child who was found.

"I need some air," Isabella told her mother and left the room as quickly as she could.

She grabbed her coat on her way out the door and cherished its warmth as the cold air hit her face. She'd been there only a few minutes when she caught the scent of cologne. Aaron.

She turned and found him standing only a few feet away. He looked worried. "Your father sent me to bring you both home. He's feeling poorly and has taken to his bed."

Isabella nodded, dread pooling in her stomach. "I'll fetch Mama."

13

Isabella hated seeing her father in such a weakened state. His face was ashen, and even his eyes had lost their luster. He was dying. She hadn't allowed herself to accept it until that moment. And it seemed accepting the truth unleashed an outpouring of guilt and regret that was hard for her to ignore.

For reasons beyond her understanding, Isabella sat awash in memories of the past even as her mother spoke of the future and her love for this dying man. She had always felt safe in the company of her father and mother, especially as a child. Thoughts of the times when Papi had come to her rescue were bittersweet. Worse still were memories of the arguments and problems Isabella had clearly instigated.

Why hadn't she known he was ill? Why hadn't they told her? She was ten years old when they forced her to leave California. She was old enough to understand that they were hopeful of a cure or at best a delay of her father's illness. They could have explained this to her, and Isabella would have understood. She might not have liked it, but she wouldn't have developed such bitterness and anger toward her parents if she had known their reasoning.

She knew she'd made her teenage years a storm of un-
pleasantries. She had been difficult and hard-hearted, hoping
they would give up and send her away. It seemed, however,
that no matter how much she alienated them, they loved her
all the more.

Was that how it was with God too? Did He love her even
when she rebelled and struck out against Him? Mama had
once told Isabella that she understood better than Isabella
might imagine. Did she? Did she understand the pain that
came from leaving?

It came to Isabella in a flash. Of course Mama understood. She lost her family, her friends, and her childhood
home when she married Daniel Garcia. It didn't matter that
he had money. She had shamed her family by marrying a man
of Spanish-Mexican heritage. Eventually her friends would
rally around her, defying their families. Isabella remembered
several times when Mama's friends had come to the estate
to visit. It was done in secret, but it had given her mother
such a lift of spirits. Eventually some of her cousins came
to apologize for the actions of their parents.

Isabella's *abuela* had always welcomed Mama. As Daniel's
mother, she might have shunned a white woman, but instead,
Violante Garcia embraced her daughter-in-law and made her
a welcomed part of the family. Isabella could still remember
the way they sat and sewed and shared stories. Isabella had
loved to be near them at such times. She had learned so much
about her heritage that way.

"*Abuelita, tell me a story about when my papi was little,*"
Isabella might ask.

"*Your papi was such a mischievous boy. He loved to play
tricks on me and sneak cookies from the jar. One day I decided to have Cook make some cookies with extra salt. I
thought I would teach him a lesson, but instead he loved*"

them. He used to ask for them all the time." Isabella could still hear the old woman's chuckles.

Isabella looked down at her father and smiled. She wished she knew how to make salty cookies.

"We'll be back to check on you later," Mama told him. "You need to rest for now."

"My girls," he said in a whisper. "I love you both so very much."

"We love you." Mama placed a kiss on his forehead.

Isabella nodded. "We do," she murmured, not able to bring herself to say the words.

She followed her mother from the room and wasn't surprised when Mama headed down the hall.

"I'm going to rest for a bit and pray."

Isabella said nothing. Even after her mother had gone inside her bedroom and closed the door, it was hard to decide what to do. With a sigh, Isabella finally headed downstairs to the music room. She had learned to play piano as a child and often found comfort in it. Since coming to New Mexico, however, she hadn't even touched the instrument.

She sat down and ran her fingers over the keys, listening to the melodic tones. The piano was perfectly tuned. Without the need of sheet music, Isabella played a Brahms piece from memory. When she finished, she felt only slightly better.

"That was beautiful." Aaron stood in the archway, smiling. "I didn't know you played."

"Since I was little." Isabella stood and walked to the fireplace. "It has always comforted me."

He joined her at the hearth. "How is your father?"

"He's sleeping now." She held her hands out to the fire, needing to do something with them. "It's hard to see him like that."

"Yes."

When he said nothing more, Isabella turned to him. "Why are you here?"

"You mean right now or overall?" He met her gaze and gave a slight smile. "Although when I think about it, both situations are wrapped up in the same reason."

"Then explain."

Aaron shrugged. "Your father wants me to take over for him. He has asked me to care for you and your mother and Silver Veil."

Isabella waited a moment, thinking anger would rise up inside her, but it didn't. Her father was a very practical man. It was completely to be expected that he would arrange for someone to handle his affairs. He had no son or brother, so it fell naturally to the one man he trusted and had done business with for years.

"And how do you feel about that?" she asked.

He looked surprised. "What, no rage? No defiant declarations of needing no one to care for you or your father's estate?"

Isabella scooted a chair close to the fire. Once it was in place, she sat. "No. I thought I might feel that way too. I'm sure just days ago I would have." She shook her head. "I find my thoughts changing."

Aaron studied her for a moment. "What caused that?"

"I'm not really sure." She stared into the fire. "Different things. I suppose knowing that my father is dying is the most influential. What purpose does it serve to continue to be angry with him? The move here was to aid his healing. I wish he had told me that—just taken time to explain why the move was necessary. I loved him and would have understood."

"Loved? Don't you still love him?"

"I do now, but for a time I don't believe I did. I certainly didn't treat him or Mama with love." She looked up. "I don't

know why I'm telling you any of this. You aren't my confi-
dante or friend."

"I'd like to be. A friend, at least." He took a seat and
continued to watch her.

"Why? I've treated you with nothing but disdain."

"It's true. You've been mean-spirited and difficult every
step of the way." He grinned. "But your father would like
us to be close."

She rolled her eyes. "My father would probably like us
to be married. You're just the kind of man he would pick
out for me."

"Yes."

Her eyes widened. "You mean . . . he has discussed it with
you?"

Aaron chuckled. "We have talked about many things. Like
I said, he wants me to take over caring for all he loves."

"And that includes arranging my marriage to you." She
shook her head. "He knew I cared about Diego Morales."

"There you go talking in the past tense again. You cared
for him. Don't you now?"

Isabella didn't know why, but she felt compelled to be
completely honest. "Something has changed in me, and it's
altering everything. I heard a woman speak at church about
her prodigal son returning to God as he died. She called it
her joy."

"The lost sinner saved."

"Yes." She fixed her gaze on the fire. "I couldn't understand it in that moment, but Mama explained, reminding
me of the prodigal son, the lost coin, and the single sheep
out the ninety-nine. I couldn't help but wonder if she was
praying for me as Julietta prayed for her boy."

"If I were to guess, I'd say yes. They love you, Isabella.
Nothing you could ever do would change that."

"I know it would please them both to put the entire world in order," Isabella said with a hesitant smile. "But especially my world."

"Yes. That's your father's desire."

"And he usually gets what he wants." She looked at Aaron as if she might find all of her answers in his face.

His smile faded. "Usually. But he can't force people to feel the same emotion he feels, or to care about the things he cares about."

"Are you speaking of me?"

"Not you alone. There are many who oppose him. Many who make demands of him and have plans for his money and future. Many who refuse to accept his counsel and wisdom."

Guilt edged in on her thoughts, and she stood, ready to leave. Something caused her to stop, however, and she looked at Aaron, who was also getting to his feet.

"Are you a praying man, Mr. Bailey?"

"I am. I think you know that, however. What is it you really want to ask?"

"Do you think God actually listens? Does He hear our prayers?"

"Absolutely." He held up his hand as she started to pose another question. "It doesn't mean, however, that He gives us everything we ask for. Otherwise, your father wouldn't be dying or even sick."

"So how do you know He hears or that He even cares?"

He considered this for a moment. "I suppose it's something I sense deep within me, in part. The Bible says He will hear us, but something in me confirms this. I don't think I can really explain it. Part of it is faith in His Word and part of it is, I suppose, His Spirit in me."

"You continue to pray even though He doesn't answer your prayers?"

"I didn't say He didn't answer. He always answers. Sometimes the answer is no. And while that's hard to hear, I do believe He always knows best and has our best in mind when we are seeking to live for Him."

"And my father dying is what's best?"

"We're all going to die, Miss Garcia. That's a part of life, but God tells us in His Word that we do not need to fear death. Your father certainly does not fear it. He knows without the tiniest doubt that when it happens, he will be with Jesus, just like the thief on the cross. Jesus told him he would be with Him that very day in paradise. Other parts of the Bible tell us that to be departed from the body is to be with the Lord."

"But I'm . . ." Her voice faded, and tears filled her eyes. "I'm not ready to lose him." Her voice broke, and a sob escaped. "I've wasted so many years in anger." She bowed her head.

"We all make mistakes, but that is why forgiveness is so important. Your father certainly doesn't hold it against you, and neither will God. Seek their forgiveness and make the best of whatever time is left."

She buried her face in her hands. She didn't want to fall apart in front of Aaron Bailey. He must think her such a child—spoiled and concerned only with her own feelings. How he must despise her for the way she'd treated him, as well as her father.

But instead of rebuke, Isabella felt the warmth of his arms coming around her. Aaron pulled her close and tenderly stroked her back. She let all thought go and gave in to her emotions. Wrapping her arms around him, she hid her face against his suit coat and let the tears come. She felt the last bits of her hard heart fall away. It had been so long since she'd allowed anyone to comfort her that she almost felt like a child again.

Almost.

Aaron wasn't sure why he'd reacted as he had. It seemed the most natural thing in the world to take Isabella Garcia into his arms, however. This broken woman was nothing like the hard-hearted person he'd met two months ago.

Apparently God had been at work on her heart. Aaron knew her parents were praying regularly for her, as was he. But to be truthful, where his own prayers were concerned, he hadn't expected results. Nor had he honestly cared as much, except that he knew it hurt his friend and mentor.

He had felt guilty for his lack of kind thoughts for Isabella, and now he felt even more uneasy at the realization that her pain was so great. Why hadn't he thought about the fact that pain often caused a person to act unfeeling toward others?

"I'm so sorry. I didn't mean to break down." Isabella pushed away from Aaron, but not far.

He kept his arms around her as she looked up at his face. "It's quite all right. This is a hard time for you."

She nodded. "More so than I ever expected. I thought I had grown up, that I had faced all I had to in order to become an adult, but I was very wrong." She sniffed and reached up to wipe her eyes on the edge of her sleeve.

The movement separated them a little more, and he finally dropped his hold on her, thinking she would move away. When she didn't, he found his heart beating a little faster.

"How much time do you think Papi has?" she asked.

Aaron shook his head. "I have no idea. The doctor thought he might die before Christmas. I think that was why he was so desperate to get you home for the holidays. I think having you here has injected new hope into him."

"I can't imagine doing that for anyone, much less him," she admitted. "I've given him nothing to hope for."

"That's not true." Aaron frowned and reached up to smooth back several strands of her black hair. "Just having you here gave him hope. Hope that you might stay. Hope that you might love him again."

"I don't think I ever really stopped, even when I was so angry. I wish he knew that, but I'm sure he couldn't, because I didn't know it myself until just now."

Aaron let his fingers linger on her cheek. "Then tell him. Don't waste any more time, because there isn't any to waste."

She nodded and spent several long moments just looking into his eyes. Aaron couldn't explain the feelings coursing through him. He'd never felt this way before and wasn't sure what it meant. When Isabella turned to walk away, Aaron fixed his gaze on the flames.

He listened to her cross the room, and then her footsteps became fainter. He let out his breath, not realizing he'd been holding it.

What had just happened?

14

Isabella sat in the courtyard. She had planned to go out early to ride, but no one had been available to act as an escort, and her mother had asked her to wait. Strangely enough, Isabella had thought of Aaron and asked if he might escort her but was told he was in a meeting with her father.

She sat and pondered what to do. She still hadn't spoken to her father about her harsh words and actions of the last few years. She'd seen very little of Aaron or her father, in fact. These last few weeks her father had been resting and doing as the doctor ordered, which meant any work was conducted from bed. As March began to warm up a bit, word came that her father was feeling much better. Isabella had visited him frequently but always held off on bringing up the past. The timing just never felt right.

"I wondered if I'd find you here," her mother said, coming to join her.

"It's turning out to be such a nice day. I thought I'd enjoy the quiet of the morning this way instead of riding."

"I'm sorry you couldn't go. It's not that this area is horribly dangerous, but there are hazards. I wouldn't want you to get hurt."

"What kind of hazards?"

"Oh, there are snakes, sometimes wild animals. Occasionally we've had a rough character show up. Usually your father is able to charm him or help him to see that he shouldn't stay if he can't be useful."

"I've always been amazed by Papi's ability to change people."

"He doesn't so much change them as help them see themselves as they are. Some people rush to become better. Others move on because they can't bear being seen for who they are."

"I understand. Maybe that's why I wanted to stay away." She looked at her mother, who seemed happier than she had in days. "Is Papi feeling better?"

"He is. He's better than I've seen him in some time. I guess the bed rest did the trick."

Isabella toyed with the leaf of a nearby plant. "Mama, I have a confession to make."

Her mother raised a brow. "What kind of confession?"

"One of apology. I've been very convicted of my bad approach to your desires for me. I've had my mind set on what I wanted to accomplish and have given little concern to you and Papi."

Her mother's surprised expression told Isabella she hadn't anticipated this confession.

"I want you to understand my heart, Mama. From the time we moved here, I felt that the life I loved was over. Even after my horse Lucy joined us, it still felt as if you had taken everything away from me."

"I know, sweetheart."

Isabella turned toward her mother, who took a seat on a wrought-iron bench to the right. "I was so angry. I felt betrayed by you and Papi. I hated you both for taking me from our home, and yet I loved you and couldn't reconcile my anger. I've been so unhappy all these years."

"But I thought you loved living with Josephina."

"I did, to a degree. But strangely enough, it did feel empty sometimes. That first year I spent the summer there, I tried to recapture the way it had all been. Nothing much had changed in the house or on the grounds, but Abuelita and Abuelito were gone, you and Papi were gone, and my terrible feelings toward you wouldn't even allow me to enjoy my memories."

"Why did you want to live there, then?"

Isabella stood and paced on the tiled walk. "Because I did love it for a while, and I suppose because I wanted to punish you by leaving you alone. I'm not entirely sure I understand it myself. Nothing felt the same after you left." She paused. "But then I began to see Diego more. I had always been fond of him. Well, more than that. I'd been infatuated with him since I was a child. He was exciting and adventurous. He told me wonderful stories, and when I returned to California all grown up, or nearly so, he saw me as a woman, and everything changed."

Mama looked sad and sat in silence, worrying her lower lip. Was she afraid of what had taken place between Diego and her daughter? Isabella sought to ease her concerns.

"Nothing has ever happened between us. You needn't worry about that." She reclaimed her seat. "We've kissed a few times, but nothing more."

"You must talk to your father about Diego. He tried to see the young man as a prospective husband, but there were just too many reasons he wasn't acceptable. I think the time has come that you should know everything."

Isabella tried for once to see it through her mother's eyes. "I'm sure you wanted better for me. Perhaps even someone here so I would stay and help with the various charities and ministries."

"We wanted you happy, and a man like Diego is only interested in making himself happy," Mama answered. "You must understand that. He may show you attention and kindness, even passion, but those things will fade. He is thirty-five, Isabella. A full-grown man, yet he talks about the trouble he's caused as nothing more than boyish pranks and sowing his wild oats. Were he only twenty-five, as you are, that might be a more acceptable excuse, but even at twenty-five, a third of his life was spent with nothing to show for it. He should have long ago taken on career responsibilities so that he could marry and have a family."

Isabella hadn't really thought of it that way. Goodness, she was twenty-five and had nothing to show for her life. Did Mama think she'd wasted her life as well? She started to comment, but her mother continued.

"Most men by your age are settled in a career, at a minimum. They've attended whatever school or training they need. Some apprentice with others or work at their father's side, but Diego did nothing. He didn't show interest in anything but entertaining himself and partying with his friends."

"What about me? I've done very little with my life. Do you believe I've wasted it?"

Mama smiled. "For women it is different. Certainly, most are married by this age, but I see nothing wrong in taking your time and making sure you marry the right man."

"But you don't believe Diego is the right one."

"I believe you must speak to your father. He's asked me to let him share what he knows, and I won't break my pledge to him."

"I want to talk to Papi and apologize," Isabella admitted.

Her conscience would not let her be. "But he's been so sick, and I didn't want to get him all worked up."

"You can see him in a little while. He said he's feeling good enough to take you for a short carriage ride. He heard about you not being able to go on your ride this morning and wanted to make it up to you."

"But surely that will be too hard on him." Isabella couldn't imagine her father should be out of bed for long, much less go anywhere.

"Your father is dying, Isabella. It's something I've had to come to terms with, and it hasn't been easy." Her mother's expression saddened, and her gaze lowered to her hands. "I've had to learn to let him go a little at a time. If he wants to spend his last hours driving, then I want him to do it." She looked at Isabella with tears in her eyes "You must let him do this. It's the only gift we can give him."

Isabella moved to the wrought-iron bench and put her arm around her mother. She had done nothing to comfort her mother prior to this. She felt it was important to show her support.

"Mama, I am here for you. I will do what I can to help you through."

Still, the idea of remaining in Silver Veil didn't appeal. She couldn't reconcile her distaste for the place, no matter how much she wanted to.

"I love you, Mama. I'm so sorry for what I've said and done. Please forgive me."

Her mother pulled away just enough to give her a smile. "You have always been forgiven, my child. I have loved you through these years with a mother's love. That never dies."

Isabella hugged her mother close. She didn't understand how her mother could forgive so easily, but it felt good to have things cleared between them.

Now, if she could just do the same with her father.

⌒

Daniel Garcia sat atop his horse by the time his daughter joined him.

"I thought we were going to take a carriage ride. Isn't being on a horse too much for you?" Isabella asked. There was great concern in her voice.

"I felt strong enough to ride, and your mother told me you had your heart set on a ride."

She looked momentarily undecided but allowed the groomsman to help her onto her mount. "If you're sure."

Daniel smiled. "I am. I'm looking forward to this."

The day was glorious. March had come in like a gentle lamb. Daniel knew it would be the last spring he'd see, and he wanted to enjoy every moment. He knew too that he wasn't really up to this ride, but he wanted to spend time with Isabella. Helena had mentioned that she was changed—that their prayers were being answered and Isabella's anger was dissolving.

The horses walked out across Garcia land. The mountain meadow was full of scrub mixed with juniper and pine. Occasional aspen offered variety, but otherwise the sandy terrain was sparse. Daniel had come to love this desolate landscape. He loved its people as well. That, he supposed, was why he was so desperate to have his daughter love it too.

He prayed silently as they made their way north. Winter melt had provided water for the streams, so they paused for a moment, letting the horses drink before heading on. Daniel could see that Isabella was trying to sort through her thoughts. She looked like she was on the verge of speaking, but then her brows would draw together, a frown would form, and she'd look away.

"Whatever you have on your mind, I hope you know you can talk to me. I won't bite," he said, laughing. Hopefully, the words would put her at ease.

"I know that, Papi." She paused. "It's just that I'm . . . I'm ashamed."

"We all have those moments. Why don't you tell me about it?"

"I've been selfish and focused only on what was best for me. I haven't considered anyone but myself." She frowned as she shook her head. "I don't know why it's taken me so long to see it. Aaron has pointed it out more than once, but I thought I was a good person."

"I believe you are."

She shook her head all the more. "No. My desires and motives have all been to benefit myself. When I arrived here and saw how much you and Mama did for others, it made me uncomfortable. I know now that it was because I had no charity in my heart—none of God's love for others.

"Ever since we moved here, I've been angry. I felt you didn't care about me or what I wanted. Again, my thoughts were all focused on me." She looked at him. "If you had just told me you were sick, I might have better understood the situation."

"I didn't want my ten-year-old daughter to worry. I don't want my twenty-five-year-old daughter to worry either." He smiled even though his pain was increasing. At least he wasn't coughing. The herbal syrup had seen to that. "The news was bad, and your mother and I deemed it best to keep it from you as long as we could. But I was wrong, Isabella. I should have told you. Maybe not when you were so very young, but as you grew up, you should have been told. I'm sorry I continued to hide the truth from you. The truth is always better than a lie, and our relationship would no doubt have been better had I just been honest with you."

She nodded. "You could have at least told me you were sick and that this place had the potential to make you well."

"The dry air here bought me a great many years. Far more than the doctor anticipated."

"But now that's come to an end?"

"Yes." He smiled. "But look at all the extra time God gave me."

"All I see is the time I wasted. Papi, I'm so sorry."

"I'm sorry too. I should have told you. I never meant for you to suffer."

"I feel the last fifteen years have been a complete waste of my life."

"Nonsense. You were a pleasure to Josephina. She often wrote of the joy she took in your company. I have to admit, I envied her."

"Again, it was my doing, and I'm so sorry."

"May I ask what brought about your change of heart?" Daniel knew she would continue in this cycle of self-blame if he didn't move their conversation in a different direction.

"Everything about this return to Silver Veil. It started at the station when Aaron Bailey came back into my life. Did he tell you about being in the room with us when I was eighteen and begged you to let me live with Aunt Josephina permanently?"

"No. He never said a word."

"That's because he's an honorable man. He was there, however. He heard my selfish rant, and after you left, he confronted me. He told me what he thought of my childish scene. It was no different when he showed up to bring me home. He was pleasant and gentlemanly, but when I became angry, he allowed me no quarter."

Daniel smiled. "That sounds like Aaron. He's always been a very practical man."

She finally smiled. "You call it practical. I called it rude and obnoxious. He rebuked me for my selfishness, and I hated him. He sang your praises and told me I owed you everything, and I hated him all the more. Nevertheless, when he mentioned that you were ill, it made me start to think. He had nothing to gain by revealing that to me except for his desire to see our relationship mended. He knew what that would mean to you, and because he loves you, it was all he wanted."

"He has come to mean a lot to me. He has always been faithful."

"Where I was not."

"I'm making no comparisons, Isabella." He turned the horses on a westerly path. "Aaron was there when I needed him most. His connection with the Santa Fe Railroad brought us together because of our mutual interests and needs, but I see him as a gift from God. The son I never had."

Daniel hoped he could get across to his daughter that Aaron was a good man and truly cared about all of them. It was what had impressed him more than once. Aaron seemed to be genuinely concerned for Helena as well as Isabella.

"Aaron comes from a good family. I don't think they show much open affection, but they serve the Lord. They don't openly speak of Him much at home, instead relegating such teachings to the pulpit. When Aaron came to me, I think it surprised him that we could openly discuss God and His Word. We have spent a lot of time studying certain passages and discussing Bible times and culture. We have prayed together too. Aaron knows about my struggles and worries over you, so no doubt he took offense on my behalf. I apologize for that, if he caused you grief."

"But I'm seeing that grief in a different light. Papi, I want to ask forgiveness for the past and for my bitterness. Please tell me you'll forgive me." She brought her horse to a stop and turned to face him. "I don't want you to die without making this right between us."

"Of course it's right between us. I forgave you long ago. In fact, the very moment you wronged me, I forgave you."

She looked confused. "But I didn't ask for forgiveness until now."

Daniel smiled. "I know, but I forgave you nevertheless. You are my child. My only child to live. I will always forgive you, no matter the wrong."

"I don't deserve your forgiveness."

"None of us deserve forgiveness. We're full of bitterness and anger. We rage in our desires to have our own way—to find self-satisfaction. You aren't the only person who has ever acted out of selfishness, and you won't be the last.

"Issy, I am so happy to have you home—and here with me." He hadn't used her childhood nickname in years. "I've worried about you and your mother. You need to be there for one another after I am gone. You need to be here for the people of Silver Veil. They are good people, but many are uneducated and know nothing about the bookkeeping and legal details that come with running this town. Many are capable of handling their own duties and upkeep, but on a larger scale, they haven't been trained. That's my fault. I didn't teach anyone. I should have. Aaron knows a great deal, so I've asked him to take over after I'm gone. I want him to keep this town moving forward, and I want him to take care of you and your mother."

He hoped the idea wasn't too offensive, but when Isabella said nothing, Daniel feared he'd upset her. "I'm sorry. I've asked too much of you."

"No. Not at all. I understand how your years of working together cause you to trust him. I know you probably wish I would choose him instead of Diego for a husband."

Daniel took a deep breath. This was the opening he needed. "Isabella, I feel the time has come for you to understand my feelings toward Diego."

"I'd like to."

His pain and weariness were increasing, and Daniel knew he needed to head back. He turned his horse around. "I hope you don't mind, but I need to start the journey home."

"I understand, Papi. Please do whatever you need to do."

"Thank you." He got the horse back on the path, and Isabella easily caught up to him.

He pondered what to say. It wasn't his desire to hurt her or push her away when they had just shared such a tender moment, but Daniel knew she needed to know the truth.

"Diego has disappointed a lot of people. He has failed to keep his word on many occasions."

"So have I. We all, as you pointed out, make mistakes."

"Yes, that's true, but Diego makes no attempt to correct those mistakes or even to clean up the aftermath. You need to understand the truth about him, Isabella. He is not an honorable man." Daniel had never wanted to share the truth with her, but there was no choice. "He has debts. He spends a great deal of time gambling and is not very good at it. His father has often had to come to his rescue and pay those expenses."

"Like I said, we all make mistakes. Surely even you have made poor choices."

Daniel didn't know whether the pain in his chest was his lungs struggling for air or his heart breaking for Isabella. "He has made more than poor choices. His indiscretions include spending time with . . . women of questionable character. He has even fathered children."

Isabella said nothing for several moments. The silence was almost more than Daniel could bear.

"If they were women of questionable character," she finally said, "perhaps they lied and the children aren't Diego's at all. Perhaps they tried to entice him, and he rejected them. This in turn made them want to seek revenge." She looked at her father. "It might all be lies."

"I suppose there is always that possibility, but Diego didn't deny what he'd done when his father confronted him."

"Even if he did those things, he wants to do better now. He wants to marry me."

"But I cannot allow that, Isabella, and perhaps not for the reasons you think."

Her knitted brows and frown had returned. "But why, then? Why can you not allow me to marry the man I love?"

Daniel knew the time for truth had come. "Because he is already married."

15

They were nearly back to the house, but Isabella couldn't leave this news without an explanation.

"What do you mean, he's already married?"

Papi looked so sad. It was clear he felt a great deal of sympathy for her. "I received a letter from his father a few days ago. I haven't even had a chance to speak to Diego about it. His father only heard it as a rumor while he was attempting to right some of Diego's wrongs. He doesn't know any more about it at this time, but he suggested I speak to Diego about it. If he's married, he's lied to all of us."

To her surprise, it was the lie that bothered Isabella more than the loss of the man she intended to marry. How could this be? She loved Diego. Yet how could she love such a man?

"Diego's father asked me to speak to him about it. He also encouraged me to keep him here working for the time being, but I don't see how I can do both. If I tell him I know about the marriage, he will realize his plots and plans are over."

Isabella found it nearly impossible to speak. She had long heard rumors about Diego but had always chosen to ignore them or silence them before the information could be given to her. It was obvious that she couldn't ignore this.

"What will Mr. Morales do?" she managed to ask.

"Esteban asked me to speak to Diego, then write to him and tell him what Diego said. He wants to know where this marriage took place and where the woman is now. Diego is joining us for dinner, and afterward I will tell him what I know and ask for the answers his father seeks." He paused for a long moment. "I'm so sorry, Isabella." He began to cough, and the severity quickly grew.

"Are you all right? What can I do to help?"

The coughing subsided. "Nothing. This is just the way it is." He gave her a sad smile. "I would have done anything for you. I wanted only your happiness, but I knew about Diego's gambling and the rumors of illegitimate children. I just don't believe Diego will change. Now we have news about this woman he's supposedly married. If they are still married, this woman must surely wonder where he is. I knew you would never make your happiness on the back of someone else's pain."

She shook her head. "No, Papi. You are right about that."

"I've only ever wanted good for you. It was the reason I let you go. I knew you were so unhappy here."

"I still wish you had told me the truth. I hate the wasted time." She hated having wasted her heart on Diego Morales, as well. His deception angered her more than her father's, to be sure, but both had conspired to make her dream of a different future impossible. Now all of her dreams were dashed.

They reached the stable, and the groomsman was immediately there to help. He assisted Isabella first, then helped her father. Once he led the horses away, Isabella went to her father.

"Thank you for telling me the truth."

"I know you're hurt by all of this. I will give you time alone with Diego to speak to him if you like." He reached out, as he often had when she was little, and gently touched her cheek.

The action reminded Isabella of when Aaron had comforted her in the music room. She put her hand over Papi's and gazed up into his eyes. "I would rather have the truth, terrible and painful as it is, than live with lies. There have been too many lies, and I want no more."

"I promise. I will be honest with you always." He hugged her close. At the sound of the mine whistle, he stepped back. "Come on, now. We should change. Diego will be here soon."

Isabella made her way to her room and found Lupe had a hot bath ready and waiting. The young woman was really very talented as a maid, and yet Isabella knew she'd never told her that.

"Thank you, Lupe. You are the most considerate of maids." Isabella pulled off her gloves and tossed them on the dressing table.

Lupe froze, her eyes wide. "Thank you, Miss Isabella."

"I want you to know that I mean it. I know I've been difficult to work for, but things will be different now." A thought suddenly came to Isabella. "I never asked if you'd prefer to return to California. I have no choice for now but to remain here. However, my father would certainly arrange for you to return."

"No, miss. Please. I want to stay." Lupe looked troubled. "I have no one there."

"I just want you to have choice, Lupe. I know I've never given you much thought before, and for that I'm sorry. I will happily give you a perfect reference and money if you prefer to find work elsewhere."

Lupe smiled. "No. I want to stay with you."

Isabella couldn't imagine why, but she didn't question it. "Very well."

After her bath, Isabella dressed in one of her many gowns, then waited while Lupe braided her hair, wrapped it in coronet fashion over the top of Isabella's head, and pinned it in place.

The clock chimed seven, and Isabella made her way downstairs, wondering how things would play out that evening. She remembered how Diego wanted her to pretend to be kidnapped for a large ransom. Could he really have been serious? She supposed a man who married and deserted his wife could do almost anything.

How could she have been so foolish? She thought about what she'd say to him. She was so mixed in her emotions, but what she felt more than anything else was regret. Regret again topped every other feeling. It seemed she'd lived a life of nothing but shame and remorse.

The others were gathered in the music room when she made her entrance. She saw Aaron first and gave him an unexpected smile. He returned her gesture.

"I don't suppose you knew I'd be here to surprise you," Diego said, coming from her other side.

"Yes, I knew. Father told me." She tried her best to keep her tone casual, but she could feel her anger building at his pretense that all was well.

"Dinner is served," Ruidoso announced from the archway.

Papi came forward and took her arm. "Allow me to escort you," he said, smiling.

She knew he understood her dilemma. She glanced over her shoulder as Aaron held out his arm to Mama. "I believe we are all ready," she said to her father.

Dinner started out well enough. The food was delicious, and the temperature in the room was perfect. Papi steered the conversation to topics mostly related to the railroad, which meant he and Aaron did most of the talking. When Aaron mentioned the town of Engle and the dam being built not far away, Isabella couldn't help but take an interest.

"Why are they building this dam?" she asked. "I would think there is hardly enough water to make a lake."

"That's in part why there's a need for this reservoir. There are always times when the Rio Grande floods, as you probably remember. By making this dam, we will have the ability to keep the community safer from floods, but also to create a way to save up the water for times of drought. Not only that, but the dam will make electricity for the area."

"That's remarkable. I should like to see it one day."

Aaron nodded. "I'd be happy to show you."

"I doubt we'll be here," Diego interjected. "Once I am able to complete my year of work, I'm certain Mr. Garcia will allow us to marry."

Silence fell over the room, and Isabella turned her gaze to the roasted lamb they'd just been served.

After a few awkward moments, Papi began talking about seeing the first signs of spring. "There were blossoms on a beavertail cactus. It won't be long until all the spring flowers are blooming."

"It's always so pretty," Mama said, smiling at Papi.

Isabella could again see what Aaron had described. Her parents looked at each other as if there was no one else in the world. She thought of her feelings for Diego. They had been nothing like what existed between her parents. Even after all these years, they adored each other.

The thought of her father dying made her sadder than ever before. What would her mother do? If Isabella left, she'd have no one. But since Isabella no longer wanted to marry Diego, she supposed she wouldn't need to leave either. It really did alter everything.

I can stay and take care of her, and Aaron will be here.

There was comfort in knowing her father had already arranged for Aaron to be around. Aaron hadn't yet decided to give up his work for the Santa Fe, however. Perhaps Isabella could speak to him. Convince him that they needed him.

When dessert was finished, Papi rose to his feet. "Ladies, if you will excuse Diego and me, we need to talk." He glanced at Diego, who was smiling. Isabella wondered if Diego thought her father was about to give him her hand without a year of working in the mine. She was almost certain he wouldn't be expecting the news to come.

"By all means," Mama replied. "I have something to see to." She rose, and that caused Diego and Aaron to get to their feet.

"Come along, Diego," Papi said, heading for the door.

The servants began clearing away the last remnants of dinner, and Aaron came to help Isabella from her chair. "Would you like to walk in the courtyard?"

"I'd rather sit and talk," she said, knowing it would come as a surprise to him.

His expression proved she had taken him off-guard.

She chuckled. "I promise not to bite." There was a twinkle in Aaron's eyes. "Shall we sit in the music room?"

"Will you play the piano?"

"Of course. After we talk. I don't know how long Papi will speak with Diego, but I know it won't be pleasant afterward."

"No?"

Isabella started for the music room. "No."

Despite the beautiful day, there was a chill to the evening air, and the maid had thoughtfully laid a fire in the hearth. Isabella took a chair and motioned for Aaron to do likewise.

"What do you want to talk about?" he asked, unbuttoning his suit coat to take a seat.

"Your place with my family."

"Oh?" He looked apprehensive.

"Don't look so scared," she said, chuckling. "I know I've been mean in the past, and I'm sorry for that. Things are changing for me."

He seemed to relax. "Go on."

"I want you to take the job my father has offered you."

Aaron's eyes widened. "You do? I thought you found me to be a pain in the neck that you would just as soon be rid of."

"I did. I also thought I hated your cologne, but over time it's grown on me."

He laughed. "Well, at least you're honest."

"Painfully so." She shrugged and looked into the fire. "Mr. Bailey, you were right. I was a spoiled child who wanted her own way. I'm no longer that same woman, however. Seeing my father sick, knowing I'm about to lose him forever . . . it's broken my hard heart." She lost herself for a moment in memories of the past. As a child she had been so happy. Why couldn't she grasp just a piece of that happiness again? "I know things will never be the same without him, but I must do whatever I can to see that his absence isn't a burden upon my mother." She met Aaron's gaze. "You can make that happen. And I will do whatever I can to make that easier for you."

"What do you have in mind?"

"Whatever it takes. I'm sure Papi would speak to the officials at the Santa Fe if necessary."

"They already know all about it and heartily approve of my taking the job."

"So what's stopping you?"

He shifted and looked uncomfortable. "My own selfish desires."

"I haven't seen any acts of selfishness on your part. I've

only observed you doing pretty much whatever my father has asked of you."

"He's been after me for over a year to take over his responsibilities. I keep putting him off. I had my own dreams and wanted to see them through. I didn't want to give up my dreams to take on someone else's."

"I understand that."

He met her gaze. "I know you do. But there's more to it than I realized at first. I care deeply for your father. He's my dearest friend and mentor. I think I'm afraid."

"Of what?" Isabella couldn't imagine Aaron Bailey being afraid of anything.

Aaron got up and walked to the mantel, where he picked up a photo of Isabella and her parents. He looked at it for several minutes.

She stood and joined him at the hearth. "That was taken shortly before we left California. I was ten years old."

"You didn't know you were leaving."

"No." She smiled. "How can you tell?"

"Something in your eyes. You look happy."

Isabella marveled at his astuteness. "I was."

He nodded and put the picture back on the mantel, but he kept looking at it as if it held some answer to his problem.

"What are you afraid of?" She touched his arm, having never felt quite so intimate with anyone as she did in that moment.

Aaron turned to face her. "If I say yes to your father . . . I think he will die."

"What?" She was more than a little confused.

"I think he's just holding on until I agree to take over. Agree to take care of you and your mother."

It dawned on Isabella that he was probably right. She gave a slight nod. "Yes. I can see that now."

"He'll hang on until I give him an answer of yes. But in giving him what he wants, I will lose him. We'll all lose him."

"You can't believe these lies," Diego said, looking at Daniel Garcia with what he hoped was a pleading expression. "I'm being falsely accused. I have no wife or child."

Mr. Garcia frowned. "I said nothing of a child."

Diego quickly realized his mistake. "I was talking of the supposed illegitimate children I've been accused of having with women of loose morals. It's all falsehoods. I'm not the beast people accuse me of being."

"And the debts? Those are lies as well?"

"No. I admit to the gambling. I knew it was out of control and stopped. But I still owed several people money. I spoke to my father about it, hoping he would take care of the matter and help me clear my name."

Of course, that was a lie, but it was clearly a matter of his word against his father's. Though Garcia would believe Esteban Morales rather than his son.

"You must see how bad all of this seems to me. I cannot have you courting my only daughter. She's a good woman, and I won't allow you to cover her in the shame of your past and the mistakes you continue to make."

"What do you mean *continue to make*?"

"I know you've been playing cards in town."

Diego had known Garcia would have spies. He should have avoided the gambling tables altogether. But there was no sense in lying about it.

"I have played, but I've been careful. I owe no man."

"I realize that, but it's still a bad habit that will lead you back into debt. Eventually it could mean that you would go through my daughter's inheritance and leave her with nothing."

"I'll stop. I'll prove to you that I don't need it in my life. I was just bored, and the fellas I work with suggested it. I don't have to do it."

"And what about your drinking? I won't have a drunkard in my family. It goes against the Word of God. Speaking of which, I never see you at church."

Diego ran a hand through his black wavy hair. "I've been exhausted, Mr. Garcia. I've never worked in manual labor before now. You know that. It's been two months of such work, and I hardly feel I get enough sleep as it is."

"Yet you have enough energy to gamble and drink."

Diego took in Garcia's expression. The older man somehow knew he was lying. It was almost as if he could see right through to Diego's soul and know the resentment he held in his heart. Not just for his father, but for Garcia as well.

"You gave me a year to prove myself, and I'm trying my best. Do I still have a job?"

Garcia nodded. "You do. I am all for you proving the truth, Diego. I encourage you to continue your work at the mine. I will leave off with this for now. Your father intends to further investigate these accusations regarding your marriage. I will keep you informed, but in the meantime you cannot be alone with my daughter under any circumstance. I believe you know why."

"Of course." Diego barely held his temper in check. "I must prove myself worthy first."

"Come, I'll walk you to the door," Garcia told him.

Diego had hoped for at least a few private moments with Isabella, but obviously that wasn't going to happen now. He obediently followed Garcia and paused at the door while the ancient butler brought him his hat.

"Isabella, come say good evening to Diego," Garcia called. "He's tired and must head back in order to get his rest."

She appeared down the hall, coming out of the music room with Aaron Bailey. She looked at Diego for a moment, then glanced away. Diego could see it in her eyes. Her father had told her everything. He wanted to yell and put his fist into both men's faces and then force Isabella to listen to his side of the matter.

"Good evening, Diego. I hope you rest well," she said.

"Good evening, Isabella. I do hope we'll have time to talk soon."

She smiled, but he could tell it was forced. "I'm sure we will."

He left the house and headed down the mountain road. No one offered him a carriage ride back to the mining houses. He was nothing but a peon, and no one was obliged to offer him anything.

Not even the benefit of the doubt.

"I thought I would have a chance to speak to Diego after you talked."

Isabella could see real anger in her father's eyes. "He lied to me about everything. Made his excuses and sounded quite sincere. I played along to give his father time to find the truth about the woman he has supposedly married."

"His father wants him to remain here?" Isabella asked.

"Yes, I think he's hoping it will keep Diego out of further trouble. I don't know what to think. His father is likely to find almost anything. Diego mentioned a child at one point. I now think there may be a baby involved."

Isabella looked at Aaron and then back to her father. "How

terrible for them both if it's true." She shook her head. "I'll say nothing. I'll avoid any contact with him."

Her father nodded. "Yes. I don't want you having anything to do with him."

"I understand, Papi." She went to him and stretched up to kiss his cheek. "I'll do as you say."

16

Diego was nearly done eating when Rudy and Jorge joined him. He gave them each a nod but said nothing as he continued eating his flapjacks. He'd hardly had any sleep the night before. All he could think about was that his father had somehow received word of the beautiful young actress in Los Angeles.

They had met at a horse race, and Diego had thought her one of the most beautiful women he'd ever met. She was alone in California, trying to find work as an actress in the new moving pictures, yet there was a naïveté and innocence about her that he couldn't resist. He had figured her an easy mark for a short period of fun. Instead, she had played hard to get, demanding they marry before she would do anything more than kiss. Her father was, after all, a minister in Kansas and would never forgive her if she turned away from her upbringing.

Diego had been so fascinated by her determination that she became a challenge to him. He talked his father into buying a small house in Los Angeles, since he often insisted Diego go to the city for business dealings related to the ranch. It was quite a distance to travel, and Diego had always hated the trip, but once the game started with his actress, he was more than happy to run errands for his father.

He had considered moving on to another actress, one of her friends, but for the life of him, Diego couldn't ignore Collette DeMeire. The more he tried to forget her, the worse it was for him, and finally he found himself proposing to the poor daughter of a Kansas preacher.

But as for being married, no, they were not legally wed. Diego had staged the whole thing. She was, after all, an actress. She should have known better. Hiring a character to play a parson hadn't been hard in a town starting to become crazy for role-playing. He'd given the actor twenty dollars for his performance and silence.

Afterwards, Diego had whisked away Collette DeMeire— whom he learned during the vows was actually Lucy Meyers—to a honeymoon hotel on the ocean. Diego then put her in the little house his father had purchased and saw her whenever he came to town. Until the day she told him she was going to have his baby. It had been a wonderful arrangement until then.

Diego had confessed his trickery just after Lucy gave birth and it became clear she expected him to be a better husband and a good father. She had been shocked and devastated when he explained they weren't really married. Her tears had come in buckets, and he honestly didn't know which had been worse, her crying or the baby's. Still, he had prided himself on not leaving her there to figure out what to do. He'd been very responsible in buying her a train ticket and giving her money for food on the trip home.

"Are you even listening?" Rudy asked, sounding frustrated.

"What?" Diego let his memories fade.

"We're wondering about that plan you had for making money."

Diego picked up his coffee mug. "I'm looking for the right time. I don't think we can count on Miss Garcia's help, however. Would you still want in on it?"

Rudy looked at Jorge, who was shoveling flapjacks into his mouth. "I don't have a problem with it," he said, nudging Jorge. "What about you?"

Jorge mumbled something with his mouth full. Diego took a long drink of coffee and considered the situation. Once his father investigated the matter with Lucy, he would know the full truth, and he would follow through on his threat to disinherit Diego. There was also no chance Daniel Garcia would let Diego marry Isabella now. This scheme might be his only chance to regain the fortune that was rightfully his.

"Empty your mouth, stupid, and then tell us," Rudy said, giving Jorge a hard jab.

"Ow. I said she'll know who we are after it's all done with. If Miss Garcia isn't going to help us, how do we keep her from identifying us?"

"You'll wear masks."

"*You'll?*" Rudy questioned, a forkful of food halfway to his mouth. "What do you mean?"

"I mean that you and Jorge will have to be the ones to kidnap her and get her to the cabin. After we get the money, I can pretend to rescue her and be the hero. You two will wear masks, and no one will know who you are. You'll kidnap her and leave her tied up and blindfolded in the mountain cabin. You'll come to work the next day as if nothing happened and go back to check on her at night."

"How's that going to work?" Jorge asked. "She'll need to use the facilities and eat and drink."

Diego grimaced. Why did everything have to be complicated? "I intend for this to last no more than twenty-four hours. We can coordinate it with the payroll coming in on the train. Garcia will have plenty of cash on hand. We'll take her and then give him twenty-four hours to deliver the money, and then I'll sweep in like a hero from a storybook and rescue her." He glanced around, hoping he'd kept his voice sufficiently low.

"The plan will only work if we have as little to do with her as possible," Rudy said thoughtfully. "We should even disguise our voices. Otherwise she might hear us sometime in town and remember it was us who took her."

"Whatever you think is best," Diego said. "The point is you two will grab her, and I will act the hero's part and rescue her."

"Grab her where?"

Diego thought for a moment. "Isn't there some sort of Founder's Day celebration coming up?"

"Yeah, in a few weeks at the beginning of April," Rudy replied. "It'll be on Saturday, and the payroll train will come in on Friday, so the money will be in the bank."

That was longer than Diego wanted to wait, but it would probably be their best bet. "Let's plan for the day of the celebration. Isabella will be a part of it, since her father is the founder."

"I heard he was sick," Jorge threw out before starting in again on his breakfast.

"He is, but not so much that he won't be there at some point for the celebration, and if not, then he will want his daughter to be there in his stead. At least we can hope for that. We will have to wait until that day to narrow down the exact way to take her hostage, but for now we can plan everything else."

"There will be a special train that day," Rudy offered. "There always is, because sometimes Mr. Garcia's friends from the Santa Fe come down from San Marcial and Albuquerque."

"How do you know this?" Diego asked.

Rudy shrugged. "I remember last year's celebration. It's a small town, and not much happens here. Even an extra train is something special."

Diego shook his head. "That probably won't work. All those officials will recognize Isabella after a day of celebrations. You couldn't just climb on and sit with them in your masks."

"Well, there will be some freight cars attached to it. They use the opportunity to bring in shipments that would otherwise have to wait for the next train. It won't be fixed only for passengers—at least it wasn't last year," Rudy said. "They'll bring in supplies like every other train."

"Then maybe we could find a way for you and Jorge to take Isabella out of here in one of the freight cars."

"That was my thought," Rudy said, looking from Jorge to Diego. "The train heads out just after all the speeches are done. If we can figure some way to grab her just before that, we can load up in one of the empty cars. The train will stop in San Marcial. We could have horses waiting for us there. I've got a cousin who will keep his mouth shut for a few dollars."

Diego glanced at the clock on the wall. "It's nearly time for our shift to start. We can talk about this later. We've got a few weeks to figure out the particulars."

Isabella felt more at home as the weeks went by. With her new outlook on life and the knowledge of her parents' reason for coming here, she could honestly say that Silver Veil was becoming dear to her. Mama noticed it first and brought it up while they were helping with one of the many church community projects. She and Mama were once again sorting clothes to give to the poor.

"You seem far more at ease these days," Mama said.

"I have to admit that I am. I think truly understanding how much this place means to you and Papi has given me a new heart. I suppose I have grown up."

Mama gave her a smile. "I'm so happy you are here. I know losing your aunt and home in California has hurt you, but I'm so glad to have you back."

Isabella pulled out a dress. "This one needs to be repaired. The underarm seams have ripped." She put the dress in a separate pile and began checking another piece for any problems.

"You know Founder's Day is coming up in April. It will be your father's last, so he wants it to be special."

"I'll do whatever I can to help, but you don't know that it will be his last. He's been battling his problems for a long time. He might get better." Isabella realized she wanted that more than anything.

"No. We know it's the end," Mama said in a tone that brooked no argument.

A woman a little older than Isabella joined them. "I've come to help you."

Isabella immediately recognized Mrs. Cameron, the pastor's new wife, and moved to make room at their table.

"What can I do?" Mrs. Cameron asked.

"We're going over each piece to see which ones need to be mended," Mama explained. "Put them in this stack if they're ready to go, and in the stack by Isabella if they aren't."

"Easy enough," Mrs. Cameron replied. "Are we worrying about frayed collars and cuffs or just rips and tears?"

Mama smiled. "All of it. We want to make them as nice as possible before passing them on."

"I'm so new to this." Mrs. Cameron sounded a little nervous. "But I love helping people."

Isabella smiled. "We're glad to have you."

"Tell us about yourself, Mrs. Cameron," Mama said, putting a pile of clothes in front of her. Pastor Cameron had only recently taken a wife from back in his hometown of Duluth, Minnesota.

"Well, first of all, please call me Millie. My name is Mildred, but that's still too formal for me." Millie gave them a sweet smile. "Tom and I have been friends for a long time. We grew up together. We fell in love with other people, but after we married, we all became good friends. His wife, Glenda, and my husband, Arnold, knew each other from church. Anyway, we were all close. After Glenda died from a bout of pneumonia, my Arnold was killed in a logging accident. I wrote to tell Tom about it because he had moved here to escape his memories. We wrote back and forth for much of the past two years. Then he proposed last December when he came up to Duluth."

"That was right after Christmas," Mama said. "I remember he said he was going north to see family and take care of something important. When he returned, he announced that he'd proposed and would marry in March."

Millie nodded, her blond curls bobbing up and down.

Mama continued inspecting a man's shirt. "We were so glad for him to marry again. He was in mourning when we hired him on to replace the church's first pastor. We felt so sorry for him, and it just seemed God wanted us to take him on. He's been a great pastor."

Isabella felt she must say something. "I think it's wonderful that you two were longtime friends."

"It was definitely an answer to prayer. We were both quite lonely." Millie picked up a dress and started checking it over.

"What about you two? How long have you lived in Silver Veil?"

Isabella laughed. "My father founded the town, so we've been here forever. Actually, that's not entirely true. Mama has been here since the start in 1897, and I was here for a time, but then nearly five years ago I moved to California to live with my aunt. She recently passed away, so now I've returned home."

"It's amazing how death has brought us together. You're not much younger than me, and I think we could be good friends."

Her comment touched Isabella, who had never had anyone strive to be her friend. No, that wasn't true. Isabella was the one who had never tried. She had isolated herself from people her own age and instead associated with older adults. Diego was the only person she knew even near her age, and he was ten years older.

"It's such an interesting and wonderful town," Millie continued. "I've never seen such cooperation between churches and people. It's like I've always wished things could be."

"We wanted that more than the silver in the mountain," Mama replied. "When we moved here, it was one of the first things we prayed about. My husband interviewed a variety of pastors interested in starting a new church here. The three he settled on were of a mindset similar to ours."

"Which was what?" Millie asked, lowering the dress.

"We wanted people to come to worship with God alone in mind, rather than religion. We knew churches would still have their philosophies and denominational beliefs, but we wanted them to be able to put that aside and instead focus on Jesus and what He's done for us, and what we can do for one another."

"That does make all the difference."

Isabella listened to Millie talk about what interested her most in the town and what she hoped to accomplish, but Diego kept coming to mind. How could she have been so blind about him? How had she not realized what he was doing?

She hadn't befriended any younger women back in California. Most were acquaintances from church or lived in town, so there was no need in Isabella's mind to get close to them. Most of their neighbors were miles away and much older, leaving her with few options for girlfriends. And frankly, she didn't want friends. Losing them was much too hard. She remembered saying good-bye to several friends from school when they'd moved to New Mexico. It hurt nearly as much as losing her horse. With that in mind, Isabella had never tried to make friends, even after moving back to her family home. Whenever there were gatherings, she always remained with Aunt Josephina or Diego. She didn't want to care about anyone else.

She could see now how God had brought her full circle. Back to Silver Veil, a place of refuge her father and mother had created for God's glory. It was their mission field. Just like missionaries who headed off to other countries, her parents had come to New Mexico. They had heard the air was better for Papi, but it was about so much more than that. Papi had seen a chance to take the family fortune and change the lives of others. He had made a plan for drawing people together to serve each other and God. And now they were taking that mission beyond Silver Veil to help the poor in other towns as well as their own.

Isabella continued to think about this on the ride home. It must have hurt her parents a great deal to do what they felt God had called them to do, yet lose their only child. They had paid the price, however, always hoping and praying that she would one day return. Like the prodigal in the Bible. And here she was.

When they reached home, the only thing on Isabella's heart was to find her father and have a long talk. She wanted to tell him that she could finally see what he had meant to do and that she wanted to be a part of it. She wanted to promise that she'd always be there for her mother, but like Aaron, she was afraid. Would saying those words give him the feeling that he could finally let go?

"Papi?" she called, coming into the house. Mama had stopped to instruct the groomsman about something she needed for tomorrow.

"Papi?" She headed to his office in the library, knowing that was probably where he was working. There was much yet to be settled for Founder's Day.

She stepped into the library. "Papi, are you here? I have something I need to—"

She stopped mid-sentence. Her father was slumped over on the desk. Blood dripped from his mouth.

"Oh, Papi." She rushed to his side and felt his head. Still warm. He was alive.

Isabella ran to the door and started screaming. "Help! Somebody help! Come to the library—it's my father!"

Aaron was the first one there. She didn't know where he'd been, but the fact that he was so quickly at her side gave her strength.

"Papi's unconscious."

"Send someone for the doctor," Aaron ordered. "I'll get him to bed."

17

Aaron sat beside his friend and mentor, hoping and praying this wasn't the end. He hadn't had a chance to tell Daniel he would take on the management of his estate. He hadn't been able to thank him for all the kindness and friendship Daniel had extended over the years.

The older man moaned and stirred. Aaron continued to pray for him. He could still see the panicked expression on Isabella's face when she cried out for help. He would have done anything for her in that moment.

Daniel moaned again, and Aaron patted his hand. "Wake up, my friend. Wake up and see what a beautiful spring day it is."

The doctor had come and gone, telling them there was nothing more he could do. Daniel would have good days and bad, but the end was drawing near.

Aaron had written a long letter to his father about Daniel. He had told his father what a blessing he had been. How he had kept Aaron faithfully attending church and studying his Bible. He explained how well they worked together and how Daniel had asked Aaron to take over his duties and watch over his wife and daughter.

He had even told his father about Isabella and how much

they had been at odds in the beginning, but that now he was actually developing feelings for the young woman. He hadn't admitted it to anyone else. He could barely face up to it himself; how could he share it? Isabella had been the bane of his existence when she returned to Silver Veil, but time had changed her. She had faced difficulties that caused her to put aside her childish ways. She had lost her aunt, and that hadn't been easy for her. The home in California had been ripped away once again. She had to accept that her father was dying and what the loss would mean to her mother. And she'd had to deal with Diego's deceptions.

Daniel had told Aaron all about the accusations and problems. He told Aaron that he worried that while Isabella was upset enough to avoid Diego for now, she might very well start to feel sorry for him and try to see him again.

Aaron didn't think so, however. He believed Isabella was a very levelheaded young woman despite the selfishness she'd exuded for years. She wasn't given to letting her emotions control her. She was actually quite sensible.

"Aar . . . Aaron," Daniel murmured.

Aaron saw that Daniel's eyes were open and smiled. "Glad to have you back with us."

"What happened?"

He was barely able to speak, so Aaron reached for the glass of water on the bedside table. "Here, have a drink."

Daniel sipped the water, then waved that he'd had enough. This time his voice was clearer. "What happened?"

Aaron returned the glass to the table. "A couple of days ago, Isabella found you unconscious at your desk in the library. You'd been working on the plans for the Founder's Day celebration, and the doctor presumes you had a bad spell and lost consciousness."

The older man closed his eyes and gave the tiniest nod.

"I remember working on the seating arrangement for the head table."

"Yes. Isabella and Mrs. Garcia are now managing that and most everything else."

Daniel smiled and opened his eyes again. "I'm glad."

For several moments he said nothing else. Aaron listened to his ragged but steady breathing, knowing that what he'd waited to say would be the best of news to Daniel.

"I want to tell you something, but I don't want you getting ideas that . . . that you can somehow go ahead and die on us." Aaron smiled but had never felt more uneasy.

"You're going to take over for me."

Aaron nodded. "Yes."

"I knew you would. God told me . . . to be patient."

"Did He also tell you that I would need you to stick around a while longer to teach me what I need to know?"

"You'll figure it out, Aaron. There's a good man who handles the silver processing and another who oversees the mine. I've told them both about you and that you would be taking over for me . . . very soon."

Aaron couldn't help but laugh. "That was pretty presumptuous, don't you think?"

"It was God's assurance." Daniel seemed to perk up a bit. "I don't suppose He's given you the go-ahead to marry my daughter, has He?"

Aaron swallowed the lump in his throat. "I don't hate her anymore," he offered.

Daniel laughed, which led to a coughing jag. Mrs. Garcia had apparently heard it, because she soon appeared at the door with medicine.

"Oh, my dear, you're awake," she said. "How wonderful. I've been so hoping you would come back to me, at least for a little while."

"I'm still here," he said, reaching for her hand.

"I can go," Aaron said, glancing at the door and starting to rise from his chair.

"No, we have too much work to discuss. My darling, Aaron has agreed to take over for me. I will put everything in his capable hands, and he will make sure no one takes advantage of you and Isabella. Who, by the way, he no longer hates." He began coughing again.

She smiled. "Thank you, Aaron. I know this will give him great peace of mind." She pulled the cork from the bottle she held, then took a spoon from her pocket.

"So long as it doesn't give him too much," Aaron replied.

Mrs. Garcia looked at him oddly, and her husband explained between coughs. "He thinks that by accepting my proposal . . . he will cause me to lose the will to live."

She nodded. "We have all had thoughts like that about various things, but I came to terms with the fact that, no matter how willful my husband can be, only God knows the number of our days. I'm content to take whatever He gives and cherish them." She poured a spoonful of syrup.

Aaron so admired their attitudes about the situation. They weren't spending their last days or hours mourning their loss. They were living life to the fullest and enjoying whatever time they had. There would be plenty of time for mourning after Daniel was gone.

Helena helped her husband take two spoonfuls of medicine and then waited as his cough quieted.

"Isabella and I are managing the arrangements for the celebration," she said as she recorked the bottle. "We're following all of your notes and instructions, so don't worry about a thing. I know you're going to have plenty to do in instructing Aaron, so just leave it in our hands."

Daniel nodded. "Thank you. I will. I know you two can manage most anything."

Helena leaned down and kissed her husband on the forehead. "I love you, my darling." She straightened and turned to Aaron. "Don't let him work too hard."

"I won't," Aaron promised.

She then surprised him by giving him a kiss on the cheek. "I hope you don't mind. You're practically family." She left before Aaron could even reply.

"She's a good woman. She gave up so much—" Daniel coughed several times, then continued. "She gave up so much to marry me."

"I don't think she lost that much, given the love of a lifetime that she gained."

Daniel struggled to sit up, and Aaron quickly jumped in to help him. Together they managed to get him propped up with pillows and comfortable enough that he continued his thoughts.

"Aaron, most of my business arrangements are straightforward. In my desk are files on all of my personal affairs, as well for my various business ventures. Each file details what you'll need to know. The most important thing I want to stress is caring for the people here. I've been a father to them and Helena a mother. They are good people. Smart too. I don't know that they really need anyone to hold their hands anymore. We've become a good town with folks who understand what it is to put differences aside and truly care for one another."

He motioned to the water glass, and Aaron handed it to him. Daniel sipped the water slowly and calmed another coughing fit. The medicine seemed to be working, as the cough was much less intense. He handed the glass back to Aaron and picked up where he left off.

"The people are changing every day. Some less-than-trustworthy characters have moved in, but you can't stop them. It's bound to happen. In the early days I had a gang of outlaws try to use Silver Veil as a place to hide from the law."

"How'd you get them to leave?"

Daniel chuckled. "I didn't. I gave them jobs and responsibilities. I told them if they were going to live here, they were going to help protect the people. For a time, they acted as guards at the silver processing mill. They would accompany any shipments when it came time to send them out. With most, I helped arrange things with the law. Some went to jail and then returned here after they served their sentences. Others moved on." Daniel smiled. "Men are often bad only for the sole reason that no one gave them a chance to be otherwise."

"I'll remember that."

"I hope so. I hope you will see what I've done here, with God's help, as a ministry unto Him. I wanted this place to be a second chance for those who had fallen from grace. I wanted it to be a first chance for those born into poverty and hopelessness. Above all, I want Silver Veil and its silver to be used not for some chance to amass fortune, but to help others. I don't live on the money from the silver mine. The silver goes toward Silver Veil and its people. I have a huge inheritance from my family to live on, and now part of that will be yours."

Aaron didn't even try to hide his surprise. "I don't know what to say. I can't take that. Your family will need every cent for their survival. Women have no other way to make their fortune, as you well know. I will manage it for them and see that no one takes advantage of them, but I won't rob them."

Daniel chuckled, but this time it didn't lead to coughing.

"I know you won't rob them, which is why I want to give it to you. I don't want you having to worry about making your living. This is my salary to you—it's just coming all at once. There will still be plenty for them. I've already discussed it with Helena and will get around to telling Isabella, as well."

Aaron felt honored and worried at the same time. Sharing Isabella's inheritance made him feel all the more obligated to follow his growing feelings for her into matrimony. But what if she wasn't interested in marrying him? What if she still loved Diego, despite all the things that he'd done?

"All right, here's what I want you to do first," Daniel said. "Go to your people at the Santa Fe and resign from your position."

Isabella enjoyed working on the plans for the Founder's Day celebration with her mother. They were able to talk about a variety of things, including Mama's family, of whom Isabella knew very little.

"My father made his fortune," her mother explained. "He was a poor farmer's son, and he wanted to go west in hopes of striking it rich with the forty-niners. He had nothing but the clothes on his back when he answered an ad from a dairy farmer who wanted to start a new life in Oregon and needed help. My father knew how to handle dairy cows and went along to help the man tend his cows on the journey. When they reached Oregon, my father bid the dairyman good-bye and went to find his fortune in the gold fields. He became quite wealthy."

"So few did. I'm impressed your father did."

"Well, he didn't make it in gold. At least not in panning for it. He went to work for a man who had a saloon and a hotel. My father made a lot of money in tips. The men of the gold rush were very generous, he told me. They would give him a pinch of dust for seeing that their drinks were refilled or for watching over their saddlebags or seeing to their horses. Sometimes they had a desire for something and would pay my father to go find it. I remember he said one man sent him in search of a pillow, but not just any pillow. This one had to be stuffed with goose down."

"Did your father find one?"

"Indeed, he did. There was no job my father wouldn't do, and he soon had enough money to invest in other things—particularly shipping. He had met a man who had his own freighting company and told my father the real money was in shipping."

"Did he buy his own ship?"

"In time he bought many, but at first he leased them. He'd hire captains to work for him, and they would bring lumber down from the northwest for building in San Francisco. That's where my father originally settled. He met my mother there, and they married after only knowing each other a few short weeks. She was the daughter of a man who owned many stores. My father arranged with my grandfather to supply most of his needs."

"I wish I could have known them." Isabella had only seen a couple of pictures of them. They had never wanted to meet her or see her mother after she married.

"They were good people, Isabella. They just didn't understand my choice to marry your father. I couldn't help that I had fallen in love. I couldn't imagine my life without him, and it hurt me deeply that they expected me to give him up without even trying to understand my feelings."

"Do you regret your choice?"

Mama shook her head. "Never once."

Maya entered the library and announced, "Señora, a man has come to see Señor Garcia."

"Did he tell you his name?"

"He's a lawman from California. Marshal Bradley."

Isabella and her mother both rose at the same time and looked at each other. Isabella could only imagine it had something to do with Diego.

"Show him into the music room," Mama said. "We'll see him there."

"Do you want me to get Papi?" Isabella asked once the housekeeper had gone.

"No, I believe you and I should be able to manage."

They made their way to the music room, where the tall man was waiting.

Mama swept into the room in her usual graceful manner. She extended her hand and smiled. "Marshal Bradley, I'm Mrs. Garcia. My husband has been very ill, so he'll be unable to join us."

"Mrs. Garcia," the marshal said, shaking her hand. "I'm sorry to trouble you, but I have some questions regarding the death of your sister-in-law."

"Please sit down. We'll answer to the best of our ability, but you must know that none of us were there when it happened."

"Yes, I realize that."

Isabella sat with Mama on the sofa while the marshal sat in the chair Aaron usually chose. She studied the long-legged man for a moment. He was tan, and his face was leathery in appearance. He seemed to be in his forties or even early fifties, with thick brown hair that was parted on the side.

"Now, how can we help you, Marshal Bradley?" Mama asked.

"I understand Diego Morales is here."

"In Silver Veil, yes. Living here at the house, no. My husband gave him a job at the mine, and he lives with the other workers."

"What can you tell me about his character?"

Mama shook her head. "Not a great deal. He is the son of our neighbor in California. He came over from time to time for issues related to the horses we raised, or to accompany his father. We left California in 1897 and haven't been back since. Our daughter, Isabella, moved in with her aunt some time ago. She and Diego became close."

The marshal looked at Isabella. She wondered what she should say. So much of what she had heard about Diego was just hearsay. The things she knew about him otherwise had always been good.

She shrugged. "Diego and I were considering marriage."

Marshal Bradley nodded. "Did you know he was the last man to see your aunt alive?"

"Yes, I did. Diego himself told me that." Isabella frowned. "I was heartsick because I knew she'd been having dizzy spells and worried that perhaps one of those caused her fall."

"We know now it wasn't a spell."

"What?" Mama asked before Isabella could pose the question.

"There was a witness to the fall. One of the young kitchen helpers. He didn't see who it was, but he heard someone on the stairs with your aunt. A man. He doesn't know if the man pushed her or not, but there was some sort of fight— harsh words. Your aunt fell, and the man apparently left her there to die."

"Oh my word!" Mama locked gazes with Isabella. "Did Diego say anything about that?"

"No, I swear he didn't. When I mentioned her dizziness, he thought it made sense that she might have fallen. But he swore he was already gone and never saw her fall." She looked at the marshal. "I presume the boy you're speaking of is Antonio?"

"That's right. He'd been sent with the menu to get Miss Garcia's approval. He was standing in the hall archway. He'd stopped because he heard arguing. He recognized Miss Garcia's voice but not the other person's."

Isabella felt a shiver go up her spine. Was Diego capable of cold-blooded murder? Perhaps Aunt Josephina was speaking to one of the servants and lost her balance. Perhaps the fall so frightened the other person that they fled the scene before anyone could find out they'd been there.

"Do you believe Mr. Morales capable of murder?" the marshal asked.

Isabella again looked at her mother. "I don't know. I've learned many things about Diego that I never thought him capable of, but I cannot say for certain with regard to murder. The other things are trivial compared to that."

"What things?"

"My father said he has debts."

"That's been established."

Isabella felt saddened by the confirmation. "He also said Diego may have . . . that he might have fathered some illegitimate children."

"We do have several women attesting to that, but because of their positions in society, there is no way of proving it."

"Those things hardly suggest murder. Did the boy see Diego leave?" Mama asked.

"No. He was too frightened and ran back to the kitchen. He didn't even tell them Miss Garcia had fallen because of his fear."

"So it might not have been Diego. He might already have gone, just as he said."

Mama's comment hinted at the possibility of Diego's

innocence, but Isabella wasn't sure he deserved it. Isabella had seen Diego's anger—particularly toward his father and brothers. He had once gone into a rage in front of her when his brother called him worthless.

"Do you know any reason Mr. Morales and Miss Garcia would have fought?" Marshal Bradley asked.

Isabella shook her head. "I don't. They got along very well in my company. Diego came over nearly every week. We'd sometimes play cards, or he and I would take turns playing the piano." She felt some of her fears fade. "I know of no reason they would have quarreled. My aunt had no business with him, and he none with her that I know of. Surely if they were fighting, Antonio would have heard what they were saying."

"He heard an exchange of words, but he doesn't—"

She interrupted. "Speak English." She turned to her mother. "He came to work for Aunt Josephina so he could learn."

"I wish we could help you, Marshal Bradley, but in all honesty, I doubt my husband would be able to offer any more information than I have. If you wish to speak to Diego, he's at the mine. I can give you the manager's name and permission to show you where he lives. You can have him brought out for a discussion."

"Thank you, Mrs. Garcia. My next question was regarding his whereabouts."

Mama got to her feet. "I'll write a note you can give to the manager. It should be all the help you need to get what you want."

After the marshal left, Isabella couldn't help worrying about Diego's guilt. Had he killed her aunt?

"That was quite the ordeal," Mama said, returning to the music room. "Are you all right?"

"I just can't believe Diego would have hurt Auntie. They

got along quite well. I know of no reason they should have fought."

"Well, it's out of our hands. Whatever Diego has done or hasn't done, God alone knows. However, I don't want him here at the house again."

"Nor do I."

Isabella thought immediately of Aaron. How she wished he were here. What if the marshal spoke to Diego and angered him? What if he felt it was their fault and he wanted to exact revenge?

"When will Aaron be back from San Marcial?" She looked at her mother, knowing her fear would be evident.

Mama shook her head. "I don't know. I'll speak to your father and let him know what has happened. If he's concerned, I'm sure he'll know what to do."

18

aron returned that evening and was apprised of what had happened with the marshal's visit. He promised he would keep a vigilant eye out for Diego. The servants were also advised that Diego was no longer welcome, and they promised to make certain he was not admitted to the house.

The marshal showed up two days later to see Isabella's father before leaving town. After speaking privately with the lawman, Papi invited the rest of them into his room to hear the news. The marshal had spoken with Diego twice. Diego had vigorously denied being there when Aunt Josephina fell, just as he had from the beginning. The marshal said there was too little evidence to charge him with murder. They couldn't determine if he'd caused her fall down the stairs. They couldn't even establish that he was the one Antonio heard arguing with Josephina. Diego denied having been there, and when confronted with the information that the boy had overheard their argument, Diego suggested perhaps Josephina had argued with one of the servants. The marshal had to admit it was a possibility. There was nothing else he could do without evidence.

Marshal Bradley left, and Papi announced that he was

going to have Diego dismissed and given a train ticket home to California. Everyone, even Isabella, agreed it was for the best.

It was funny, Isabella thought. She'd fancied herself in love with Diego—had planned to spend the rest of her life with him—yet now that it had fallen apart, she wasn't that upset. What did that mean? Was it never love?

It seemed the more she matured, the less attractive he grew. Then, when she considered his lack of responsibility toward money and people, Isabella found herself repelled more than ever. It was probably a good thing he was already married. That way he couldn't come to her begging and pleading she be his wife as she had promised.

On the other hand, there was Aaron. He and Isabella's father worked together every day. Papi was determined that Aaron know every intimate detail of his business dealings. Together they drafted letters to various business associates, then accompanied it with a letter from Aaron as well. One letter explained the transfer of power and Papi's illness, while Aaron's letter gave them an introduction to him and his vision for working together.

Papi got a little stronger, but it was clear he would never have the strength to do much but rest. Aaron had arranged for a wheelchair for him and could often be seen pushing Papi from his bedroom, which had been moved to the first floor, to the library and back.

Isabella didn't like that they spent so many long hours going over her father's investments and business dealings, but she knew it was necessary. Papi wouldn't be with them much longer, but that was the very same reason she wanted him all to herself. As the days passed, Isabella found it impossible not to become teary when she considered that each one brought them closer to her father's death. As much as

Isabella wanted to honor him by not mourning the coming loss, it was hard to ignore.

Sometimes she had a good cry in her bath, and other times she would cry into her pillow at night long after everyone had gone to bed. She wasn't even sure she was mourning her father or if it was more so the time she'd wasted. Now they faced a future without Papi, and Isabella wanted him to know how much she loved him and how sorry she was. But he always seemed busy with someone—usually Aaron.

Mama had overseen all the arrangements for Founder's Day, sticking to Papi's plans completely—with one exception. She allotted a time during the big picnic lunch for people to share stories about what Papi had done for them. She and Isabella agreed that while it might be embarrassing for Papi, he needed to hear the people, and the people needed to be able to say good-bye.

Isabella thought perhaps she would also use that time to tell her father how much he meant to her—how she regretted their time apart and wished she had understood the blessing of having him and her mother as parents.

The morning of the Founder's Day celebration dawned without a cloud in the sky. Isabella dressed in something different from what she usually wore. Her mother thought it would be fun for them to dress as most of the other women did, in a simple skirt and a lightweight blouse. The skirts were made of a colorful print that matched the embroidered flowers on the white blouses. Isabella had decided to add a wide black belt to show off her tiny waist.

She hoped Aaron might notice. Lately she was rather happy for his company. She wouldn't call it love, but then again, she knew everything had changed between them. She had feelings that she couldn't deny. Feelings that were nothing like what she had felt for Diego.

Isabella considered all she'd gone through with Aaron and had to admit that he had always been honest and forthright with her. He hadn't been afraid to deal with her emotions, and above all, he seemed constant. That was important to Isabella. She needed consistency now more than ever. Aaron represented that and so much more. He loved God and wasn't ashamed to admit it. He really was quite a man. Isabella didn't know why she hadn't seen it sooner.

She made her way downstairs, knowing her mother was waiting for her. Isabella wondered if she should speak to her mother about Aaron and how she felt about him.

"There you are, and aren't you pretty," Mama said, looking just as lovely in her own colorful skirt.

"I can return the compliment." Isabella kissed her mother's cheek.

"Pablo brought the carriage around and will drive us down," Mama said, heading to the door. "Papi and Aaron will come later."

Isabella knew her father wasn't coming to the celebration until lunchtime. He would stay for the picnic, and then Aaron would bring him home to rest so that he might return in the evening to speak one last time to the people of Silver Veil. With that in mind, Isabella and her mother climbed into the carriage together, with only Pablo for company.

It seemed strange not to have Lupe at her side, but the young woman had gone to town early to help set up with a group of friends from church. She was truly blossoming here in Silver Veil. And why not? Isabella had kept her so isolated in California. This was the first time Lupe had really had a chance to make friends her own age. Isabella felt guilty for that. When her father moved them to Silver Veil, Isabella had been determined not to make friends. It had hurt so much to leave her friends behind in California, and

216

she was determined never to feel that kind of pain again. Now, Isabella could see that she'd imposed her feelings on Lupe.

"You're awfully quiet," Mama said as the carriage started the short drive down the mountain road.

"I was just thinking of how I worked very hard not to have friends here in Silver Veil."

Her mother gave her a sympathetic smile. "I always worried about you not allowing yourself friends."

"I didn't want to care about anyone ever again. It hurt so much to say good-bye."

Mama shook her head and took Isabella's hand. "I know it did. I suffered too. I never told your father because I didn't want the move to hurt him more than it already did."

"I never thought of Papi hurting."

"He had to say good-bye to his mother and father, his friends, and his sister. I think he knew he would never see his parents again."

"I honestly never considered how anyone else felt. I'm so sorry. And I fear I've imposed my fear of caring for anyone else onto Lupe."

"I think she's making up for it now," Mama said, smiling. "She has a great many friends at church."

"I know. That's what started me thinking about all of this. My hard heart punished her for no wrong whatsoever. I feel so guilty and full of regret, but thank God I have changed. Or at least I'm trying to change."

Mama squeezed her hand. "You have a good heart, Isabella, and I see the change."

"I think working with you and the ladies at church, as well as spending time with Papi and learning the truth, has transformed me for the better. I actually prayed the other night. It's been so long because I just didn't think God cared, but now I see that He does. And even if His answers to my requests are no, I now believe He does answer."

Her mother pulled her close and hugged Isabella. Their straw hats collided, and they laughed. "We're going to be all right, Isabella. God will see to it. I just know He will."

Isabella nodded and felt compelled to bring up the other topic that consumed her thoughts. "Mama, what do you think of Aaron?"

"In what way?"

"I suppose . . . well, I know Papi trusts him completely. I think Papi even wishes that I would . . . that we might . . ."

"Marry?"

Isabella gave a nervous laugh. "Yes. I know it sounds silly."

"Not at all. Your father believes that Aaron is the man God intends for you to marry. He has prayed on it for some time."

Isabella couldn't contain her surprise at her mother's words. "I had the feeling Papi wished I would consider Aaron instead of Diego, but how could he know that God wants us together?"

"I'm not entirely sure, but we've prayed for your husband since you were born. We have always wanted an honorable man who loved God, one who would put God first and you a close second. There was no one, however, who we thought could fill those shoes. We considered Diego when you were younger, but he was so impetuous and unreliable, so your father didn't look at him for long. Then Aaron came into our lives, and Papi started spending more and more time with him. They valued each other's opinions and studied the Bible together and prayed. One day your father told me that he felt Aaron was the one to become your husband—that God had laid that clearly on his heart. Of course, we knew at the time that you two couldn't stand each other. We had hoped in sending Aaron to bring you home that the past would be forgotten and you two would find something of interest in each other."

"And instead, I acted horribly spoiled and was angry that you had sent someone to watch over me." Isabella shook her head.

"Why do you ask about our thoughts toward Aaron?" Mama questioned.

Isabella shrugged. "Things have changed between us. I'm not sure I entirely understand my feelings toward him. I thought I understood love, but it's so obvious that my feelings for Diego weren't really love, or I wouldn't be able to cast them aside so easily."

Mama nodded. "Sometimes we build up dreams and feelings in our head, and they're based on nothing but illusions. Ask God to help you figure out your feelings for Aaron, one way or the other. He will. I promise."

A little before noon, Aaron brought Daniel down to join the fiesta. There were tables full of food in the center of the plaza, where people were already lined up to help themselves. Father Eduardo got everyone's attention and offered a prayer of blessing for the food and the man who had made it all possible. When he finished, he gave instructions for an orderly feast and turned the people loose to eat.

Aaron helped Daniel up the few steps to the raised table at the front of the park. Most of the townspeople were spreading blankets on the ground for a true picnic, but here and there, tables had been set up for the elderly or those who preferred not to sit on the ground.

Once Daniel was seated, Aaron put the wheelchair behind

them at the side of the bandstand. He was about to join Daniel at the table when Helena and Isabella showed up, both holding large plates of food.

"We've brought you lunch," Helena declared. "We didn't want either of you to have to wait in line."

"What about you, my dear?" Daniel asked.

"I took care of that as well. Lupe is bringing our plates."

Just then the little maid showed up, carrying two plates with more modest portions of food.

Helena sat to the right of her husband while Isabella took the seat to his left. Aaron wasn't sure if his place had been predetermined, but he wanted to spend time with Isabella, and seeing as how she had his food, he sat down beside her.

"Here you are," she said, placing the food in front of him. "I hope you like it all. I tried to remember whether or not I'd seen you eat these things before."

"That was very considerate."

She smiled at him and took her plate from Lupe. "Thank you, Lupe. Now, go have some fun and enjoy the rest of the day with your friends. Oh, and thank you for coming early to help set up."

"It was my pleasure," the younger woman replied. She all but danced away.

"I think Lupe has a young man paying her court," Helena said in a conspiratorial fashion. "Perhaps we'll have a wedding soon."

Aaron kept his focus on the food. Daniel had already asked him about that possibility with him and Isabella. Aaron could only assure Daniel that they were at least getting along and enjoyed each other's company. Daniel had chided him that he was taking much too long to win his daughter's heart.

The lunch was as delicious as Aaron had come to expect

from these town gatherings. He enjoyed Silver Veil's celebrations, and he was surprisingly content working for Daniel. As he became more and more familiar with the way Daniel did things, he could see that the older man was extremely thorough in his business practices. He was a cautious investor overall but not afraid to give something new a chance. When Daniel's lawyer came to the house to update his will, Daniel had arranged for Aaron to join their meeting. He insisted Aaron needed to hear what he had to say and how his last will and testament would be set up. It made Aaron very uncomfortable, but he stayed. He listened to Daniel tell the lawyer how he wanted things specified. It was just as neat and orderly as the rest of his business. He explained that he was adding Aaron to his will, and the lawyer asked why. Aaron could still hear his explanation.

"Because I want to. He's a good man and has been a great friend. Not only that, but I fully intend that he will be my business partner."

Aaron knew now, without any doubt, that Daniel also intended him to be a part of their family. Daniel Garcia intended him to marry Isabella.

The idea of marriage to Isabella was becoming all too real. It was a little disturbing, given the fact that the thought didn't bother Aaron like it used to. Isabella had softened, grown sweeter. She had learned to open her heart to others. He was impressed with the way she'd been treating Lupe and the other servants. He'd even caught her helping Ruidoso carry groceries. The old Isabella would never have stooped so low.

"You seem completely lost in your thoughts. Is something wrong?" Isabella asked.

"Quite the contrary. I was just thinking of all that's happened and how right it seems. However, none of it is what

I originally planned for my life when I first came here years ago."

"When you met a very spoiled girl giving her father an intolerable time," she countered.

"Yes, but that girl has grown up, and the changes are remarkable."

Isabella laughed. "That's a kind way of putting it."

Aaron stopped eating and just looked at her. She looked like one of the peasant women with her traditional clothes. But she was radiant, and despite knowing that her father was dying, she had a genuine glow of happiness to her overall countenance.

"You've impressed me," Aaron finally said.

"Well, you did play a role in that change. Had you not berated me over and over for my selfishness and self-focus, I might not have realized just how others saw me."

"I could have been kinder."

"You were brutal, but I prefer the truth every time over a lie. If you'd been kinder, I might not have listened."

"I'm glad you did. I enjoy the company of this Isabella." He smiled, then turned back to his food.

Others joined them at the table, and it wasn't long before everyone had their fill and Mrs. Garcia rose to speak.

"Thank you, everyone, for your hard work and participation in making this the greatest Founder's Day ever." She clapped, and everyone else joined in. Once they calmed, she continued. "Today is rather bittersweet for us. As most of you know, my precious husband is very sick. The doctors tell us he won't be with us much longer."

The people's expressions seemed to sadden in unison.

"But while he's still here," Mrs. Garcia continued, turning to Daniel, "I wanted a chance to tell him how wonderful our years together have been. I cannot imagine my life without you, Daniel, but I will endeavor to make you proud. Our marriage has not been without its difficulties, but the love and joys we've shared have far outweighed those troubling times. I want you to know that I do not regret a single moment."

Daniel reached up and took her hand. "Nor do I."

She smiled and turned back to the audience. "Our daughter asked to say a few words as well, and then if any of you wish to share your thoughts, you are welcome to do so."

She sat next to her husband as Isabella got to her feet. Aaron could see her hands nervously twisting the material of her skirt. Figuring no one could see, thanks to the large flower arrangement on the table, Aaron closed his hand over hers and gave it a squeeze. She looked down at him, her eyes wide in surprise. He winked and squeezed her hand again before letting her go. She smiled and turned back to the audience.

"I am so glad to have this opportunity to tell you how important my father is to me. From the time I was a little girl, we shared a special relationship. Unfortunately, when I grew older, I damaged the love we shared with bitterness and anger. I was selfish and inconsiderate of both my mother and my father, and many of you witnessed that. For that, I want to apologize to you as well as to my parents. Especially you, Papi."

She reached down and took his hand. "I am so sorry for the wasted years. I know I've told you this before, but I cannot forget the sadness I brought upon us. Forgive me, Papi. You deserved so much better. You too, Mama. I cannot bear the thought of losing either of you. You've been so dear to me these last few months, and it only makes me more aware of the wasted time."

Isabella turned back to the audience. "I hope, if you have a similar situation in your life, that you will remedy it as soon as possible. Lately, I've come to see that God is all about reconciliation. And for that, I'm eternally grateful, for while I was ignoring and hurting my parents, I was doing the same thing to Him." She wiped a tear from her eye and smiled. "But like the prodigal in the Bible, I have returned to beg forgiveness and start anew."

The audience burst into applause as Isabella took her seat. Daniel leaned over and embraced his daughter while Aaron looked on. She really was quite remarkable. There weren't many who would make such a public confession of their sins.

Señora Rosa Martinez stood at a nearby table. "I am so grateful for the help the Garcias gave to my family. I came here in the early days of Silver Veil. My husband was dead and my children grown. My brother, who is considerably younger than I am, had heard there was a need for mine workers here. We were in Albuquerque at the time, and he showed me the advertisement that stated there was free train fare and help with housing for those who wished to relocate. So we came."

She looked up at Daniel and Helena. "It was the start of a new and good life for me. Even after my brother decided to move on, I stayed and have never regretted it. In all my seventy-four years, I never felt so loved and cared for as I did by you. I remember the first Christmas after my brother moved away. You came to see me, bringing a gift and some food. You wanted to make sure I had what I needed, and when you saw I had very little, you continued to watch over me like a son to his mother. You even paid me to make tortillas for your mining company, though I'm sure you didn't need my help. It gave me a living and saved me from embarrassment. Then, when my brother returned"—she looked at the man sitting beside her—"you hired him right back and, in fact, gave him a position that paid better. I am very grateful for what you have done, and I hope my words of thanks will let you know how much you have blessed me and my family."

She reclaimed her seat, and the audience again applauded. Others rose and spoke of their gratitude, and Aaron couldn't help but be impressed. Daniel Garcia would always be remembered as a great and loving man. The service he had given to God had in turn brought him much love and affection.

After nearly an hour of various people sharing their memories and thanks, Daniel finally stood to acknowledge the people—his people. Aaron knew that once he was gone, this town would never be the same, but it had gotten an incredible start in love, and hopefully that would carry forward into the future.

"My family and I have been so blessed to share in your lives. Silver Veil has been a wonderful place to live, and I thank each of you for your kind words and for the part you have played in my life.

"Years ago, God spoke a dream into my heart, and Silver Veil is the result. I pray for this town every single day, and I pray for each of you. I will speak more later tonight, but for now, I want to stress this. Do not be afraid. God is with you. Do not be hateful and bitter. God's love is strong and can change even the hardest heart. And please, do not mourn me when I pass, for I am going to a better place to be with our Lord. I won't be sad, so don't you be sad either."

He looked at Helena and smiled. She gave a slight nod, but the look of serenity on her face was enough to put tears in Aaron's eyes. To his surprise, Isabella reached for his hand and held it tight. Their gazes locked for a moment, and then they both turned back to her parents.

"That was beautiful, Papi," Isabella told her father as he slumped down in his chair. She leaned over and kissed his cheek.

"Thank you, my dear." He drew in a ragged breath and began to cough. When it subsided, he looked past her to Aaron. "I think it's time for me to go home."

Aaron got to his feet, still holding Isabella's hand. Daniel noted this and glanced up to smile at Aaron. There was no use trying to hide it. Aaron knew seeing him draw closer to Isabella was more pleasing to Daniel than if God had offered him more years of life.

"I'll help you stand, my darling, and we'll all go home," Mrs. Garcia said, getting to her feet.

"No, I want you to enjoy the day. I'm fine. Aaron will see me back, and then I'll return to spend part of the evening with you." Helena looked at him with great apprehension, and Daniel laughed. "I promise I won't die while you're gone."

Helena chuckled, and even Isabella smiled. "Very well, my dear. So long as you promise."

"I do. Now, go and have fun."

The day had turned out just as Daniel had hoped. He smiled as Aaron pulled the coverlet over him and turned to grab his Bible off the bedside table.

"I'm thinking you probably want this," Aaron said.

Daniel nodded. "I do. I want to spend some time reading before I take my nap."

Aaron handed the Bible to him, then checked to make sure his glass had plenty of water. Seeing that it did, he turned back to Daniel.

"Go on, now," Daniel urged him. "You've got me all propped up, and I have everything I could possibly need. Go find my daughter and see if you can't get past the hand-holding stage."

"I just started holding her hand."

"I haven't got time for you to take this slow," Daniel said, grinning. "Maybe explain that to her and apologize for being pushy."

Aaron laughed. "I don't know what to think about all of this. I wasn't looking for a different job or town to live in, and I certainly wasn't looking for a wife."

"Well, you've managed to take care of the first two, so move on to the third and let me die a happy man."

Aaron sobered at this, and Daniel could see the concern in his eyes.

"Aaron, we both know what's going to happen, but as I've said all along, so long as I have things settled for my girls, it will be all right. I'm not afraid to face my Maker, and I don't want you to be afraid of my going."

"To be honest, my worries are rather selfish. I fear that I won't be the man you need me to be."

"I want you to be the man God called you to be, and then you will be what I need. You've already been the son I never had. I've so enjoyed our years together. Don't be afraid of this next step."

"But you won't be here to make sure I do things right."

Daniel smiled. "You won't be alone. Put your trust in God, Aaron. He's the one who mapped this out for the both of us. I think we can trust Him to see to the details."

19

It wasn't too late to make Diego's plan work. In fact, Daniel Garcia had made it easier for him in some ways. Firing him from the mine weeks before and giving him money and a train ticket back to California had all worked to aid Diego in his plan to kidnap Isabella.

He had confided in Rudy and Jorge as to what had happened and pretended to take the train out of Silver Veil for home. When he reached San Marcial, however, he slipped off the train as a dozen or more Santa Fe officials boarded. They were boisterous and full of railroad talk, making it easy for Diego to leave unnoticed. Knowing Daniel Garcia and his relationship with the Santa Fe, Diego wouldn't have put it past him to have someone watching him. But all seemed calm as he disappeared into the night.

Just as he'd arranged, the boys were there to meet him with a horse, and together they made their way back to the mountain cabin above Silver Veil. And that was where Diego had stayed, biding his time until today.

With the Founder's Day celebration in full swing, he had finalized plans with Rudy and Jorge and sent them to Silver Veil. They would grab Isabella when an opportunity presented itself and get her out of town. Since things had changed, the boys had agreed it would be simpler just to sneak her up to the cabin rather than try to take her out on the train. Diego had found out for himself that it wasn't easy to get up to the cabin, and he figured no one would think of looking there. The boys were going to grab her and, if possible, try to leave one or two signs of her having been taken by train. Diego suggested that if she had a hat or a scarf, they could tie the ransom note to it and leave it at the train depot. Hopefully no one would notice it until the train had gone, but even if that weren't the case, it would start the search in that direction.

Diego had to let go of his idea of being the hero since Mr. Garcia had banished him from town. Getting the money would have to be enough. He knew from overhearing conversations in the office when he was given his final pay and train ticket that payroll and bank money would be coming into town the day before Founder's Day. This meant Garcia would have plenty of cash at his disposal, so asking for it in a ransom wouldn't make for an impossible situation or force a delay. Garcia would leave the money along the tracks at a place Rudy and Jorge had chosen. It was an isolated place where an old rancher named Garrison had once lived, and where there was a rocky mesa where the money could be hidden.

Rudy and Jorge would get the money, and Diego could be gone before anyone found Isabella in the mountain cabin. And, just so she wouldn't be stuck there alone, Diego had even decided he would stay with her until Rudy and Jorge brought the money. They would divide the ransom as he'd promised, and then he'd send Rudy and Jorge on their way so they wouldn't be blamed. Then he would take his horse and leave. That way he would be long gone before Isabella could make her way down the mountain on her own. She would either tell everyone about him or keep his secret, but either way, it didn't matter. He had plans to go to South America, where no one knew him.

If they were able to keep their identities hidden, Rudy and Jorge would go back to work at the mine on Monday as though nothing had ever happened, and Diego would ride out to a new life.

Isabella wasn't surprised when Aaron joined her later that afternoon. She couldn't deny that things had changed between them, and quite rapidly. Her father had apparently known what was good for both of them, even when they didn't know it for themselves.

"How is Papi?" she asked as Aaron drew near.

"He was tired but seemed in good spirits. I think he's looking forward to tonight. When I got back to town, your mother had some things for me to take care of, so I was delayed in finding you."

"You were looking for me?"

He smiled, and Isabella felt her heart skip a beat. "I was. I promised your father I would look out for you and make sure you weren't bored."

She laughed to hide her disappointment that he hadn't wanted to find her for himself. "I'm not sure a person could get bored on Founder's Day. I remember all the games and vendors from when I was a girl and am glad to see it hasn't changed."

Aaron offered her his arm. "Shall we check out some of the vendors or games?"

Isabella slid her hand into the crook of his elbow. She was

so uncertain of her emotions. Diego had never made her feel this way. She had never anticipated having feelings for Aaron Bailey, yet here she was.

They strolled around the plaza park and hadn't gone far when they ran into Pastor Tom and Millie. Isabella felt flushed at their greeting. Would they assume something was going on between her and Aaron?

"Are you enjoying the Founder's Day celebration?" Pastor Tom asked.

"We are," Aaron answered before Isabella could speak up. "How about you two?"

"This is the first time I've fully enjoyed Founder's Day. Before now, Millie wasn't here with me. I find everything has gotten a whole lot better with her by my side."

Aaron nodded. "I'm glad you're having fun. I've attended quite a few of these celebrations and have to admit that this one is my favorite as well."

He glanced over at Isabella, who nodded. "Yes. It's been a wonderful day, although bittersweet."

They all sobered, and Pastor Tom spoke first. "Your father is a good man. Everyone here has much to be grateful for because of him."

Isabella didn't want the moment to become morose. "He would tell you they should be grateful to God rather than to him. He was just the servant doing his master's bidding."

"I haven't known him long," Millie added, "but he was so sweet when he welcomed me. He told me if we needed anything to come see him straightaway."

"He's been that for everyone," Pastor Tom added. "Even when he called me to the house to talk about his funeral, he was more concerned about the church and whether or not we would have enough money for the new pews."

"That sounds like my father." Isabella wished they could change the subject.

"Well, if you'll excuse us," Aaron said, pulling Isabella just a little to the left, "we are off to look at the handweaving. I want to send a gift to my parents."

"There were some beautiful mantel scarves," Millie said as they started to walk away.

"We'll be sure to check it out," Aaron called over his shoulder.

They were about ten paces away when he leaned down to whisper in Isabella's ear.

"You can loosen your hold now."

Isabella realized she'd been gripping Aaron's arm so tightly that her fingers had gone white. "I'm so sorry!" She dropped her hold altogether. "I don't know what came over me."

"I'm sure it was the talk about your father's funeral."

"I'm sure you're right." She felt awkward and glanced around, wishing a hole might open up and swallow her.

"You don't have to stop holding my arm." He reached out and drew her hand back to his side.

"Thinking about Papi dying is so uncomfortable." Her eyes dampened despite her best efforts not to cry. "Oh, I'm such a mess." She reached into her skirt pocket for her handkerchief.

"It's all right. We don't need to think of that right now. How about we talk about us?"

His question put all thought of her father from her mind. "Us?"

He was the one who looked uncomfortable now. He ran a finger under his shirt collar. "I thought that might do the trick, but I have to admit I'm not sure where to go from here."

She shook her head. "I'm not either."

A large group of squealing children ran past them with pinwheels twirling in the breeze. Their laughter and excitement made most of the people around them laugh, but Isabella only felt more confused.

Aaron pulled her away from the vendors and all the hubbub to one of the side streets. It was quieter here, although not by much, as a band of strolling musicians had started up not far from them.

Isabella gave a nervous laugh and dabbed her eyes. "It would seem that everyone is conspiring against us."

"It would seem that way." Aaron shook his head and began walking again. "I suppose we could head back to your house. It's pretty deserted on that mountain road."

"Especially when the mine's shut down. However, I think we'll be just fine walking here by the houses instead of right on the plaza."

"I suppose we will."

He looked straight ahead, and Isabella thought he seemed to be searching for words. She decided to take pity on him.

"My father believes we are meant for each other. How do you feel about that?"

He stopped mid-step. "No easing into the conversation, eh?"

"No need to. We are both big on honesty, so why play around with words?" She smiled. "If it helps, I'll go first. I never intended to marry anyone but Diego Morales." Aaron frowned, but she continued. "However, in better understanding who he really is, I could see that my desire to marry him was built on nothing but lies. I was relieved when my father sent him away, because I realized I didn't want to marry him. I didn't love him. In fact I didn't have any feelings for him whatsoever, except maybe feelings of contempt."

"I see." Aaron started walking again, and Isabella carefully kept step with him. "So Diego is gone for good?"

"Yes. Happily so."

"I'm glad. I could see he only cared about what he could get for himself. I don't think people like Diego ever really love anyone but themselves."

This time Isabella stopped. She turned to look Aaron in the eye. "I don't care who Diego loves."

"Nor do I."

She smiled. "See. There's one point on which we agree."

They began to walk again. The light was starting to fade, and Isabella knew it wouldn't be much longer before Aaron would need to pick up her father. If they were going to have any meaningful conversation about their relationship, they needed to get on with it.

"Aaron, do you have feelings for me?" She paused and added, "Besides your irritation when you showed up in California to bring me home."

To her surprise, he stopped and pulled her into his arms. She hadn't anticipated kissing Aaron Bailey that day, but it wasn't at all to her distaste. Neither was the cologne he wore. Funny how she found it so appealing now.

When he pulled away and looked into her eyes, Isabella couldn't help herself. "I love your cologne."

He shook his head. "Don't you mean you love me?"

Her eyes narrowed as she cocked her head to one side. She remembered long ago when hate had been the topic of that question rather than love. She nodded, amazed by the truth that settled in her heart. "I do."

He kissed her again, and Isabella wrapped her arms around his neck and kissed him back. She did love him. She honestly loved him. Never had she expected to confess such a thing on this day. She had only intended that they might at least agree to consider her father's desire for them to be together.

When the kiss ended, Isabella had only one thought on her mind. She searched Aaron's face for the truth. "Do you love me?"

"I thought that was evident, but let me make myself clear. I do. I never intended to, but I've fallen in love with you."

"Well, that makes it easier. And one more thing on which we agree." She wondered what he would say next. Would he ask Papi for her hand?

"I need to go get your father for dinner." He started walking her back to the plaza. "I'll talk to him about our mutual feelings." He grinned. "If you're all right with that?"

"I am." Isabella searched the crowd. "I'll find Mama and tell her."

He dropped his hold on her. "Isabella, are you sure about this?"

"Are you?" she countered.

"Surprisingly enough, yes." He shrugged. "I think your father could see something that neither of us could. We fit together perfectly."

Isabella nodded. "We do." She laughed. "Mama said God told Papi we belonged together."

Aaron nodded. "I guess He's told us as well."

"I wish He would have done it sooner."

Aaron laughed. "It probably wouldn't have mattered if He had. We would have both ignored Him." He seemed as hesitant to leave as she was to let him go. "Look, I've got to go. I'll be back as soon as I can."

"See you at dinner."

She waved good-bye with her handkerchief, awestruck by all that had just happened. They had known each other for years but ignored each other because of their feelings of contempt. How strange to see that contempt transformed into love.

Without warning, her vision went black as someone pulled a hood over her head. She tried to yell, but a hand quickly covered her mouth. Panic flooded through her.

What was happening?

20

"You what?" Daniel asked again.

Aaron laughed as he helped the older man into the wheelchair. "I would like to ask for your daughter's hand in marriage."

"How did this happen? Does she want this too?"

"Yup." Aaron secured a lap blanket across Daniel's legs. "You told me to speed things up."

"I did. Still, I didn't expect this."

Aaron sat on the chair Daniel had just vacated. "To be honest, neither did I. When I returned to the celebration and found her, Isabella was eager to discuss our feelings for one another."

"I see." Daniel sounded more than surprised. Still, there was joy in his face. "Tell me everything."

"I suggested we talk about us, and she agreed. She mentioned right from the start that you believe we belong together. She asked me how I felt about that."

"And what did you say?" Daniel asked, chuckling.

"I kissed her."

Daniel slapped his leg. "A man after my own heart. Good for you. Did she approve?"

239

"Enthusiastically."

"This is truly the happiest news I could have. I knew you two were meant for each other. God has kept that ever present in my mind."

"Well, there was a lot of contempt on both our parts to overcome first. Hate seemed to blind us both."

"Nonsense. It wasn't hate. It was just passion. You are both passionate people—like Helena and I. You feel things deeply." He looked at Aaron, suddenly growing serious. "You do love her, don't you?"

"Yes, and I told her so."

"And did she return your love?"

"She actually told me first." Aaron smiled.

"She's so like her mother. Brazen couple of gals. Always speaking their mind." Daniel shook his head, still grinning. "Let's get to this party so I can give my final speech and pray a blessing on you and Isabella."

When they reached the fiesta, Helena was near the bandstand, talking to Aaron's former Santa Fe supervisor. She was nodding and smiling, so the conversation must have been pleasant. Aaron wheeled Daniel up to join them, and Helena stopped chatting to greet him.

"My darling, it's so good to have you back. Of course, you know Mr. Wright."

"Good to see you again, Joseph," Daniel said.

Aaron gave Wright a nod, and his former boss looked him up and down. "It would seem," he declared, "that working for Mr. Garcia has been good for you."

"Very much so."

"It's even gaining him a wife," Daniel said, then lowered his voice. "But don't tell anyone just yet. My daughter doesn't know I've given my blessing."

Helena looked surprised but pleased. Her eyes were wide

as she turned to Aaron. "Is this true? You two have declared for one another?"

Aaron laughed. "Yes, it's true. It happened rather quickly. She finally approved of my cologne and then me."

They all laughed at this, but Daniel stretched to look beyond the group. "Where is she, by the way?"

"When I came to get you, she was headed to find Mrs. Garcia."

Helena shook her head. "I haven't seen her."

"She probably got waylaid," Daniel said, settling back down. "I'm sure she'll join us at supper here in a few minutes."

But she didn't. Aaron sat beside her empty seat for fifteen minutes before pushing back from the table.

"I'm going to see if I can find her. She may just be busy talking to someone, but I know she'll want to hear your speech," he told Daniel.

"I'm sure it's nothing to worry about, but go right ahead. I understand."

Aaron left the raised platform where they were sitting along with several other dignitaries. He had never craved the limelight, but Daniel wanted to introduce him as the man who would take over the Garcia holdings. Daniel wanted to assure people they could come to Aaron as they had him, and Aaron wanted that too. But right now, all he could think about was finding Isabella.

He made his way through the crowds, looking for any sign of her. She seemed to have completely vanished, though. He searched along the line of vendor booths, but there was no sign of her. Retracing his steps from earlier, Aaron had a difficult time seeing in the dim light. He was about to the place where he'd left her when he spotted something white on the ground. Picking it up, he recognized it as Isabella's handkerchief. He remembered it from earlier when she had been tearful over her father.

Frowning, he tucked the piece of fabric into his coat pocket and continued to search. After twenty minutes, he wondered if perhaps she'd gotten ill and had gone home. It was a long shot but the only thing left that he could think of.

He found the carriage he'd come in with Daniel, but the driver was at the celebration. It didn't matter. He climbed in, releasing the brake in the same fluid motion. He grabbed the lines and snapped them, taking the horse back onto the road for home.

He found the house empty. Everyone was at the fiesta. Daniel had given them all the evening off so they could enjoy the fireworks and food. Roasted pig was on the menu, and no one wanted to miss that.

"Isabella!" he called. "Are you here?"

There was no answer. A sense of dread began to form in his stomach. "Isabella!"

He searched the entire house and stables. There was no sign of her. He climbed into the carriage and headed back down the dark road. Where was she? Surely she wouldn't have gone off with someone without telling anybody.

The sense of dread intensified. Had she been upset by their declarations of love? Maybe after he'd left, she regretted what she'd said. Aaron shook his head. No, that couldn't be the case. She was just as happy as he was.

He made it back into town and parked the carriage where it had been before. For several minutes he just sat and considered the situation. Where could she be?

He didn't want to upset Daniel and Helena, but the matter was too important to say nothing. Besides, they would expect her at dinner. Aaron made his way back to the plaza and once again climbed the few steps up to the head table.

He sat in the chair that would have belonged to Isabella, and Daniel looked at him oddly. "What's going on? Where is she?"

Aaron shook his head. "I don't know. I've looked everywhere, even the house. I found her handkerchief where I left her when I came for you."

"Where was that?"

"Third and Washington."

Daniel turned to Helena. "Did Isabella say anything to you about not being here for dinner?"

"No, of course not. She knows you're going to speak tonight and wanted to be here. Why?" She looked around her husband to lock gazes with Aaron. "Where is she?"

"We don't know."

"I'll make an announcement," Daniel said.

"Yes, do." Helena looked out across the crowd. "It's possible she's helping someone with something. A team of women were making last-minute batches of tortillas. Maybe she's lending a hand."

Daniel struggled to his feet with Aaron's help. "Attention, everyone!" The crowd quieted marginally, and he called again. "Could I have everyone's attention?"

This time most of the partiers fell silent and looked toward the platform.

"We're missing someone. Has anyone seen my daughter, Isabella?"

There were murmurings and whispers among the people, but most shook their heads. The lanterns that had been lit for the party revealed their faces. No one seemed to know anything.

"Does anyone know where the group of women went who made the extra tortillas? We think perhaps Isabella was helping with that."

"She wasn't there," Rosa Martinez said, standing. "I was one of the women, but Isabella wasn't with us."

"And no one remembers seeing her?"

Just then the station manager from the depot came running. He held a woman's straw hat in his hand. There was a piece of paper pinned to the band. "I just found this at the train station." He waved the hat. "There's a note addressed to you pinned to the hat."

Daniel motioned for him to come up and bring the hat.

Helena snatched it from the station manager's hands. "This is Isabella's hat."

A heavy feeling settled over Aaron. "What does the note say?"

Daniel unpinned and unfolded the paper. He looked up at Aaron, a look of horror on his face. "They've taken her."

"Who? Who has taken her?"

Daniel handed him the note. Aaron scanned it quickly and read it aloud. "'We have Miss Garcia. Leave $100,000 in the rocks by the Garrison's Chute tonight, and we'll return her tomorrow.'" Aaron looked at Daniel. "Who could have done this? Do you have any enemies?"

Daniel shook his head. "Only one person comes to mind."

Aaron nodded. "Diego Morales."

Isabella had no idea what was happening except that she had been taken from the party and then thrown facedown over a horse. Every step was jarring and painful. She wasn't able to breathe very well because someone had tied something around her mouth over the sack they'd put on her head. She tried her best to fill her lungs, but it was nearly impossible. More than once she moaned, hoping her captor would take pity on her, but no one ever did.

Finally, she fell silent in order to better pay attention to the situation. They were moving at a fast clip, and there was the clear sound of another horse beside them. Whether or not it had a rider, she was unsure.

She tried to figure out how long they'd been riding, but the pain made it seem like hours, and she couldn't be sure. After what seemed like forever, they slowed and began an upward trek. They were clearly climbing into the mountains, but she had no idea where they were.

The sack over her head was thick enough that she couldn't see through it, but not so thick that she couldn't tell it was now completely dark. The light had already been fading when the man snatched her away from Silver Veil, and that had been around suppertime.

Isabella tried to think, but the lack of air was making her dizzy. What if she passed out? She fought against that, doing her best to take deep breaths whenever she could. What had happened? Was this a joke? This entire situation was so outrageous. It left her in a state of shock, and that alone made thinking difficult.

Who would want to steal her from the party? She thought of Aaron, but he'd never pull a prank like this. No, this was clearly someone who had bad motives—but what? She tried not to think of all the ugly things that could happen.

The horse misstepped, and Isabella felt herself falling. She was sure she would hit the ground, but the man on the horse grabbed her by the waistband of her skirt and pulled her back across the saddle. She cried out as she hit hard against the saddle horn, hard enough that she might have broken a rib.

They rested two different times, with the man dragging Isabella off the horse to sit on the cold ground. She was so grateful for the change that she wasn't about to protest. Not that she could. She listened carefully, hearing two people whisper to each other. She presumed from the sounds that it was two men. No doubt they were discussing the situation. Before her muscles could even fully relax, the trio was back on the road. This time the pace was much slower.

Isabella began to pray. She chided herself for not having done that first thing, but in her defense, this was new to her. She'd only reinvested her trust in God over the last month or so. She was certain, however, that God understood.

I don't know what's happened here, Lord, but I sure need your help. Please keep me safe and unharmed. Well, no more harmed than I already am.

She paused. It was hard to pay attention to her surroundings as well as pray. Still, there was really nothing to see or hear. Nothing had changed in some time. They were climbing. It was cold. And she had no idea who had taken her hostage.

Please, God, don't let my mother and father worry too much. This might rob Papi of the little strength he has. Please help him. I know Aaron will be looking for me, so maybe just help him and whoever else he might get to look for me. The people really don't know or care for me as they do my parents. I didn't give them any reason to, and for that I'm sorry.

I'm actually sorry for so much, Lord. Please forgive me and help me.

Daniel Garcia briefly mentioned to the people what the situation was before nearly everyone in the audience volunteered to look for Isabella. Groups of women with their children in tow went from house to house, checking inside and out. They went together, figuring there was safety in numbers, while their men gathered at the Garcia house to form search groups and make a plan.

Aaron formed a group of searchers on horseback. Daniel suggested they use the Garcia horses. They were shod and would probably have better traction and distance capabilities. Within an hour of finding the note, Aaron was organizing the search while Daniel and the sheriff tried to figure out what to do.

"The drop for the money is in the middle of nowhere. You can see folks coming and going from a long way," the sheriff said. "Except on the back side coming in from the east. I could slip in there around the rocks and wait for them to come for the pickup."

"Someone might be watching, though," Daniel said from his bed, fearful that it could cost his daughter her life.

"Daniel, you know me," Zed Jones replied. "When I want to, I can be downright invisible."

"It's true," one of the other men said. "He'll never be seen."

"Let me go in there while someone else is depositing the ransom—or the stack of newspapers Lucas suggested. It's being cut up as we speak. While all the attention will be on the money, I'll already be in place. I'll leave immediately and make my way there. No one will be the wiser."

"All right." Daniel knew that if Diego Morales was involved, he'd be hard-pressed to keep Isabella under control, get the money, and make a getaway all at once. That was, unless he had friends. "Has anyone seen John Briggs? I want to talk to him."

"He's going with Aaron," one of the other men replied.

"Stop him. I want to talk to him first. We need to find out about Diego's friends."

The man took off in a hurry.

"Diego?" the sheriff asked.

"Diego Morales. He was here for a short time. He thought he'd marry my daughter."

"Oh yeah, I remember him now." The sheriff walked to the window. "They're still down there. Trying to get organized with lanterns and such."

"I have some Eveready lights," Daniel said. "Pablo, go get those and have Aaron hand them out. Make sure there are batteries in each one. We have extra batteries in the pantry."

"Sí, Señor Garcia." The boy took off at a run.

"So what about Diego Morales?"

"We didn't part on good terms," Daniel said, falling back against his pillows. "He's the only one I can think who would want to harm me—who would want to harm Isabella. He's in a desperate state."

"We'll find him no matter his condition. I promise you, Daniel." The sheriff headed for the door. "I'm going to get the things I'll need and head out to the drop site. Hopefully this will all be over by tomorrow."

Daniel closed his eyes but nodded. "I pray you're right and that she'll be home safely."

21

As soon as there was enough light to see, Isabella sat up and looked around the room. It was a big one-room cabin that looked oddly familiar.

After a minute or two, it dawned on her that this was the cabin Papi had built with the help of some men in Silver Veil. It was created to be a simple respite for those times Papi wanted to pray or take his family to enjoy the cooler mountain temperatures and wildlife.

She thought back to the night before—the uncomfortable ride. She stretched and moaned at the pain in her side. She was still tied with her hands behind her, and her ankles were tightly wrapped in rope. The men had carried her from the horse and dumped her on the bed, removing the sack from her head before leaving her there with the order not to move. Somewhere in doing her best to obey their order, she had fallen asleep. Now she was wide awake and frantically wondering what to do. Where were the men? How could she escape them?

It had been ten years, maybe more, since Isabella had been here, and yet it looked untouched. She was almost expecting

Papi and Mama to come through the door at any minute. Instead, only silence greeted her.

For several minutes, Isabella struggled against the rope that tied her hands. It was definitely snug and immovable. She tried to put her legs down over the side of the bed but found herself tangled up in the covers and her own skirt. She tried to roll back and forth to loosen the materials, but she was getting nowhere.

She stopped moving and tried to think. At least it was now daylight. That would make it Sunday. There was no possibility that she'd slept longer than the night. She thought back to the two men who had taken her. Who were they? They never spoke except in whispers to each other, and they were never loud enough for her to hear their voices.

She heard noise outside the cabin window. Could it be an animal or perhaps the men who'd taken her? Isabella wondered what she should do and decided to pretend she was still asleep. She'd try to get a good look at the assailants and judge what she could do to help herself.

But the noise faded, and no one came into the cabin. Isabella shook her head. Now what? Whoever had kidnapped her—

Kidnapped. She hadn't thought of that term until just now. Diego had talked about kidnapping her so they could get money from her father and run off to be married.

This was his doing.

Isabella didn't even question it. She sat up in bed and called his name as loud as her voice would allow.

"Diego! *Diego!* Where are you? Come here right now!"

She waited and listened. The noise outside the cabin returned, and the front door opened.

Diego Morales strolled into the cabin as if they were doing nothing more than sharing the day together.

"I see you're awake."

"Diego, untie me right now. How could you? I should have known it was you."

Isabella was angrier than she'd been in some time. In fact, the last time she'd been this mad, the focus of her emotions had been Aaron Bailey.

"I demand you untie me. This is ridiculous. Do you know what this stunt has probably done to my poor father? You know he's dying. How could you?"

She fought against the entanglement of covers and nearly rolled off the bed. Diego came to her side and caught her before she could fall.

"Whoa. Hold on now. Just hold on." He pushed her back and unwrapped the blanket from her skirts.

She fixed him with what she hoped was her most intimidating stare. She clenched her mouth closed to keep from saying anything more. How could she have ever thought herself in love with this man?

"Now, look," Diego said. "You aren't going to be hurt. I wanted to give you one more chance to slip away with me—to elope."

She said nothing but watched him carefully as he sat down on the edge of the bed. He put his hand on her lower legs to still her.

"Please listen to me, Isabella. I love you."

"That's a lie." She couldn't refrain from speaking her mind. "You stole me away from the people who honestly love me to bring me here. I thought I was going to die on that horrible ride up the mountain. Whoever helped you—or maybe it was you yourself, and that's why you never spoke because you knew I'd recognize your voice—sorely mistreated me. Threw me over the horse like a bag of oats. My body is probably black and blue."

"I am sorry for that, Isabella. Sorry too that you were frightened. I never wanted that but didn't know how else to get you here. I know you have deep feelings for me, and I wanted us to have a chance to talk and perhaps still move forward with our plans."

"And just how are we supposed to do that? You haven't got a penny to your name. Your own father won't have anything to do with you because you have debts and a wife."

"I don't have a wife! We were never legally married. She was just a loose woman I pretended to marry. She tried to obligate me by having a child. I don't even know if he's my son."

"So you deserted them and came after me, and when that didn't work out, you killed my Aunt Josephina."

"I didn't kill her. I *did* argue with her. I wanted desperately to get a job so my father wouldn't turn his back on me. I went to her house that day to check on you but also to ask her to hire me on as her foreman. She told me the place was sold and that she didn't need anyone. I argued with her, but I didn't kill her. I reached out to stop her from leaving, and she jerked away from me and lost her balance. I was too stunned to move when she began to fall. It all happened so fast, and then suddenly she was there at the bottom of the stairs, bleeding."

"And you didn't even attempt to help her?"

"She was dead already. Don't you see?"

"You didn't know that, Diego. You ran off and left her there to die."

"I'm telling you she was already dead. She wasn't breathing. I couldn't see her breathing at all."

At least now she knew the truth of what had caused her aunt's fall. "So if you weren't guilty of pushing her, why didn't you clear that up with the marshal? Why did you leave in the first place?"

"I needed to be with you. I knew losing your aunt was going to be devastating."

"Yes, it was, but believing her to have possibly been murdered was even worse."

"I'm sorry." He ran his hands through his wavy black hair. "I know I made a mess of everything, but this will work out for the best. You and I can leave together and get married. We'll be able to go anywhere. We could even live abroad." He looked at her with such a hopeful expression that Isabella thought him mad.

"Diego, my father is dying. This might have even killed him. I won't desert my mother in her hour of need—especially not for you. You mean nothing to me but heartache."

"I never meant to hurt you. I made mistakes, it's true. But never to purposefully hurt you. Please believe me."

Isabella looked at him for a moment. "Oddly enough, I do believe you. I don't think you ever gave me a single thought in all of this. You only thought of yourself and your own needs. Just as you're doing now."

"I'm thinking of us. Both of us. We belong together."

"No. We don't. We never did. I don't know what I saw in you. I suppose it was a little girl's infatuation with love, but you definitely didn't deserve my affections."

"Look, I demanded a ransom be left in place last night. My men will pick it up today, and then we can go."

"Go where, Diego? Do you not realize that my father will have every man in Silver Veil looking for me? I'm surprised no one's come here yet to check out the cabin. The whole town knows it's here."

"Yes, but who would think a kidnapper foolish enough to stay so close to the scene of the crime?" He smiled. "Hiding right under someone's nose is often a benefit."

Isabella sighed. "Diego, this will not work. I will not go with you nor marry you."

Diego shrugged. "You're overwrought right now, and I'm sorry for that. We'll discuss it later when you're feeling more yourself."

Isabella fumed at his condescension but decided to play along. "Thank you. In the meantime, won't you please untie me? I need to use the outhouse."

"Of course." Diego reached for her feet. "You must understand, though, that I will have to keep you under guard. I know you too well. You will try to escape."

"And go where? I don't know my way around here. I don't think I'd even know how to get here. I haven't been to this cabin in ten years—probably more than that. All I remember is that it is up in the mountains."

Diego got up and grabbed her by the shoulders. He pulled her to her feet, and Isabella couldn't help but moan in pain. Her ribs were so sore where she'd hit the saddle horn.

"I'm sorry. Did I hurt you?" he asked.

"It's from the ride up here." She didn't want to say anything that would cause him to stop untying her. "I nearly fell off the saddle at one point, and one of your men managed to catch me and then slammed me back across the horse. I may have broken a rib."

"The fool. I am sorry, Isabella. I meant no harm to come to you."

"And yet it has. Diego, you can have all sorts of good intentions, but that doesn't mean no one will be hurt."

Her hands came free, and she drew her arms forward. There was a slight ache from having had them tied in that position, but as Isabella took account of her body, and despite the pain in her side, she was fairly certain she could run for it. If the right situation presented itself.

Aaron had never been so angry at himself or at Diego Morales. Perhaps it was wrong to assume Diego was involved, but who else would act in such a brazen manner? Who else had a desire for revenge against Daniel Garcia?

They had searched until midnight for Isabella, but there had been no sign of her anywhere. Aaron had no idea where they'd taken her. Finally, someone suggested they wait until morning so they could see tracks better. But with so many gathered for the fiesta, there were tracks everywhere.

"I suppose they could have gotten down to the railroad and hitched a ride on the freight train. It stops there to off-load goods sometimes, and they might have taken that opportunity to sneak into one of the empty boxcars," someone suggested.

Someone else countered, "If that's the case, they could be well away from here by now."

"Aaron."

He turned to see Jim Jensen. "Oh, Jim!"

The two men embraced.

"I heard about Isabella Garcia and decided to come see what I could do. Have you figured anything out yet?"

"No. We can't find tracks or even a hint at which direction they might have gone. I figure Diego Morales had something to do with this, but so far there's been no sign of him either."

Jim nodded. "Well, I'll try to help you figure it out."

"Thanks, Jim. You're a godsend. I don't know what I'll do if something's happened to her."

"Whoa, now. Sounds like she's not just the boss's ornery daughter anymore." Jim grinned.

"No, she's not. She's the woman I love and intend to marry."

Jim let out a laugh. "If that don't beat all. The last time we talked, you said—"

"Forget what I said. I just didn't know my own heart, but now I do. I don't want to lose her."

His friend sobered. "So what do you know so far?"

"Not much. She was taken yesterday just as the sun was setting. I was up here at Garcia's, getting Mr. Garcia ready to take down to the party. He had been resting and was supposed to attend the supper and give a speech. We got back to town, and supper was served, but Isabella was nowhere to be found. The station manager at the depot found her hat with a ransom note pinned to it."

"What did that say?"

"They demanded one-hundred-thousand dollars be dropped off at Garrison's Chute in the middle of the night. Sheriff Jones went around through the back country to come up on it from the east so no one could see him. He's still lying in wait, as far as I know. He's good at what he does, so I think he'll be able to catch whoever comes for the money."

"Good. Then maybe we can find out where they've taken her."

"I hope so, Jim."

Jim put his arm around Aaron's shoulder in a brotherly fashion. "You know God has this under control. I've been praying for her and for the entire search. Others are bound to be doing the same. We've got to keep the faith, Aaron."

"I know, and I'm doing my best. I just didn't realize how much she meant to me."

"Aaron, Daniel is asking for you," Helena Garcia said, coming to join the two men.

Aaron made the introductions. "Helena Garcia, this is my good friend Jim Jensen."

"Mr. Jensen, it's good to meet you. Will you be here long?"

"I came to help with the search for your daughter."

"Oh, thank you. I cannot begin to tell you how much it means to me that everyone has come to help. Do you have a place to stay?"

"No, I just arrived and haven't yet looked for a room in town."

"Then you must stay with us, since you're Aaron's friend. I insist." She turned and called for the housekeeper. "Maya, please show Mr. Jensen to one of the guest rooms. He's come to help in the search."

"Go with her, Jim," Aaron encouraged him. "I'll speak to Daniel and return here to find you."

Jim nodded and picked up his bag.

"Mr. Jensen, have you had breakfast?" Maya asked and then checked if he had other luggage.

Aaron smiled. It was so like Jim to help in their hour of need.

He made his way to Daniel's room, where the sick man commanded the search from his bed. Aaron was amazed. Daniel would fight with every ounce of strength left in him to save Isabella. Aaron would too. Seeing her in danger made Aaron all the more certain of his feelings.

"Aaron, I'm glad you came to see me before you left again," Daniel said.

"Have you had word yet from the sheriff?"

Daniel shook his head. His skin was a pasty gray, and his eyes were sunken in from lack of sleep. "Where are you starting out the search this morning?"

"Your own backyard. We're gonna start here and then go down the road to where it branches off for the mine. We'll search around the mine and make sure they didn't decide to hide there since things are shut down. If it was Diego and his friends, they would know that area very well."

"It's probably a long shot." Daniel started coughing, and Aaron wasn't surprised when Helena rushed in with a bottle of medicine.

"You have to rest, Daniel, or you won't even be here when they bring Isabella home." She poured the medicine, and Daniel took it obediently, then fell back against his pillows.

"Find her, Aaron. Please find her."

"I will. You can be assured of that."

Daniel coughed again and struggled to get his breath. Aaron knew his time was very short.

"You must rest and be here for her when I bring her home." Aaron met his mentor's gaze and gave a nod. "And I *will* bring her home."

22

Diego waited outside the privy while Isabella relieved herself. He looked at the scenery, wishing he could enjoy it. In another place and time, he might have come here with Isabella as his wife. She was really the most beautiful of women, and she would inherit a fortune when her father passed on, which was imminent. With Isabella he could have it all. Why hadn't he seen that sooner? He should have proposed long ago. She was naïve enough that she would never have suspected him of wrongdoing. Now, people had changed her mind about him—poisoned her thoughts. If only he could turn back time.

Isabella came out of the outhouse and made her way to the small mountain stream without asking permission. She washed her hands and face and then scooped up the icy waters to drink. Diego had done something similar only an hour or so before she'd awoken.

"It's very cold, isn't it?" he said.

"It is." She straightened and returned to where he stood.

Together they made their way back to the cabin. Isabella looked around when they entered.

"I don't suppose you brought food for us, did you?" she asked.

"We didn't figure for this to last much past noon. I have a few tortillas with beans that Ru—one of my men brought, and some apples."

Isabella continued to poke through the room's nooks and crannies. It was almost as if she was searching for something specific.

"What are you looking for?"

"Memories," she replied, walking back to where he stood. "We used to come here all the time when I was a little girl. Papi and some of the men from town built this cabin. Did you know that? Maybe your friends told you?"

"It's not important."

"Well, it is to me. I have many happy memories here, despite the sorrow of leaving California behind. I don't know why I enjoyed being here so much. Maybe because Papi wasn't caught up with work." Isabella ran her hand along the table where they had taken their meals. "Funny, I thought this table was much bigger."

Diego was uncertain what to say or do. He took a seat at the table, hoping she would sit as well. "Please sit and talk to me. Let's make plans for our future."

Isabella looked at him for a moment, then took a seat opposite him. "What kind of future can we have, considering this will probably kill my father?"

"He's dying anyway." Diego shook his head. "You hated him for so many years. Why do you care now?"

"I guess because I realized I was the one at fault. Papi and Mama moved here because of Papi's health. I learned that the doctors told Papi the arid desert would help his lungs. Someone told him about this territory and how there was plenty of land for the taking. He came to visit it and was shown where the silver would be easy to mine."

"Nobody just gives up a silver mine," Diego countered.

"Nobody did. This old man just told Papi that he had a feeling there was silver—maybe even gold in this area of the mountains. And there was. Papi never saw the man again and sometimes suggested he was an angel. Wouldn't that be something if an angel actually showed Papi where the silver was?"

"Since when do you believe in angels?"

She looked at him for a moment. "I know I didn't have much to do with God when I was younger. I blamed Him as much as I did Papi for making my life miserable, but that's changed now. I understand better why things were done the way they were, and I'm no longer the ungrateful daughter."

"You were never ungrateful. You deserved to have all the wonderful things the world could give. You deserved the beautiful clothes and furnishings. I do too. We are just that kind of people, Isabella."

"No, we don't deserve anything of the kind. We are fortunate—blessed to be born into wealth, Diego. So many of our people are hated and abused because of our darker skin. You know it full well."

"That doesn't mean we don't deserve riches. Some people just do. My ancestors and yours worked the land and worked hard. They left us the results of their labor. That money should be ours, and we should be able to enjoy it."

"But we did nothing to earn it, Diego." She was smiling, and for some reason it irritated him.

He slammed his hand on the table. "I am the son of Esteban Federico Morales, who was the son of Miguel Federico Morales. I am entitled to share in their bounty."

Isabella cocked her head to one side. "Why does that entitle you to anything? You didn't work for it."

"I have done much for my father, you know that."

"Yes, I suppose you have. But I haven't done much for mine

but give him a hard time and withhold my love. I certainly don't deserve any inheritance."

"But you have money already from your grandparents, and you will soon have money from your aunt. They adored you. You must have brought them joy or they wouldn't have given it to you. We can marry and live on that money, and when your father dies, you will inherit his money as well."

"And that's all that matters to you, Diego? Don't you want a wife who will love you? One who will admire and esteem you? What about the woman you tricked into thinking you had married her? There must have been something about her that made you want to be with her."

"I only wanted her for the good times we could have together. I didn't want a wife or a son."

"But you got them nevertheless."

"It wasn't a legal bond," he protested, not sure how they had gotten back on this subject.

"But it should have been. You have a son, Diego. A son who needs a father to love him."

He frowned. "I had no father to love me. He was always much too busy with my brothers or his horses."

"Yes, and look at how miserable you are—how you are now facing criminal charges and prison. If you get the money as you hope, I want you to take it to wherever that woman and your son can be found. Marry her genuinely and raise your son with love."

"Once they know it was me, they will hunt me down unless we are married." Diego settled his nerves and memories. "You and I will leave here as soon as we get the money, and we'll be married first thing. Then you can tell them how it was just a romantic gesture—something I did to show you how much I wanted to marry you."

"Everyone from here to Albuquerque and El Paso will

know what happened by now. No one is going to marry us. There is no hope of taking the train to escape, and we would probably die trying to navigate the desert. Besides, I don't want to marry you anymore. I'm in love with someone else."

"That Bailey fellow?"

"Yes. Aaron and I are in love and plan to marry. I'm sorry. I realized that my feelings for you were just girlish infatuation. There was no real foundation for love."

"But I love you."

"I think you love my money, Diego, but you hardly know me well enough to love me." She shook her head and went to him. "Diego, this is quite hopeless unless you give up. I will speak on your behalf and tell them what a troubled soul you are. I'll even assure them that you didn't kill my aunt, because I honestly believe you. I don't think you are a killer, Diego."

"They won't believe you."

"I think they will."

Diego tried to sort through her words, but his head was beginning to hurt. "Stay here. I have to check for the boys. Don't attempt to leave. I know this area quite well and will easily find you. Besides, I'll have this place in my sight line the whole time."

Aaron and Jim walked along the road, looking for any sign of Isabella. Aaron supposed it was too much to hope that she could have left them a sign. The man or men who took her probably had her tied up.

"There's been so many horses and people stomping around that tracking anything is impossible," Jim said, shaking his head. "I'm sure sorry."

"She has to be here. Surely someone would have seen them

if they managed to jump the freight train. They might be able to ride it to San Marcial or Socorro without being seen, but surely one of those stops would have had someone checking the cars. There's no way they could have gotten all the way to Albuquerque."

"Probably not, but if they went by horse, it could be otherwise. If it's Morales like you figure, he probably hired someone who knows the area to help him. There are all sorts of hiding places around here, and you know that full well."

"Yeah, I suppose I do." Aaron pushed back his hat and looked across the Garcia property to the valley below. "I feel like I've failed her. I've failed Daniel. I promised I'd keep her safe."

"It won't do any good to ponder your actions at this point. You didn't do anything frivolous or dangerous. You weren't out playing around and ignoring the risk. They took her right out of town in the middle of a party."

"I know."

Jim continued to walk, leading his horse. Aaron caught up with him after a few minutes.

"So when did your feelings for Isabella change?" Jim asked.

"To be honest, I think it started when I picked her up in California. I don't know what it was about her. She was still as self-focused as ever, but there was an attraction I couldn't deny. I don't know if it was the same for her. And I did my best to ignore it." He looked at Jim and smiled. "I kept telling myself I hated her, but I didn't."

"Hate and love walk a fine line together."

"I suppose they do. Plus, Daniel was always there, encouraging me to join him—to take care of her and his wife. Even then I knew that was where I was going to end up. I tried to fight it. I tried to convince him and myself that my place was with the Santa Fe. I wish I'd given in sooner. I would have had more time with him to learn everything."

"It was time enough, Aaron. It's all God's timing. We need to learn that. We don't control things down here. If we're living a life yielded to God, then we don't need to worry about those kinds of things. God will direct us to the places He chooses. It seems to me that when we fight against it, it never works out well for us."

"Maybe that's why Isabella has been taken. Maybe she was taken so I'd realize just how much she means to me."

"Men have evil in their hearts and do stupid things. That's most likely why this happened, but I'm not going to try to second-guess God. I've learned my lesson where that's concerned. Now, come on, we need to get back to the house and see if anyone else has found anything. It's nearly suppertime, and I'm starved."

"I can't bear the idea of her being gone another night."

"Maybe she won't be. Maybe the sheriff caught whoever was coming for the ransom and found her too."

Aaron mounted his horse, and Jim did the same. "I'm going to find her." It bolstered his spirit just speaking the words aloud.

Jim smiled. "I know you will."

There was a great deal of commotion when they returned to the Garcia house. Maya came running from the kitchen door to greet Aaron.

"They caught the men who demanded the money. Sheriff Jones caught them, and they're here."

Aaron nodded and jumped from his horse. He handed her the reins and ran for the house. He pushed past several men standing in the foyer, drinking lemonade, and raced down the hall to Daniel's bedroom.

Bursting through the door, Aaron pushed several people

aside to get to the sheriff and the two men who looked absolutely terror-stricken as they stood at the edge of Daniel's bed. Aaron didn't recognize either man.

"Just tell us where she's being held," Daniel said. "We've already guessed this is Diego Morales's plan. Tell us where she is, and we'll take it easy on you."

Aaron didn't wait for them to speak. Instead, he went up to the first man and took hold of him by the collar. "Tell me where she is, and maybe I won't put my fist through your face."

23

P lease help me," the man said, looking to the sheriff. "I didn't hurt her. She's safe."

The other kidnapper nodded. "She is safe. Diego wouldn't hurt her. He wants to marry her. He just wanted the money so they could go away."

Jim put his hand on Aaron's shoulder, and Aaron let the man go. It took everything he had not to hit him. The very thought that he knew where Isabella was and refused to talk was making it hard to contain his anger.

Daniel Garcia fixed the man with a hard stare. "Rudy, Jorge, you were both petty thieves when I first met you. I gave you a second chance to make a good life, and this is how you reward me?"

"Diego can be very persuasive," the man called Jorge replied. "He was very sure this would work and we would all get money."

"Money was that important?" Daniel reached for his wallet and threw the contents of his wallet into the air. Bills of varying denominations rained down on the bed. "Take it. Take the money. Just tell me where my daughter is. She's all that matters to me right now."

The men exchanged a look. "What will happen to us?"

"If you tell us where she is, the judge will take that into consideration when deciding your punishment," the sheriff said. "It'll go a whole lot better for you both if you tell the truth."

Rudy nodded. "She's in the mountains. Beyond the old mine road. There's a cabin way up there."

"My cabin?" Daniel asked. "My family's cabin?"

"Yes." Rudy looked ashamed and bowed his head.

Aaron moved up next to Daniel's bed. "Where do I go, Daniel? How do I get there?"

"Give me paper and a pencil. I'll draw you a map."

The sheriff took hold of Rudy and Jorge. "I'm taking these two down to the jail." He looked at first one and then the other. "I hope you boys know that if Morales does anything to harm Miss Garcia, you two will be accessories to the crime."

"We didn't want her to get hurt," Rudy protested as the sheriff dragged them away. Jorge was pleading the same and doing his best to keep up with the sheriff's long-legged strides.

Aaron turned back to Daniel to see Helena giving him a pencil and paper.

"It's a little tricky once you get up past the mine," Daniel explained. "Look for the white post I put in as a marker. You'll take a left immediately. It starts right up the rocks higher into the mountains."

Aaron looked around at the few remaining men in the room. "Whoever wants to go with me is welcome to. We don't want any gunfire, however. It'd be too easy for Isabella to get hurt."

The men nodded. "I'll tell the others," one declared. "I know they'll want to help."

268

"That's fine, but we'll do this my way," Aaron said.

He waited for the map, and when Daniel had finished, he handed it up. Daniel pointed to the path. "It's not an easy road, but if you leave the trail at this point, you can sneak up and surround the cabin. There's a stream off to the east of the cabin. There's an outhouse over here and a woodshed to the west of that. Plenty of places to hide, but it'll be dark, and the road up isn't easy."

Aaron nodded and took the map. "Don't worry. We'll find her and bring her back. It's going to be all right, Daniel. I promise."

Daniel smiled for the first time since Isabella had disappeared. "I know you'll find her."

Aaron marched from the room with Jim close on his heels. "What's the plan, boss?" Jim asked.

"I'm open to suggestions." Aaron looked at his old friend. "I want all the advice I can get."

"I didn't want to say anything in front of Daniel, but we need someone who has been up there before."

"I know the way, Señor Bailey," Pablo said, coming from seemingly nowhere. "I will take you to the cabin."

A sense of relief washed over Aaron. "Thank you, Pablo. You are exactly the man I need." The young teen smiled. Aaron gave him a nod and continued heading outside, where everyone was gathered. "All right. Let's go make a plan."

Isabella was hungrier than she'd been in a long time. She'd missed the fiesta supper where her father planned to say good-bye to everyone. She'd had one of Diego's apples, but the beans wrapped in tortillas looked filthy, and she had no desire to eat them. Now it was a full twenty-four hours since she'd been taken, and she was starved.

I'm just spoiled, she reminded herself. *It doesn't hurt me to miss a meal or two. A lot of people get so little to eat, and they never know when their next meal might be.* She shifted in the chair. She was tired of just sitting around, waiting for Diego's friends. There had to be a way to get out of here.

She thought about the lay of the land. Their small creek ran through their property and then off the side of the mountain in a small but beautiful waterfall. Using that for navigation would do her no good. There were several small trails, mostly made by animals, and they too would be of little help. She would have to stick with the main road.

"Do you mind if I make a fire now that it's dark and no one will spot the smoke? It's cold in here, and I'm freezing," she told Diego.

He looked at her and frowned. "Go ahead." He got up for the twentieth time and went to the door. He opened it and stepped outside. He'd done this all evening. He was clearly anxious for his men to return, but so far there'd been no sign of them.

"They should have been here this afternoon," he said, coming back into the cabin. He left the door open, which irritated Isabella.

She said nothing, however. It had been a long time since she'd had to build her own fire, and she wasn't sure she could do it. Papi had taught her to make one when she was a young girl, but since then it was a job servants did for her.

She grabbed a handful of kindling and dried straw. Next, she took the matches from the mantel and knelt down to arrange things in the hearth. There was only one split log in the firebox. She supposed she could get Diego to get more wood, but if he'd let her get it herself, she could use the opportunity to escape.

A sense of excitement started in her toes and worked its way up her body. She had been looking all day for a chance to escape, and now she had a great idea. She knew the path picked up on the other side of the woodshed. This would loop around to the main road. Of course, that was only a little more spacious than the path, and it was pitch-black outside. The moon was only a sliver and would hardly offer any light. But that was probably a good thing. Diego wouldn't know his way around like she did.

It had been a long time since she'd been up here, but Isabella felt confident she could manage, despite having told Diego otherwise. She'd only said those things to make him believe it was safe to leave her untied.

To her surprise, the straw and kindling caught, and healthy flames flickered up. She grabbed the split wood and arranged it as well, leaving plenty of space for air, just as Papi had instructed.

She straightened and dusted off her hands. "We're going to need more wood. There's only this one piece. We'll need to get more from the woodshed. I can go, if you like."

Diego appeared to consider this. Isabella was ready either way. If he told her to go get it, she would make a run for it in the darkness. If he told her to stay while he fetched it, she would leave the cabin as soon as he entered the shed and run through the darkness, making her way to the road. The only real problem was if he wanted to go with her.

She made a decision there and then. "But it might be better if you get it. My ankle has been troubling me all day. I think it got hurt when you tied me up."

Diego shook his head. "I never meant to hurt you."

"I know that. I'm not saying it to make you feel bad. I just need your help with the wood." She rubbed her shoulders for effect.

"Very well. You stay put."

"Hurry. I'm cold."

He walked through the open door. "Don't close the door. I don't want to have to stop to reopen it with my arms full."

Isabella nodded. "I won't."

She gave him a few seconds' start to the shed and grabbed the blanket off the bed. She really was cold, and the night air would just make it worse. It would take quite a while to get down the mountain, especially being careful not to be caught by Diego or his men, who could return at any time.

Poking her head out the door, Isabella could see Diego had almost reached the woodshed. She pulled the blanket tight around her shoulders.

He opened the door. She drew a deep breath and held it.

He stepped inside the shed.

Isabella slipped out of the cabin and raced around to the side. She hurried along the edge of the creek and behind the outhouse. She had to time this just right so that she didn't draw his attention as she came near the woodshed. She slowly let out her breath, then panted softly into the folds of the blanket.

She saw him step from the shed, his arms full of wood. Diego headed toward the cabin, and once he'd reached the corner of the house, Isabella took off at a run. She crossed the distance between outbuildings, slipped behind the woodshed, and found the path she knew would lead her to the main road.

Diego's voice bellowed into the night. "Isabella, where are you? Come back here at once!"

She ignored him and pressed on. Something tripped her, but Isabella righted herself quickly and slowed her pace. She didn't know the way as well here, and she had to be careful or she could fall and get hurt. She stopped momentarily to get her bearings, then continued along the path.

"Isabella!" he called again, and this time his voice was louder—closer. "You know you won't find the way. You haven't been here for a long time. Let me know where you are. I don't want you to get hurt."

She wished he would be quiet and stop distracting her. She needed to focus. There were sheer drops off the side of the road in some places, and she needed to be careful. Knowing he was right on her heels made her nervous—agitated. It was the kind of thing that caused mistakes.

God, help me, please.

Mother had once told her not to pray only in times of trouble, but also to spend time in praise and thanksgiving. Isabella hadn't prayed much at all the last several years and hoped God would hear her desperate pleas.

She found the main road but then worried about what was to come. There were rocky ledges along the roadway, and rocks often tumbled down onto the road. If she tried to run in the dark, she could trip over debris. On the other hand, if she didn't pick up her pace, Diego would catch up with her. Fear snaked up her spine. There were also places in the road where the side of the mountain just dropped away. One misstep and she could fall to her death.

She swallowed the lump in her throat and did her best to calm her nerves. She heard something off to her left and hurried farther down the road. She hadn't gone far, however, when she heard Diego's voice louder than ever. The glow of lantern light flashed in the darkness behind her. Apparently he'd gone back for a light. Isabella edged closer to the rocks. If she could just find a crevice to hide in, she might still escape him.

Feeling her way with only the tiniest bit of vision in the blackness, Isabella got off the road and worked her way up the rocks. There was no crevice, but the rocks were large. Hopefully if she got behind them and flattened herself against the ground, Diego would never see her.

He was closer than ever. She could hear his footsteps. Isabella closed her eyes, afraid that if she could see him, he could see her. She began to pray, knowing that God was her only hope.

Please, Lord, don't let him see me. Don't let him hear me. Please, God.

He was nearly to the place where she had left the road. When she dared to open her eyes, she could see the dim glow of lantern light down below.

"Isabella, I know you're out here somewhere. You're going to get hurt. Come on, call to me. You know I won't hurt you."

She held her breath until she could no longer stand it, then let it out, muffling it once again in her blanket. Breathing in deep, she caught the faint scent of something she knew quite well.

Aaron's cologne. She'd never smelled anything more wonderful.

"How about you come and deal with me, Morales?" Aaron called out. "I have a dozen men here with me."

There was nothing but the sound of someone hurrying away. Isabella figured Diego was probably trying to disappear into the brush or back to the cabin. If he wasn't careful, he might lose his way and fall off the side of the road. She bit her lower lip and waited to hear what might happen. She knew the men would eventually capture him if, as Aaron said, there were a dozen with him. She hoped he wasn't exaggerating.

Someone cried out in pain, and there was the sound of a scuffle. A man called out, "I've got him, Aaron."

Isabella got to her feet in the dark and began to work her way back down the rocks. "Aaron! Where are you?"

"Isabella? Keep talking. I'm close."

"I'm here. I'm here by the rocks." She heard movement and smelled him. "I do love that cologne."

He caught her in his arms and held her tight. "I just love you. You and you alone." He buried his face in her hair and held her for the longest time.

Isabella relished the warmth and strength of his arms. She felt safe there despite the growing ache in her side. Bruised ribs could wait. She laid her head against his chest, knowing that everything would be okay now that he was here.

"Are you all right?" he finally asked.

"Yes, but my ribs are sore from the ride up here."

He loosened his hold. "Are you hurt anywhere else?"

"No. They weren't mean or ugly with me, just threw me over the horse like a bag of grain. My ribs took the brunt of it."

He brushed hair back from her face and found her lips. Isabella felt his tender kiss and dampness on his cheeks. Was he crying? She reached up and touched his wet face. She wasn't sure that any man, save perhaps Papi, had ever shed a tear over her.

Aaron took hold of her fingers and pressed a kiss to them. "I apologize if my tears are distasteful to you."

"They aren't. I'm deeply touched that you care so much. I was just thinking that the only other man who might cry over me would be Papi. No one has ever loved me like this."

"Aaron, are you out here?" a voice called. "Have you found her?"

"I have her, Jim. She's safe," Aaron yelled back.

Isabella heard something, and a light came on. The man holding the Eveready laughed. "These are mighty convenient."

"I don't know," Aaron said, looking at Isabella. "We were doing okay without it." The man laughed but kept the light shining on them.

She smiled and put her arm around Aaron's waist. "I want to go home."

Daniel and Helena sat awaiting news of their daughter. They had prayed off and on throughout the night, knowing there was nothing else they could do but also knowing that through prayer they'd seen God move mountains.

Helena had gotten into bed fully clothed beside Daniel. She sat against the headboard and held his hand. He knew she was there as much for him as for herself. They had always turned to each other in times of difficulty.

"I'm sure he'll find her and she'll be safe. Diego wouldn't hurt her," Daniel said, giving his wife's hand a squeeze.

"I know. I feel certain of that too." She squeezed back.

The minutes became hours, and still they waited. Neither had ever known so grave a time, but they found strength in God and in each other. Daniel couldn't help but wonder what his precious wife would do once he was gone. She was too young to follow him quickly in death. God willing. He prayed she'd have a long and fulfilling life—live to see their grandchildren and tell them stories of their grandfather—but doing it by herself would be lonely.

He turned to her. "You know, if God allows it, I will always look after you. And if not, the Bible does say there are angels who watch over us and that God will never leave us nor forsake us."

"It won't be the same, but yes, I know what the Bible says."

Daniel looked at her. "I've fought all these years to remain at your side."

She continued to stare straight ahead. "And now that fight is coming to an end."

"Yes, but my love for you never will. You must always carry that in your heart. Still, if there should come a time when another man enters your life . . . to love you, promise me that you won't dismiss him."

This made her glance his way. "There will never be anyone but you, Daniel. You know that very well. I will be your widow and carry your love to my grave."

Daniel started to speak, but there was a commotion in the hall and then a loud knock on the door.

"Come in!" he called, anxious for any word.

Pablo burst into the room. "Señor Aaron has her. The men have found her and captured Señor Morales. They are coming down the mountain. Señorita Isabella is all right. She is safe."

24

Isabella had never been so happy to see the lights of home. She hurried inside, knowing her parents would be anxious to see that she was safe.

Maya stood in the foyer and pointed down the hall. "They are both in your father's room."

Isabella called to them as she ran the distance. "Mama! Papi! I'm home! I'm here!"

She burst into her father's room through the open door and found him sitting in a chair by the fire. Her mother stood behind him. Both were crying tears of joy and smiling.

Knowing how worried they'd been, Isabella began to cry as well. "I'm so sorry." She embraced her mother, who cradled her close like a baby.

"We're so glad you are safe. We feared the worst at first, but God calmed our fears, and we knew Diego wouldn't hurt you."

"No, he didn't hurt me. Neither did the other two." She pulled away and leaned down to hug her father. "I hurt my ribs on the ride up, but otherwise I'm fine."

Papi held her in a tight grip, but then his strength gave way and his arms fell to his side. "I'm so glad you're home."

"Aaron told me you caught the other two men—that you didn't lose your money."

"I wouldn't have cared if I did, so long as it meant you'd come home safe," her father declared. "You know that nothing matters to me save your mother and you."

Isabella met his gaze and nodded. "I do, Papi. I thought a lot about that while I was a prisoner in our cabin."

"Tell us what happened." Her father looked at her and then Aaron as he stepped into the room. "Tell us everything."

Aaron smiled. "I'll let her start. She was already on the run when we got there."

Papi laughed. "That doesn't surprise me."

"I just kept looking for a chance to escape. When the men first took me, I had no idea who was behind the scheme, but then I realized it had to be Diego. He had actually spoken to me of just such a plan months ago. He wanted me to run away with him and get married against your will. He said we'd stage a kidnapping and get the money. He would pretend to save me, and that would cause you to agree to our marriage. And if that didn't work, we could just run off and elope. I told him the whole idea was ridiculous and that I'd have no part in it. Partly because of what I feared it would do to you, but also because I no longer wanted to marry him."

"So what happened? How did they take you? Rudy and Jorge are the ones who grabbed you, but they've said very little. I'm sure they're going to confess everything, however. We promised to go easier on them if they cooperated."

"Papi, I don't want you to charge anyone. I don't even want Diego to go to jail." She raised her hand as he started to protest. "I know he broke the law and caused so much trouble, but we both know he isn't really a criminal. He's just lost. He has shirked so many responsibilities and ignored the truth his entire life."

"That's why I think he should go to jail," Papi replied. "He needs to learn that there are consequences for his actions. All of his life he's managed to avoid them. I love that your heart is so tender, but I think he needs to learn his lesson."

"So do I. He could have killed you like he did your aunt," Aaron said.

Isabella could see his anger. "He didn't kill Aunt Josephina. We talked about that. He admitted they did argue on the stairs and that he grabbed her arm. She pulled away, however, and lost her balance."

"And you believe that?"

"I do." Isabella nodded. "The way he told me, it wasn't as if he were making excuses or trying to get out of something. It was just the facts, and I believe him."

"He still could have stopped to help her."

"I agree. He should have." Isabella took a seat on the edge of the bed. "He acknowledges that running away was cowardly and wrong. I think the shock was too much. It's hard to tell what any of us might do in the same situation."

"I'd stay and help," Aaron said firmly.

"I'd like to think we all would," Isabella continued, "but I can't be sure I would have. Fear and surprise often make us act in ways we might not otherwise."

"He's done a lot of wrong—hurt a lot of people beyond what happened to your aunt," Papi said. "Diego needs to face what he's done. He knew taking you by force was wrong. He knew demanding money for your return was equally wrong. He deserves to be tried and convicted of it all."

"Absolutely," Aaron growled.

Mama seemed to understand, though. "We all deserve conviction for our wrongs. Thankfully, we have a Savior."

"Yes, but Diego has no interest in God," Papi declared.

"Has anyone bothered to share God with him?" Mama asked, looking from person to person.

Isabella shook her head and pushed aside her guilt. "I've only just made things right with God myself. I certainly haven't been a good example or a godly witness to Diego or anyone else."

Aaron met her gaze and looked away as if ashamed. He was clearly wrestling with his feelings about the matter.

"We should have been better to him. We should have shared about Jesus," Mama said.

"We should have," Papi agreed. "And maybe one of you will while he awaits his trial in jail, but he must face his consequences."

Isabella knew she wasn't going to convince her father otherwise. "Well, I'm just glad to be home. I'm going to find something to eat and then take a nice hot bath."

"None of us have eaten," Mama said, moving around Papi's chair. "I'll go see what we can prepare in quick order. I'll have Maya bring it here, and we'll celebrate. Aaron, can you get Daniel back to bed?"

"Of course." Aaron went to Papi's side.

Isabella got out of the way. Her father was barely able to sit up. He looked so weary. No doubt this entire situation had taken a toll on him. When she considered how it had caused him so much worry and fear, she almost changed her mind about Diego.

Before Aaron had Daniel back in bed, Lupe ran into the room in her nightgown and robe. She squealed at the sight of Isabella. "I'm so glad you're home. I was so afraid for you." She hugged Isabella despite the difference in their stations.

Isabella moaned but hugged her back. "I'm glad to be home, Lupe. So very glad."

"What can I do to help you?"

"I'm going to eat something, and then I would love a bath, but I don't want to make you work. Maybe just a pan of hot water."

"No. I will make you a bath. You deserve it after all you've been through. You eat and then come upstairs. I will have it ready." The maid all but danced out of the room, leaving Isabella to shake her head.

"She must be in love. I've never seen her so happy."

Her father laughed as Aaron arranged the pillows behind his head. "Is that why you're so forgiving? Because you too are in love?"

Isabella cocked her head as she considered her father's words. "Being in love does make me feel better about most everything, so perhaps. But I want to learn to be a very forgiving person no matter what." She glanced at Aaron. "I've had to forgive some, but I've had to be forgiven much. It's time I learned to forgive easily and without such a battle."

It wasn't long before they were eating cold tamales and fried chicken, along with barely warmed refried beans and tortillas. Maya had arranged the food on the small table in Daniel's room and brought in extra chairs. Isabella thought nothing had ever tasted so good, but exhaustion was starting to take its toll. As was the pain in her side.

When she reached for another tortilla, she couldn't help giving a yelp of pain. She grabbed her side. "Sorry."

"I think the doctor needs to check you over," Mama declared.

"I agree." Aaron had mentioned on the way down that he thought a doctor should check her ribs, but Isabella hated to be fussed over after everything else that had happened.

"I'm sure I'm fine."

"The doctor will be here in the morning to see your

father. He can look at you too." Mama smiled and passed the tamales to Aaron. "More?"

Aaron shook his head. "I think I'm going to clean up and go to bed."

Isabella nodded. "I feel the same way." She glanced at her father and saw that he was already sleeping. "He's so much weaker, isn't he? This has cost him his last reserves of strength. I'm so sorry."

Mama gave her hand a squeeze. "He will rest easy now that you're safely home. Whatever time he has left, it will be spent pleasurably, knowing you are here."

Isabella felt she had barely gotten to sleep when Maya was waking her back up. "Your mama said to come. Your papa . . ."

She didn't need to say anything more. Isabella got up quickly and pulled on her robe. The pain in her side gave her pause, but only for a few seconds. If Mama was sending for her, it must be the end.

Isabella hurried down the stairs. Aaron was already at the bottom, waiting for her.

"Is he . . . ?" She couldn't bring herself to ask if Papi was dead.

"It won't be long now." Aaron put his arm around her shoulders, and they moved as one to her father's bedroom.

Isabella bit her lip to keep from crying. She wanted to be happy for Papi. He was not going to suffer anymore. He wasn't afraid of leaving them now that Aaron had agreed to take care of everything, so she didn't want to show any fear or sadness.

Mama sat beside Papi on the bed. She was holding his

hand and smiled when Isabella and Aaron came through the door.

"Look, my darling, Isabella and Aaron are here to see you off."

Papi opened his eyes, and a smile formed on his lips. "I love you all." His words were raspy and barely audible.

Isabella sat on his other side. "And we love you, Papi." Tears came unbidden, and try as she might, she couldn't contain them. "I promised myself I wouldn't cry. I know you are going to a better place, but I will miss you so much. I wasted so much time." The tears slid down her cheeks as she leaned forward to kiss her father's forehead.

"I wish," her father said, trying his best to reach up to touch her, "I could have walked you . . . down the aisle."

Isabella took his hand and drew it to her cheek. She held it there so he wouldn't have to spend his own strength. "I wish you could have seen us married, but you put us together, and now God will do the rest."

"She's right, you know," Aaron said, setting his hands on Isabella's shoulders. "Neither of us would have considered the other for a mate had it not been for you and your prayers."

"And his drive to see it done," Mama said, smiling. "Many a blessing has come out of his drive to see something done."

"When God . . . gives a vision," Papi said, sounding more and more distant, "He gives the . . . the . . . power to . . . see it done." He looked at each of them, then closed his eyes. "I'm . . . going . . . to see you . . . again."

"Yes, Papi. You will see us again." Isabella's voice broke, and she gently placed his arm at his side.

"Oh, my darling, it will be so hard without you." Mama leaned forward and kissed Papi's cheek. "I love you so."

"I love . . . you."

He continued to breathe, but the breaths were slow and very shallow. It was as if they were all frozen in time, waiting, watching.

Light was just edging the horizon when a gurgling sound rattled from Papi's throat. Isabella waited for him to draw another breath, but he didn't. She looked to Aaron, who pulled her into his arms.

"He's gone," Mama whispered. She laid her head on his chest and nodded. "Gone."

Sobs broke from Isabella, and she buried her face against Aaron's shoulder.

After seeing Isabella and her mother taken care of and back in bed, Aaron rode for the undertaker.

The sheriff was just heading to the jail when he saw Aaron and gave a wave. "How are things up at the house?"

"Mr. Garcia just passed an hour or so ago." Aaron climbed down from his horse. "I'm coming for the undertaker."

Sheriff Jones nodded. "Definitely a big loss for these people. You have some huge shoes to fill."

"Don't I know it. I have no idea how to be even half as helpful to this town as he was."

"Just do what you can and trust God for the rest."

"I know trusting God is the only way I'm going to get through this. In the past when things were rough, I would pray and then go to Daniel for advice. With him gone, I feel such a huge loss." He shook his head and tied off the horse. "I'd better go. My first official duty awaits."

He had started across the street when he spied a man on horseback coming down the mountain road from the house. It was Jim Jensen. Aaron had wanted to talk to him this morning, but since Jim had been up all night helping to rescue Isabella, Aaron had decided to let him sleep. But now his friend was here, just when Aaron needed him.

Jim pulled his horse up alongside Aaron's and dismounted. "Maya told me about Mr. Garcia." He tied the reins around the hitching post.

"Yeah. We were all with him, and it was an easy death."

"I'm glad for his sake and for all of you." He gave Aaron's shoulder a squeeze. "You should have woken me up."

"You needed rest after being up all night. I knew I could have woken you, but frankly I needed a few minutes by myself."

"You want me to go back to the house?"

"No. I had my time on the ride down here. I'm glad to see you."

"You're going to do a great job, Aaron. Mr. Garcia was obviously a great judge of character, or he never would have fought to have you join him."

"He must have seen something in me that I can't see for myself." Aaron shook his head and looked down at the sandy roadway. "I loved that man like another father—or maybe better still, a brother. An older, wiser brother."

Jim smiled. "Kind of like you are for me."

"I'm younger than you," Aaron said with mock affront.

Jim chuckled. "I'm just teasing."

Aaron shook his head. "Here I am, five years younger than you and soon to have responsibility for an entire town."

"And a wife."

"Yes, and her mother. Since I can hardly foist them off on you to take care of, how about you move down here and help me with the town?"

Jim's eyes widened. "You serious?"

"I am, and before you ask, the job will pay a whole lot

better than stockyard keeper." He shrugged. "I don't know anybody else as well as I know you. I know I can trust you and that you love God. Who could ask for a better right-hand man?"

Jim looked around at Silver Veil. "I think I'd like to move here. It's a pretty little town. Most of the time everything in mining towns looks stripped away, but Garcia made Silver Veil a pleasant place." He paused and leaned in. "What about cafés and places to eat? Any good ones?"

"Well, there's no Harvey House, but yes. We have a few excellent places to grab a bite. However, you'll probably take most of your meals at the Garcia house. There's a small guesthouse you can live in on the property. Daniel offered it to me, but now I won't need it. It's small but has everything you'll need."

"Small just means less to clean."

"Oh, the housekeeper will come and clean up after you, so no worries there."

Jim laughed. "Then I accept. I've never had a housekeeper or folks to cook for me. Better still, I've never gotten to work with my best friend."

"There's just one more thing I have to ask."

"What's that?"

"Will you be my best man?"

"When's the wedding?" Jim asked, grinning.

"Not sure. I want Isabella and her mother to have all the time they need to get through their grieving. I've left it in Isabella's hands. When I know more, you will too."

"Well, I guess that makes it all the more important to take the job. So yes, to both."

25

I know your father wouldn't want you to wait very long to marry Aaron," Mama said.

Isabella had joined her mother in the courtyard to plant flowers. Mama wanted to plant a tree and flowers in honor of Papi so that every time she came out here, it would remind her of him.

"It seems bad to wed too soon. People are grieving the loss. It's April, so maybe in September."

"If that's what you feel is right."

"We'll have this mess with Diego settled by then."

Mama dusted off her hands and looked up. "When did the sheriff say the trial would be?"

"The second week of May. The judge will come in on Sunday the twelfth, so the trial can start on the thirteenth. He doesn't think it will last long."

"Perhaps Diego will plead guilty and save the town the time and trouble of a full trial."

"I plan to encourage him to do so," Isabella admitted.

"You're going to see him?"

"Yes. I'll probably take Aaron with me." Isabella stood up and pulled off her gardening gloves. "I want Diego to know

I'm not angry but that he needs to be honest and truthful. He needs to own up to all he's done."

"Señora," Maya called as she entered the courtyard, "a letter has come for Señor Garcia." She looked as though she might burst into tears.

"It's all right, Maya. There are bound to be more letters that show up. He ran a great business." Mama took the letter and opened it. "Speaking of Diego, this letter is from his father." She scanned the lines, then handed it to Isabella. "Why don't you read it aloud."

Isabella took the letter and sat down on the nearest bench. "'Dear Daniel, I wanted to write and tell you of my progress. I traced the woman Diego is said to have married. I found her in Kansas. Her name was Lucy Meyers. Her stage name was Collette DeMeire, and they met when she was an actress.'" Isabella looked up and met her mother's gaze. "He says 'was.' Do you suppose she's dead?"

"Why don't you read on, my dear?"

Isabella nodded and returned her gaze to the letter. "'Apparently the marriage was a sham performed to trick the poor girl into believing she was legally wed so that Diego could take advantage of her.'" She looked up. "That's exactly what Diego told me he'd done."

Her mother nodded, and Isabella turned back to the letter.

"'She lived with her father in Goddard, Kansas. She died from a fever not long before I arrived. In fact, both she and her mother passed away just days apart. Her father was in a bad way, having neither his health nor family. However, there was the matter of his grandson. My grandson.

"'His name is Lawrence Miguel Morales, and he's the spitting image of Diego. Mr. Meyers told me the boy had been named for him and for my father because Lucy couldn't remember my name. The baby is only a year old, and Mr.

Meyers asked me to take him to raise. He said he knew he didn't have long on this earth. He has some sort of heart ailment.

"'I hired a nurse and brought the boy back to California with me. There is no doubt he is my grandson. I would like for you to share this news with Diego if he is still in Silver Veil. He needs to know he owes this child a responsibility. I have my doubts that he will come home and do his part, but I want very much for him to know that is what is expected.

"'Daniel, I blame myself for letting Diego go his own way. I should have been more of a father to him. I should have guided him more, but I was so busy with all that life required of me. Now I regret ignoring the boy. I pray he will come home to my forgiveness and that he will forgive me. When I look into the eyes of my grandson, I know we all owe him that much.'"

Isabella shook her head. "He can't go, of course."

"No. We don't have any idea what will happen at the trial."

"I still want the judge to be lenient with Diego. He's not really a bad person."

"We did agree to leave it in God's hands," Mama replied, "but I wonder if we should show the judge this letter. Perhaps we can talk to him about all that's happened and how we feel about it."

"I think we should. It's not taking it out of God's hands." Isabella reasoned the matter in her head. Surely it wasn't wrong to give the judge all the facts. After all, he would determine Diego's future.

Her mother nodded. "Then we should talk to him and let him read this letter before the trial starts. Perhaps we can even persuade Diego to plead guilty and show his remorse."

"That would surely impress the judge," Isabella said with an enthusiastic nod. "Let's do it."

⁓

"I want you to plead guilty, Diego. Everyone knows it was you, and it will only take up more time if you claim you didn't arrange the kidnapping."

Diego looked at Isabella through the bars of his cell. He'd never once been in jail before now. He had always been able to bribe his way out of trouble, but not this time.

"Mama and I plan to talk to the judge and encourage him to go easy on you. You aren't a bad man, just misguided."

There was a time when he might have been angry at her comment, but Diego had no energy left to give to such things. He was desperately afraid of where this was all going to lead.

"Do you think the judge will listen?" he finally asked.

"I hope so. Sheriff Jones says Judge Breidenbach is a good man." She paused and worried her lower lip. She'd always done that when struggling with how to tell him something.

"Just say whatever it is that's troubling you." He folded his arms.

"We had a letter from your father. He found where Lucy was living with her folks in Kansas. I'm afraid she's dead. She came down with a fever and died. Her mother too. Her father was in a sickly way and asked your father to take your son back to California with him."

Diego's mouth went dry, and he stumbled back to sit on his cot. He didn't know what to think. Lucy dead. His son being raised by his father.

"Your father asked my father to send you home. He thinks you should come back to raise your son." Isabella paused. "I think you should too."

"And how am I supposed to do that? I'm a prisoner."

"That's why I want you to plead guilty—tell the judge you weren't thinking clearly, which is obviously the truth. I don't know why you did what you did. Perhaps it really was for the sake of loving me, but it doesn't matter. I want the judge to be lenient but fair with you, and you must answer for what you've done. Still, your son needs you." She smiled. "His name is Lawrence Miguel Morales. Lucy named him for her father and your grandfather. Your father says he looks just like you." Isabella came closer to the bars. "Please do right by him, Diego."

The weeks he'd spent in jail had caused Diego to rethink much of his life. Lucy and the baby hadn't been uppermost on his mind, mainly because he knew they were better off without him. Now things were different, and Diego was hard-pressed to figure out what to do. His father wanted him to come home and help raise the boy. Could they manage to do this together? Would his father still allow him to work for the family?

Diego had spent over three months working in a silver mine. He'd never worked so hard in his life, and all to give him time to figure out how to get Isabella and her money. Now none of that mattered. She was going to marry Bailey and remain here in Silver Veil to oversee the town's needs and care for her mother. There was no future for them, so why not give it to his son?

"Did you hear me, Diego?"

He looked up and shook his head. "No, I was thinking. What did you say?"

"I said I'm leaving, but I'll be praying for you."

He studied her for a moment. She really was the most beautiful woman he'd ever known . . . but she would never be his.

"Thank you for your prayers, and I will think on what you've said." He rose and came to the bars. "I really did love you, Isabella. It wasn't just about the money."

She gave him a sad smile. "I believe you, Diego."

Isabella sat with her mother in front of a kind-looking old man. He was a little on the stout side with a mass of thick white hair.

Judge Breidenbach raised his gaze to Isabella. "Are you saying you don't think he's a danger or likely to try this kind of thing again?"

"I don't think he's a danger to anyone," Isabella declared. "He was struggling with a lot of problems. But he's just found out he has a son and the boy's mother has died."

"And where is this son now?"

"Living with Diego's father in California," Mama answered. "Please understand, Your Honor, we know Diego did wrong. We know there are consequences for wrong actions. We're just asking that you be lenient."

The judge glanced from Mama to Isabella and then looked once again at the papers in front of him. "I will take everything into consideration. You do know that he plans to plead guilty and has thrown himself on the mercy of the court?"

Isabella nodded. "We encouraged him to do that. We were hopeful that if he admitted to his wrongdoings, it would go better for him."

The judge nodded. "We shall see. Tomorrow in court, I will announce the sentence."

It was hard knowing that Isabella planned to ask for leniency on behalf of Diego Morales after all the trouble he'd caused. Aaron had argued that people could have been killed, but Isabella had explained that she had needed forgiveness for her wrongdoings and Diego was no different. Jim had agreed and reminded Aaron that he had won Isabella's heart and all that Daniel Garcia had blessed him with, so perhaps he could afford to be charitable. After much prayer, Aaron agreed.

The judge entered the small room and took a seat at a table the sheriff had positioned near the front wall. When everyone had retaken their seats, the judge gazed out over the gathering as the case was announced and Diego was asked to stand and give his formal plea.

"I am guilty as charged." Diego lowered his head.

Aaron liked to think he was ashamed of what he'd done. No doubt his actions had hastened Daniel Garcia's death. That was the part Aaron had a hard time forgiving. Isabella agreed it was difficult to think of it, but she knew Diego hadn't kidnapped her with that purpose in mind. His selfish ambition had driven him, not a desire to commit murder or cause harm.

"Mr. Morales," the judge began, "I have had several people speak on your behalf. It seems especially touching that your victim should ask for compassion for you. What you did, however, was most grievous, and therefore the consequences must also match the crime. So many things could have gone wrong, and your victim could have even met with death.

"However, as I mentioned, those who have spoken on your behalf believe you to have learned your lesson. I am also told you have a small son for whom you will be responsible. It is not the desire of this court to see you separated indefinitely.

Therefore, I sentence you to three years in prison with a chance of parole for good behavior." He pounded his gavel.

Aaron looked at Isabella. She smiled. "That seems fair," she said as people around her began getting to their feet.

They rose together, and Aaron offered her his arm. "It does seem fair, and as the judge said, he might be able to serve even less time if he conducts himself well."

Aaron offered Isabella's mother his other arm. Helena smiled and shook her head. "I want to speak to the pastor for a moment. He's going to talk to Diego."

"We'll wait outside." He led Isabella from the room before she could suggest they join her mother. They found themselves immediately at the center of attention when they exited the building.

"Are you happy with that sentence, Isabella?" one woman asked.

Another pressed in. "I think the judge went far too easy on that man."

Isabella raised her gloved hand. "I prayed about this matter, and I believe God has made His will known through the judge's actions."

The women fell silent. After all, how could one argue with the will of God?

As the crowd thinned a little, Isabella turned to gaze into Aaron's eyes. "I've been thinking about our wedding date."

He was surprised by this but smiled. "And what did you conclude?"

"I was worried about marrying too soon after Papi's death for fear of offending folks. You know how people are with their traditions, and I didn't want to do anything inappropriate. But I think there's no reason to wait. Papi wouldn't have wanted that. He would have seen me married to you years ago."

Aaron chuckled. "Yes. I know he would have done exactly that."

"Well, I'm just thinking—unless, of course, you are against the idea—that we could marry next month. I'll need to give Mama a little time to plan things."

He sobered and gazed into her dark eyes. "I'd like that very much."

Isabella smiled. "I would too."

Mrs. Garcia rejoined them and seemed to realize that something important had just happened. "And just what are you two scheming?"

"We've decided to get married next month," Isabella said, reaching for her mother's hand. "Will that give you enough time to plan a wedding?"

Her mother gave Isabella a hug. "It will. Oh, you've made me very happy. We will be a family together as your father always dreamed." Her eyes grew teary. "I know it would please him."

"I know it would too. That's why I thought we should go ahead with it rather than wait. Tradition might suggest otherwise, but Papi would say, 'Phooey on tradition!'" They all laughed.

"Is this acceptable to you, Aaron?" Helena looked to him for an answer.

"I would have asked the judge to marry us after he passed sentence on Diego if I thought I could get away with it. But I know Isabella wants a church wedding with all of her friends."

"And a big party at the house."

"Why not in the plaza?" Helena asked. "Then everybody can come and enjoy."

Isabella looked at Aaron. "That seems only right, now that you've become the town's manager." She turned to her mother. "We'd best get to planning. We're going to need all the ladies from all the churches to help. Maybe we could even be married in the plaza rather than the church so that anyone who wants to join us can."

Aaron glanced heavenward. "I didn't know we were going to make this a town event, but I suppose I should have expected as much." He looked at Isabella, falling more deeply in love with every passing moment. "I'll get word off to my parents right away."

The wedding took place on the fifteenth of June. Isabella didn't know when she'd ever been so happy. The ladies from the Bible Church made her a gown of ivory silk with a full skirt that rounded out in the back to trail behind her. The bodice was well-fitted with a high neckline of lace, and sleeves of the same. The ladies from the Catholic church created a veil and a bouquet of pink roses, while the Methodist church women made the wedding cake. It was quite the ornate piece, done with six tiers and several small cakes surrounding it. They had decorated it in white icing and trimmed it with pink roses to match those in Isabella's bouquet.

All of the women had worked together to create a luncheon feast fit for a king and queen. Isabella couldn't be happier, and Aaron seemed equally pleased. With the ceremony behind them and the luncheon being readied, Isabella couldn't help drawing Aaron off behind the bandstand for a few moments of privacy.

"We're going to cause a scene sneaking off. Someone's bound to notice," Aaron teased.

"Let them. We're man and wife," Isabella said, throwing herself into Aaron's arms.

He pulled her close. "I'm glad we decided to get married in the morning. It's going to be a scorcher today." He lowered his mouth to hers and kissed her.

Isabella sighed and melted against him. "I love you so very much."

"And I love you, Isabella Garcia Bailey." He grinned and then kissed her again.

"And not just because I have money?" she asked, laughing.

He held her at arm's length. "As I told you, my father has a great deal more money than your father."

"But that's your father, not you." She raised a brow as if daring him to contradict her statement.

"Well, it just so happens that upon my wedding day, I inherited a large trust my grandfather set up. So I don't need your money. Feel free to spend it on whatever you like."

"You inherited money because you married me?"

"I did." He grinned. "And you inherited money because you married me."

She laughed. "I did."

He swept her into his arms once again. "But we both know that was never the reason for our union." He nuzzled her neck. "You married me because you love my cologne."

She giggled. "I've been found out."

"Here you two are," Mr. Bailey said.

Isabella jumped at the sound of her father-in-law's voice and hurried to extricate herself from Aaron's arms. Aaron would have none of it, however, and held her fast to his side.

"Hello, Father. You're interrupting a very important conversation." Aaron wagged his finger at the older man.

His father smiled. "I'm sure I am, but you have an entire town full of people who want to eat. I suggest you come and join them, since you are the guests of honor. You can *talk* later." He gave Aaron a wink, then turned and walked away.

Aaron's mouth had dropped open, and Isabella laughed. "What's wrong with you?"

"So am I." Isabella leaned against him with a smile. "So am I."

Tracie Peterson is the award-winning author of over one hundred novels, both historical and contemporary. She is often referred to as the "Queen of Historical Christian Fiction," and her avid research resonates in her stories, as seen in her bestselling Heirs of Montana and Alaskan Quest series. Tracie considers her writing a ministry for God to share the Gospel and biblical application. She and her family make their home in Montana. Visit her website at www.traciepeterson.com or on Facebook at www.facebook.com/AuthorTraciePeterson.

Sign Up for Tracie's Newsletter

Keep up to date with Tracie's news on book releases and events by signing up for her email list at traciepeterson.com.

More from Tracie Peterson

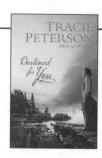

These sweeping historical romances set on the shores of Lake Superior explore nineteenth-century Duluth, Minnesota, and the dangerous world of shipping on the Great Lakes. In these compelling novels, three women encounter adventure and romance, and must rely on their faith to see them through.

LADIES OF THE LAKE: *Destined for You, Forever My Own, Waiting on Love*

⬧BETHANYHOUSE

 Stay up to date on your favorite books and authors with our free e-newsletters. Sign up today at bethanyhouse.com.

 facebook.com/bethanyhousepublishers @bethanyhousefiction

 Free exclusive resources for your book group at bethanyhouseopenbook.com

You May Also Like . . .

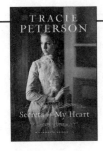

This follow-up to the beloved HEART OF THE FRONTIER series features a new generation of women striving for a life of purpose. Nancy Pritchard, Faith Kenner, and Constance Browning wrestle with issues of the heart, their faith, and cultural injustice in these stirring novels.

WILLAMETTE BRIDES: *Secrets of My Heart, The Way of Love, Forever by Your Side* by Tracie Peterson
traciepeterson.com

Del Nielsen's teaching job in town offers hope, not only to support her three sisters but also to better her students' lives. When their brother visits with his war-wounded friend RJ, Del finds RJ barely polite and wants nothing to do with him. But despite the sisters' best-laid plans, the future—and RJ—might surprise them all.

A Time to Bloom by Lauraine Snelling
LEAH'S GARDEN #2
laurainesnelling.com

When three kids go missing from the children's home, Lillian Walsh and Grace Bennet will do all they can to find them. With the future of the children's home in question, and everyone struggling to determine their paths forward, they all begin to realize that sometimes loving well means making difficult choices.

Unfailing Love by Janette Oke and Laurel Oke Logan
WHEN HOPE CALLS #3

BETHANYHOUSE

More from Bethany House

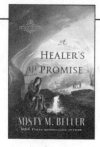

British spy Levi Masters is captured while investigating a discovery that could give America an upper hand in future conflicts. Village healer Audrey Moreau is drawn to the captive's commitment to honesty and is compelled to help him escape. But when he faces a severe injury, they are forced to decide how far they'll go to ensure the other's safety.

A Healer's Promise by Misty M. Beller
Brides of Laurent #2
mistymbeller.com

Libby has been given a powerful gift: to live one life in 1774 Colonial Williamsburg and the other in 1914 Gilded Age New York City. When she falls asleep in one life, she wakes up in the other without any time passing. On her twenty-first birthday, Libby must choose one path and forfeit the other—but how can she possibly decide when she has so much to lose?

When the Day Comes by Gabrielle Meyer
Timeless #1
gabriellemeyer.com

While Brody McQuaid's body survived the war, his soul did not. He finds his purpose saving wild horses from ranchers intent on killing them. Veterinarian Savannah Marshall joins Brody in an attempt to save the wild creatures, but when her family and the ranchers catch up with them, they will have to tame their fears if they've any hope to let love run free.

To Tame a Cowboy by Jody Hedlund
Colorado Cowboys #3
jodyhedlund.com